Ki's Redemption

Book 3 of An Alien Exchange

Keri Kruspe

For those of us who have been betrayed by the people we trusted the most. Chin up, achieved success is the sweetest revenge. And, for those of us who've made mistakes along the way, redemption is already within you... all you have to do is be brave enough to embrace it and yourself.

CONTENTS

CHAPTER ONE

Ki

The Mineral Wealth Industries on Reinus45; 106 solar years prior

"But *nytsa*!" Young fourteen-year-old Ki whined to his gentle mother as only a youth his age could. "I've made plans with my friends! I can't watch Yn'eo tonight." Now came the pout and soulful eyes. Worked every time.

Gah! Except now. Pitiful eyes and begging wasn't working on his normally agreeable mother, Jexa.

"Now, now, my strong little warrior."

She wagged a finger in his direction.

"You were well aware your father and I had to go to the awards dinner tonight. There's no excuse for you to make other plans."

"Don't you want to be with me, *mihr*?" His six-year-old baby sister, Yn'eo, asked with a quivering voice. Her wide eyes filled with tears covering her dual-colored irises, a mirror image of his own navy blue surrounded by hunter green. "I thought you loved me."

Now came the manipulative sniff. *Danka shit!* Yn'eo was better at this than he was. With a heated face, he clenched his fists under crossed arms. An annoying sprite, she'd had their parents twisted around her little finger since the day she was born...and knew it too. Ki gave her a narrow glare and a slight shake of his head in warning.

She returned his threat with a twinkle before the shimmer of tears spilled out.

"*Nytsa...* Ki is being mean to me!" Yn'eo put her fists on thin hips and stomped a foot. Her dark mahogany hair unraveled and floated around her disheveled head as if to emphasize her distress.

"Ki." The gravelly voice of their father Tror'yrc rumbled as if he talked through a cluster of boulders. The terse words delivered through his deep tone commanded instant obedience.

With pangs of bitter acid churning in his stomach, Ki let his arms drop as he turned toward their glaring sire. Game over. Ki's shoulders drooped. "Yes, sir."

The elder E'eur, a full foot and a half taller than Ki, widened his legs while he crossed his massive arms over an equally massive chest. Everyone who first met him assumed he was a soldier or a mercenary, not a bureaucrat—a paper pusher for the mining company.

Due to his Crart birthright, Tror'yrc could be more dangerous than any soldier or mercenary in the known nine systems. Part of his genetic heredity enabled him to fuse an impenetrable battlesuit at the cellular level whenever he wanted.

Thank the Goddess, he wasn't going to wear it that night. For whatever reason, his father planned on leaving it behind. Which gave Ki a once-in-a-lifetime chance to take the suit and show that bully Drirux and his gang a thing or two. Those disgusting *puntnejis* had insulted him for the last time. If only Yn'eo would spend the night at her friend's house. The spoiled little monster refused to cooperate, and he was stuck with her. *Gah!* She was such a pain.

No matter. He'd just sneak out after she fell asleep. The only thing to worry about was how to get the dragon to cooperate since the symbiont who lived in the suit hadn't been transferred to him yet. No...he'd come. Yeah, the dragon didn't have a choice. After all, Ki was the eldest E'eur, next in line to inherit. It'd be perfect. He imagined the looks of terror on Drirux and his gang when they got a load of him when he morphed into the dragon. First thing he'd do was blow fire at their sorry asses.

No way would those jerks mess with him again.

With a brave front, Ki stared back at the narrow look his *nytso* gave. He began to shake. What if his father suspected what he planned on doing? His mouth dried. But he had to do something! The constant harassment at school was starting to get out of hand. Oh, at first their taunts and name-calling were easy to ignore. But lately they'd taken to surrounding him on his way home from school. Hiding bruises and cuts from his vigilant mother was getting harder to do. So, he'd made an agreement to meet with them that night and settle everything once and for all. If he didn't show up... He shuddered. He couldn't begin to imagine the horrors he'd have to put up with at the tutorial academy the next day.

"Yn'eo has already had dinner and I've made your favorite for you."

His mother interrupted before Ki hyperventilated and passed out from his scary thoughts.

She spoke in her normal, whisper-soft voice. "Be sure to clean up the food prep room after you eat and don't forget to finish the assigned lessons from your instructor." Jexa reached over to brush his long hair over his shoulder before caressing his cheek.

The comforting scent of her floral fragrance calmed him.

Her smooth forehead creased as she studied him in her typical annoying, mother way.

Ki gazed back. Earlier that year he'd reached her height and before long would tower over her petite form. Gently, he laid a larger palm over hers and squeezed with a sheepish smile. Was there any other female in the universe more beautiful than his *nytsa*?

She had thick alabaster-white hair, its heavy length wrapped in a large bun at the nape of her slender neck. A dark, black ring separated her equally colored dual-emerald irises. While green eyes might be normal for a Zerin, ususally the inner ring had a darker color than the outer. So, when she met people for the first time, they commented on her strange, matching shades of green eye color...that is, until they caught sight of Ki's father.

Tror'yrc E'eur had the same basic characteristics of any Zerin, with slightly pointed ears and russet-brown skin overlaid by an iridescent sheen. His three fingers were the same length accompanied by one thumb. Ki inherited his dark-mahogany hair from his father, who had braided his long tresses in a tail that reached the back of his knees. A smattering of yellow at his temples denoted his advanced age, a respectable 256 solar years with no sign of slowing down.

Ki hoped he looked half as good when he reached his maturity.

The colors of his father's eyes gave away his genetic anomaly. He'd inherited dark and light navy-blue irises from his father's alien grandfather, a Crart.

Ki also ended up with weirdly colored irises, one navy blue, and one hunter green. That was the very reason Drirux and his merry band of *aHxxjt* assholes kept harassing him at the tutoring halls. Past time to show those *puntnejis* he wasn't someone to mess with.

"Don't worry, *nytsa*," Ki reassured his mother. "I'll take care of everything."

"See that you do." The unyielding baritone of his father left no doubt of the severe consequences if Ki ignored him. "Come, *yofie-na.*" Jexa was enfolded in a tight hug as his father's rumbling tone changed to a silky-smooth croon. "We'll be late if we don't leave now."

Their foreheads rested together, showing the matching swirls of their MalDerVon scrolls on their temples and upper cheeks. Heir crystals nested in the middle of the purple ink at their temples winked clear and brilliant in the light of the room.

His mother's emerald eyes returned her mate's loving gaze and she pressed closer.

Ki fought to keep his face from twisting in disgust. Goddess, did they have to do that in front of him? *By the father of all...* they weren't the only people in the room... *gah!*

Tror'yrc straightened and sent him a warning glare.

Ki held his breath and breathed a sigh of relief when they finally left. He barked at Yn'eo to join him in the preparation room while he ate. He might as well get her a frozen treat to keep her from bugging him.

Several macroclicks later, Yn'eo whined her last complaint and finally went to bed. Normally she was a sound sleeper and wouldn't wake until sunrise.

When he was sure she was out for the night, he rushed to his father's study to the cocoon the suit lay in. Having watched his *nysto* unpack the suit countless of times, he mimicked the movements to free the garment. He gave a grunt when he picked it up. It was heavier than he thought.

With an eager hand, Ki tore off his clothes and put the black matte suit on feetfirst. A whiff of animal musk reached his nose. Sheesh, what a snug fit. With a wiggle, squirm, and hard tug, he pulled it over his thin form. How did his huge father put the damn thing on? That was a mystery for later. After he put his arms through, the front closed automatically. A light sensation similar to an arm falling asleep after laying on it too long traveled from the top of his head down to his toes. An echo of "*hatchling*" made him pause, but the sound passed before he could process it. Shaking his head to focus, he snuck out of the house so Yn'eo couldn't hear him leave.

It was time to give those guys the butt kicking they deserved. They needed to be taught a lesson, and he was just the professor to give it to them.

All too soon, Ki arrived at the prearranged grove where the bullies waited. They didn't waste any time surrounding him.

The stupid *puntnejis* with their predictable taunts made him leer with arms crossed. The idiots should come up with something else besides calling him a freak and a loser as they teased him for showing up. Their lack of imagination was laughable.

Dressed in the impenetrable battlesuit, Ki let the five males shout their stupid words all they wanted.

When he didn't respond, they jabbed him with either fingers or rocks they'd picked up from the grassy ground. When they didn't get any reaction, shoves began, and fists flew. Emboldened, the bullies attacked.

With glee, Ki reached deep inside to access his Crart heritage to let the Solaherra dragon have free rein.

Nothing happened.

His stomach knotted as his knees became weak. While the suit protected him from the harshest blows, some fists made their mark on his face and hands. He covered his head to protect himself when a searing pain ripped inside, throwing his hands wide as he screamed in terror. Every nerve exploded as they reformed around muscles that bulked and expanded beyond his control. His bones broke apart before they sucked together in a denser form.

What scared Ki most was the loss of control. His consciousness was thrown into a metaphoric hole, locked away from any decision-making ability. *Oh, Goddess!* What if he couldn't change back?

"Hatchling."

A deep, powerful voice boomed and echoed in his skull.

It was Grirryrth, the dragon. *"Wherever is your sire?"*

Huh? Sire? It was hard to focus. Drirux and his buddies were making too much noise as they ran away and screamed like the whiny little babies they were.

"Yes, hatchling. You are not supposed to be with me until your sire deems it to be so."

Ki made a lame attempt to respond when a loud, screeching noise pierced his ears. He'd have covered them if he had any. Looks like being incorporeal had more than one disadvantage.

"Tror'yrc!" The booming internal voice of the dragon was full of anguish. *"No! He is in mortal danger, we must go to him!"*

With the dragon's cry, an overwhelming panic choked Ki. *Oh my Goddess!* Something had happened to his father! The next thing Ki knew, he was weightless in winged flight as he and his newly changed body took to the skies and headed home.

Over the dusty, hole-ravaged landscape of the mining planet they flew.

Ki sat in the back of the dragon's consciousness, quaking like a coward. If he concentrated, he could see out of the dragon's eyes. With a detached air, he watched the zooming black landscape pass by at a dizzying rate. Good thing he and the dragon weren't in his body, because he'd have thrown up by now.

Then, there was home right in front of them...but something was wrong. Black, billowing smoke stained the sky from the back of the house. Roaring flames licked the structure with greedy mouths of destruction.

Ki scrambled to take control, but the dragon kept a firm grip on their reality.

He swooped down and landed with a loud boom when his hind legs touched down. Wings flapped behind as the beast ran toward the home on gargantuan legs that shook the ground. When they reached the two-story house, the dragon grabbed the roof, pulled it off, and threw it away.

The first thing Ki saw was the twisted, broken body of his dead six-year-old sister.

Her head lay facedown at one end of the room while her body was crumpled in a heap at the other end like a piece of trash.

"NO!" Ki gave an internal scream while the dragon bellowed his sorrow with him.

A desperate war cry caught the dragon's attention, and he twisted toward the sound.

There was Ki's father, unsteady on his feet as he clutched his blood-soaked tunic with one hand.

Next to his father was his beautiful mother, bloody and broken. Her neck was bent at a perverse angle, her elegant silver tunic ripped, exposing her nude body to the horrific last moments of her life.

At the dragon's answering roar, his father looked up. His face became red as his brows furrowed and his lips thinned. "Grirryrth... destroy!" Tror'yrc's thunderous war cry followed as he gestured at the seven ragged criminals surrounding him.

The dragon inhaled, filling his massive lungs with the air he needed to blow an inferno. Within nanoclicks, the thugs were gone, consumed by a fire so hot, their powdered ashes blew away in the wind. The bite of sulfur lingered.

Tror'yrc continued to stand on unsteady legs in the middle of the burning ring. When the flames died out, he dropped to his knees.

Time gripped Ki in its frozen grasp. *Nytso?*

The dragon's snout reached his father who rested a bloody hand on him. With white lips, he spoke to the large dragon. "Take care of my son, Grirryrth." A gasping, gurgling sound came out of his father's throat. His large body folded, and he fell to the hard, blackened ground on his side.

Let me out...let me out! Ki gave an internal shout. *I have to go to him!*

Hatchling, I fear it is far too late. My friend and brother is all but gone from this world. The male dragon croaked the horrific words. The weight of his sorrow squeezed the mammoth beast.

I don't care...let me go! Ki was desperate. He struggled within the confines of his Solaherra prison.

Between one heartbeat and the next, Ki stumbled in his own body. The battlesuit protected his knees but not his hands when he hit the ground. Ignoring the stinging pain, he rushed to his father's side.

"*Nytso!*" Ki screamed and reached for his fallen parent. "*Nytso*, I'm here. I'll get help." He pulled his father's head on his lap and with trembling fingers tried to brush away the blood that seeped out of the corner of his father's mouth.

"Ki, my beloved son," Tror'yrc E'eur whispered with a pinched mouth and eyes. "Thank the Goddess you're safe."

"What happened?" The smoke from the burning house singed his nose and lungs. Ki watched the massive destruction of his home in detached fascination. When his gaze slid to the broken body of his mother, tears blinded him. "Who were those people and why did they attack?"

"While I was at the awards banquet, they came to steal the battlesuit," Tror'yrc uttered faintly as a roll of thick crimson flowed past his lips. "They are xenophobic fanatics who have hunted our family for generations, determined to destroy the last Solaherra dragon. And they'll stop at nothing to kill you and Grirryrth, now that I'm gone."

"Gone...no! If I hadn't taken the suit, Grirryrth would have been here for you. *Nytsa* and Yn'eo would be okay." Ki wailed as sobs tore through his throat. "I'm so sorry, *nytso...* I'm so sorry. Don't leave me...please don't leave me, *nytso!*"

"You must be strong, M'alalu." Another wet, bubbly hack. "I have no choice; I must join my TrueBond and your sister." His voice gurgled low and faint.

"NO!"

"Son...listen to me." Tror'yrc took in a rattling breath and grabbed Ki's shoulder with a blood-soaked hand. "You must leave here and never look back. Run as far and as fast as you can, get off this planet. You are the last of the Crart line and solely responsible for the Solaherra dragon, who depends on you." A weaker cough. "He must never fall into the hands of others. *Trust no one with this secret!*" The last sentence came out hard. "Promise me, on the eternal souls of your sister and mother, you will guard him with your life." He gave a gurgling choke as he gasped out the words. "Promise!"

Ki nodded. His heart squeezed as tears blinded him and rolled down his cheeks. "Yes, I promise, *nytso.*"

The beloved face turned serene, his father's eyes and mouth softened.

"Grirryrth, by the blessings of the Eternal Goddess, I leave unto you my only son, M'alalu Ki E'eur. M'alalu, by the blessings of the Eternal Goddess, I leave unto you Grirryrth, the Solaherra Dragon, and the pride of our Crart heritage." A rattling inhalation. "What I have wrought, may no one put asunder."

As he forced out a wet exhalation, a dark blue mist left Tror'yrc's body and floated in front of Ki. Thin tendrils of smoke wrapped around the youth before dissipating to his skin through the battlesuit. Ki's ears popped as the heavy strength of the dragon settled deep in his bones.

"There, it is done." A bare smile crossed Tror'yrc's ravaged face. "I love you, son, and have always been proud of you." A slow breath. "The Goddess and Grirryrth will protect and bless you." His dual-navy irises became blank as he died with a shallow puff of air through bloodstained lips.

A ragged sob tore out of Ki before grief thundered through a raw throat. He closed his eyes and cried, clutching his dead father's body.

Hatchling. Grirryrth's voice was insistent. *We cannot stay...we must leave right away.*

"No, leave me alone," Ki yelled. He tried to see his father's beloved face through the puddle of tears that clouded his vision. "I've gotta take care of them."

Yes, hatchling.

Ki had a hard time understanding the dragon's voice in the long, dark tunnel he was in.

But our enemies have friends and they will be here in less than five clicks.

An infusion of warmth flooded him, which created a sense of calm. Instinctively Ki knew the emotion came from the dragon to steady him.

If we do not leave, others will come, not only to kill you but they will *find a way to imprison me. Let us honor your family and mine and not allow their tragic deaths to come to naught.*

"Tragic?" Anger replaced the calm. "Their deaths weren't tragic! They died because of me." Shame tightened Ki's face and clogged his throat. "If I hadn't taken you to show off to those bullies...you'd have been here for him to stop them!"

The words no sooner came out of his mouth than a large war cry ripped the air as something plowed into him. Ki went flying; his face hit the dirty ground and his breath whooshed out. The weight on his back made it hard to breathe. Thick fingers pulled his hair in a painful grip and exposed his vulnerable neck.

"Disgusting hybrid piece of *danka* shit!"

The male's sour breath roared into Ki's ear as a flash of steel swooped down toward his throat. Reacting on instinct, Ki pulled to the side. Too bad his undeveloped body was no match for the grown male trying to kill him. Just as the razor-sharp blade made its way down to slice him again, a surge of power from Grirryrth infused Ki's muscles. Now he had the strength to fling the male over his head. The attacker landed with a loud thud in front of him in a cloud of dirt and grass.

The mature Zerin male twisted to his feet and waved a broadsword in Ki's direction. "You're gonna die, *abomination*." The pockmarked face of his adversary hardened as he raised the weapon above his head and swung it toward Ki's skull.

Ki dodged the killing blow but didn't move fast enough to avoid it completely. Fire and ice exploded across his face as the sharp steel sliced his skin from the top of his forehead, skipping his left eye as it dug across his cheek. Blood streamed into his eyes; he wiped the burning liquid away with the back of his hands.

Enough! Grirryrth blasted a charge of power into the battle suit.

The extra boost gave Ki the strength he needed to throw a punch at the male's head. The blow was hard enough to pop it off his neck. Shocked and disgust warred within Ki as he watched the head of his attacker bounce and rolled away. Absorbed in the sight, the brutal pain of his wound faded slightly.

That was the last of this bunch. Time for us to leave, hatchling, his inner companion declared. *I will fly us far away from here. Once we find a suitable place, we will coordinate our next move.*

Jolted back to reality, Ki went over to the body of his father and collapsed to his knees. He leaned down to hug his father's cool neck for the last time. "But we can't leave them like this!" Fresh grief welled as he held on to his sire. "We have to take care of them!" He refused to look at the wreckage of his beautiful mother.

Rest, little hatchling. The dragon's deep voice soothed Ki's raw, ragged emotions. *I will take care of everything.*

Ki sat back on his heels. With a moan, he dragged a sleeve across the river of tears that mixed with the steady metallic taste of blood from his face wound. He squeezed his eyes shut with a twisted grimace. Unable to speak, he gave a nod. With a weary heart, he opened his eyes and stood. With trembling steps, he backed away, not losing sight of his dead parents.

Ki experienced once again the bone-shattering transformation as his body changed from his Zerin form into the massive bulk of his dragon companion. Settling in the back of the dragon's mind, he wallowed in his grief, too wounded to care what happened next.

He watched with mind-numbed interest as Grirryrth detonated the smoldering remains of his home.

All too soon, the bodies of his family and the last attacker disappeared in a white-hot inferno.

Before the flame died, Grirryrth spread his bladed wings. The thick skin scooped the dry air as they fanned to lift the large body into the sky to head away from the civilized section of the mining colony.

With detached despair, Ki watched as Grirryrth's flight took them away in the frigid night air from the only home he'd ever known. He was responsible for everything that happened that night. To honor his family, he vowed he would keep the deep scar across his face and go against the Zerin custom of wearing his semi-sentient hair long. He'd endure the pain of getting it cut... proudly wearing the shame for all to see.

Ki made another vow. While he'd honor his father's request to protect Grirryrth, he wasn't going to let his selfish character flaw pass to another generation. He'd never claim his TrueBond and father children. It was far better the Crart heritage died out when he did.

Chancellor U'unk

Chancellor's Palace, present day

The Chancellor of the Federation Consortium, Shon U'unk, prided himself on being a pragmatic, unemotional individual. Emotions were for the weak and ignorant, and he was neither. Surprisingly, the last visit with his captive twin unnerved him. To combat the swell of unknown frustrations, he went to his "playroom" to visit a female Runihura he held captive. There he used his favorite whip until the fog in his mind cleared, which allowed him to take a cleansing breath of her sweet blood, keeping his mind from reverting into chaos. With a frown, he wiped the silver-laced blood from his hands on a cleansing cloth and stepped back to admire the ragged welts on her midnight-colored body. Satisfied he'd accomplished his goal, he sent a command to his personal equerry, Fritjof, to clean her up and place her in a healing pod. Without waiting for his subordinate, he headed to his personal quarters on another part of the palace in the space station.

Although U'unk wasn't one to second-guess his decisions, he had to consider he'd been using his prisoner a bit too harsh. The Runihura female's responses had been nonexistent and her blank stare only infuriated him. It was past time to replace her or leave her alone long enough for her to heal. He would have to contemplate that decision.

Entering his personal suite, he ignored the opulent surroundings, tossed the soaked towel onto a nearby table, and headed for the shower. Once under the multi-layered fountainheads, he let the hot water rinse the blood and grime from his body to swirl down the drain. He tilted his bald head and allowed the soothing spray to trickle over his face and took in two gulps of the refreshing liquid before he straightened. He blanked his mind before he waved the cleansing water off and stepped out into the swirl of steamed air.

Walking into his sleeping chamber, U'unk allowed his body to dry without using a cloth or the full body dryer. Placing a palm on the ID indentation to open his closet, he pulled out a long burgundy robe. With automatic movements, he slipped his arms through smooth Wyht silk before tying the front with the belt.

Just as he was about to call for food, a chime announced a message. He frowned. Only a handful of allies knew that particular channel.

"Go." He blinked the request in his personal ODVU.

A 3D image appeared of an unknown human woman who glared at him. She was attractive enough for a human, with short reddish-brown hair and a lush bust line in a compact body. Her eyes were unusual, however. Instead of the normal single-colored irises of a human, hers were white with a vertical, red slit in the middle.

Ah, maybe a unique candidate to replace the broken Runihura female.

U'unk crossed his arms. "Who the *fruk* do you think you are, calling me on this frequency?"

"Now, Shon," admonished the female. Her deep tone sounded peculiar coming from a female. "Is that any way to greet a longtime friend and ally?" She grabbed her full breasts and mashed them together before flashing a lascivious grin. "Even if my outer body is a bit, ah, different, than when we first did business together."

"You have five nanoseconds to get to the point before I terminate not only this communication but you for using it in the first place."

"Oh, I do love it when you threaten me," the female purred.

What kind of game was she playing? Several possibilities ran through his mind before she spoke.

"So tell me, how's Lok doing?"

It had been a long time since someone made U'unk speechless. No one alive knew anything about his twin...except the only being in the galaxy left alive who'd helped incarcerate the pest. "Who are you?" A new suspicion formed.

The female snorted in a contemptuous tone no one used at him and lived. She dropped the hold on her chest. "You know exactly who I am." The red slit in her eyes widened as a sneer crossed her full lips. It made her attractive features twist into something ugly.

"Maynwaring?" But, how could this be? The Dread Pirate was a prisoner in his globe, tucked away in his fortress on FiPan. U'unk was quite aware of how safe the pirate was, he'd tried to have him eliminated enough times.

"Yay, give baldy credit where credit is due." Maynwaring clapped her palms together.

"How did you end up in a human woman's body?" When confronted by the impossible, it was always best to open one's mind before proceeding. Maynwaring being loose in an organic body was not good.

Especially for U'unk.

"That's not important," she retorted. She put hands on her slim hips and widened her stance like a male. "I have some information you need to know concerning the coup of the Federation Consortium you've got going." She leaned forward from the waist. "And if you don't do exactly what I say, you *are* going to lose everything."

Sherri

Aboard the AI spaceship "Elemi" on the way to Earth... present day

Being possessed sucked.

Yep, she, Sherrilyn Marie Cantor, was possessed—like "demon taking over your body" type of possessed. Instead of housing a spitting-pea-soup demon, Sherri endured an unwanted galactic gangster fighting for domination of her body and mind. From the moment the bubble housing the Dread Pirate Maynwaring popped over her face and his essence entered her, she'd been fighting for control. So far she'd kept a tight lid on things, but the whole situation was turning out to be a huge pain in the ass.

But, bright side, she had help from her Zerin shipmate, Ki. He'd taught her how to access the memories of her unwanted guest while at the same time keeping him locked away. Jeez, the spirit called himself Dread Pirate. What kind of name was that? Apparently, that wasn't his original name, but something he'd adopted after hearing the story of *The Princess Bride* from a human slave. He'd become so enamored of the dread pirate character he changed his title.

What a snowflake.

What'sss a sssnowflake, human? He asked it in his normal, hissy tone.

How a disembodied entity had a tone was a mystery to her. He sounded like a snake with a speech impediment. She created a visual of sticking his stupid forked tongue between his teeth and clamping his mouth shut then taping it closed. And, if he called her *human* in that derogatory manner one more time....

Ki's training kicked in. Instead of imagining the pain she'd rather give, she created a dark, dank pit to throw his happy ass in.

No...no, don't sssnd me there again!

Sherri imagined throwing his bright orb down a bottomless cavern before rolling an avalanche of sharp, heavy rocks to cover the hole. Dust billowed up and down before it settled in a thick layer to create a mountain to contain him. Then she pictured the mountain folding upon itself, repeatedly, until it was a speck of light flashing out of her thoughts.

Unfortunately, this exercise never held him for long. One minute he'd be gone (treasured silence), and the next, he'd be right back butting in and making snarky comments every chance he got. You'd think he'd be smart enough to keep his mouth shut so she didn't know he was there.

Whoa...where'd that creepy idea come from? Sometimes the hair on the back of her neck broke out in chill bumps as if someone looked over her shoulder. What if...what if she wasn't aware when he wormed his way out? Was he spying on private intimate things she was obsessed with...like say, a certain tall, well-built, sexy-as-sin Zerin named Ki...

Damn it! She shook her head to get rid of that image. She didn't trust people outside of her body, much less the asshole inside. Only constant vigilance on her part would keep the alien in the hole she'd put it in. *Shit*, no wonder she was tired all the time.

Sherri sat with her feet over the side of the comfortable bed she'd slept in. She had to admit, she was happy enough with the accommodations aboard the organic AI ship called "Elemi." Still, she could do without the snarky attitude the female contraption gave her all the time. The sleek 11-15 ship apparently came with a load of baggage, and not the kind Sherri liked to use on vacations.

Her friend Lora had tried to warn her.

Once assigned to a particular male, Elemi latched on to him like a jealous lover.

Lora said Elemi barely tolerated her when she'd been on board and would ignore any request she made. Only when D'zia was in the room would the ship talk to her in a semi-polite manner.

At first, Sherri thought Lora was kidding. Who's to say her friend hadn't suffered a weird personality shift when she changed from a human to a Zerin?

Humph, it didn't take long for the crazy ship to talk to Ki in a sultry, sexy voice that made Sherri's eyeballs pound in frustration. Not that she was jealous or anything, she hardly knew the man...er, male...um, alien. Whatever.

"Oh, is her highness finally going to get up?"

And cue in the wonderful wake-up call from the bitchress herself. Great, things were looking up. One thing Sherri learned on the trip was nothing pissed Elemi off more than being ignored. So, what did Sherri do? Yep, every chance she got, she pretended Elemi didn't exist.

Sherri surveyed the room she slept in. It might be small, but it had everything she needed during the journey. She had a comfortable bed and a nice bathroom, complete with a tub and shower that used actual water. She could program any clothes she wanted, provided by a replicator available in a hidden compartment in the wall. She even had a small desk with an inboard computer screen that floated above the surface.

"You're not going to wear that...are you?" The condescending tone from Elemi was awfully thick that morning.

Sherri gritted her back teeth and kept quiet. She'd pulled out a pair of skinny blue jeans and a soft pullover sweater in a swirl of fall colors. A low-heeled pair of faux-leather brown boots completed the outfit. A tunic over billowy leggings might be the preferred dress aboard the *StarChance*, but she was happy to be back in normal clothes.

Besides, it'd be a cold day in hell if she let a bossy ship tell her what she could and couldn't wear. Once she learned how to program the replicator, her wardrobe decisions were all hers. With a critical eye at the vid mirror in the bathroom, Sherri fluffed her short auburn hair, now growing out of the edgy bob she normally kept. She smoothed her wispy bangs. First chance she got, she'd figure out how to get a touch-up.

Sherri studied her reflection. Even without her normal makeup, her image remained the same, no different from when she'd left Earth. The edgy bob of her dark reddish-brown hair framed her brown eyes, surrounding her long mink lashes and trimmed eyebrows. A tan long since faded had left her skin lighter than before. She chuckled wistfully. It was a little hard to bask under the sun on a spaceship. Her disgruntled semi-frown caught her eye. Damn mouth had always gotten her into trouble. The cupid bow of her lips gave a lush appearance that most men fixated on, that is, until some jerk pushed her to the limit. Then her mouth became a weapon to cut them down. She had a hard time suffering fools and had no problem verbally eviscerating those who deserved it.

Even as a young child, she'd received deferential treatment because she was pretty, but she didn't care how she looked; she'd never counted on her physical appearance to get by. The only thing to rely on was hard work and goals kept in focus. Success didn't become a reality through magic or wishful thinking.

She wasn't going to get anything handed to her, it was up to her to get what she wanted. Abandoned as a small child by her alcoholic father after her mother's death, Sherri shuffled through too many foster homes to count. Instead of wallowing in her misfortune, she worked hard to gain a full scholarship to college. Once she graduated *summa cum laude*, she received her doctorate in business management. Then, she and her college roommate, Natalie, created an app that merged Mac and Windows programs to be used on either system. With the money from that program, she and her partner developed another app that combined all rewards cards into one QR-Quick Response code. Almost overnight, Sherri went from being a penniless orphan to someone worth millions.

Just her luck, Natalie embezzled from the company and instigated a hostile takeover. At the same time, she had evidence planted against Sherrilyn to frame her for the federal offense.

Arrested, charged in an airtight case, and facing up to 20 years in maximum prison, Sherrilyn became desperate. When the Zerins offered the prospect of attending the Exchange, she didn't think twice and left Earth behind.

As she took one last glance in the 3D mirror, Sherri's frown deepened. While she didn't regret her decision to leave home, she wished things would have turned out the way the Zerins had promised. While she might still appear the same, inside she was someone, or rather, *something* different because of the pirate in her noggin. Finding a mate, alien or otherwise, was the last thing she needed.

"No, really." The female voice of the ship yapped. "You look like a child in those clothes. No one will ever take you seriously."

Sherri's mouth quirked into a slight smile. *Ha!* She'd gotten under Elemi's skin if the ship resorted to lame insults. Better slurs had been thrown at her in grade school. The obnoxious AI ship couldn't even begin to upset her.

After leaving the sleeping chamber, she went down the narrow, cool corridor to the dining area. At first, the ship with its dim, narrow interior had made her nervous. The only thing that made it bearable was the warm glow from the pores of the walls, like being wrapped in a friendly cocoon. Now if only that cocoon came with a pleasing personality instead of Elemi's snarky one, life would be pretty damned good right about now.

Being possessed by the pirate notwithstanding.

She stopped in mid-step.

Ki was sitting at a small table used for eating, an empty plate and a hot beverage cup sitting in front of him.

Every time she saw him, her body shot into hyper-drive. Her breath would catch, her nerves strung tight, and she sweated. Hardly attractive.

Ki was in deep discussion with his Zerin friend, D'zia. Next to the light-haired male sat his mate? Girlfriend? Wife?

The Zerins called it a TrueBond. At least that's what her friend Lora—a former human who had been forcibly converted into a Zerin female—told her. She'd met the woman aboard the *StarChance,* when they both left Earth to attend the Exchange to meet an alien soulmate. Yeah well, at least that worked out for Lora.

The holographic images of the two appeared to sit at the same table as Ki. Every time they communicated with the two, she had to remind herself they were thousands of light-years away and not in the same room. The realistic way the Zerins communicated by hologram was far superior to Skype any day.

She made a beeline to the food initiator and programmed a cup of coffee, her mouth watering as she waited for the much-needed shot of caffeine. She glanced at Ki before filling the cup with freshly brewed coffee, the nutty flavor perfuming the air. His steady gaze unsettled her, especially when he was talking to someone else as he watched her.

After a few tense moments, he gave her a nod and turned his attention back to his holographic friend, never breaking their line of conversation.

Sherri gripped the warm coffee cup. The dual navy/hunter-green stare amped her nerves a little tighter. Not one to ignore a challenge, she squared her shoulders and placed the steaming cup of coffee on the table, then sat across from him. He wasn't going to intimidate her, no matter how distracting his gorgeous appearance was. She returned his nod before she took a small sip of the scalding liquid.

His dual-colored eyes widened, showing off the dark navy-and-hunter-green irises that surrounded the green iridescent pupils. Ki resumed his steady regard as he agreed with something D'zia said.

Sitting back in the chair, Sherri took the time to study him as his attention went back to the conversation with the others. *Sigh*, she had to admit; the man...er...male was magnificent. Why was she so drawn to him? For God's sake, he rarely smiled. But she'd always been a sucker for tall men, and Ki fit the bill. His seven-foot frame dwarfed her average five-foot-six. With his height and wide chest, he could satisfy any girl's fantasy.

Masculine, roped muscles were on prominent display in the formfitting clothes. Bulky, yet not so blocky to be offensive. Ki's dark, mahogany hair was shoulder length, with a small braid at his right temple. There the strands had a wave of buttermilk yellow that boasted of his more mature age. The tips of his pointed ears poked through a curtain of thick hair.

His regal nose was that of a conqueror of old, while a black, short-cropped beard and mustache surrounded full, sensuous lips. His deep, rich golden tan skin tone was overlaid with the normal Zerin pearlescent sheen that reflected a rainbow in the low light.

The large, deep scar that bisected his face might have overshadowed his masculine appeal, but instead, it intensified his attractiveness. The gash started at the top of his hairline, passed his left eye, and ended across his cheek to taper off at his jawline, just under his ear. While the facial hair hid some puckered skin, it only covered the tail end of the old wound.

While the pain behind the scar had to have been horrendous, Sherri was proud that he didn't cover it up or have it replaced. The Zerins obviously had an advanced civilization and she didn't doubt he could have had it erased a long time ago. It didn't matter to her why he kept it, she admired him for keeping the memento for whatever reason.

Overall, he was a handsome devil who made her shudder like a preteen in the throes of her first crush. Bad enough she had to ignore her own reaction to him, but with the pirate squatting in her brain, it was a struggle to keep her attraction to the Zerin hidden. The last thing she needed was the annoying pirate in on her secret. She'd never hear the end of it.

"Hey, Sherri!" Lora gushed. She leaned toward her.

How wonderful to see Lora in Earth clothes.

Instead of the Zerin tunic and pants, Lora was sporting a large bright-red sweater over black leggings tucked into black ankle boots. "How's it going with the hitchhiker in your noggin?"

Sherri gave Lora a wide smile at her apt description. "Just great! How's it going being an alien?"

Lora whooped. "Ha! You only wish you had it as good as me." Her wide grin flashed fangs when a happy expression lit her face.

No doubt about Lora's contentment, her friend's body thrummed in joy with every movement.

Her friend had gone from being a human to becoming a Zerin alien due to the diabolical machinations of a crazy alien Erkek scientist. When Sherri first met her, Lora had been a pretty, full-figured woman with dark-blonde hair. Now her tresses were mixed with the soft-brown shade the same color as D'zia's, and reached the top of her butt. While Lora's body retained its prior shape, her fawn skin boasted a pearlescent sheen that reflected softly in the light. Her hands had also changed, from a normal human's four fingers and a thumb to Zerin three fingers, all the same length.

Lora's cheekbones retained their scattering of freckles but were higher and sharper, and her ears had a slight point at the tip. Her gray eyes were now dual colored with a dark-gray ring surrounded by a lighter-gray color and iridescent dark-green pupils.

The most striking feature was the unusual tattoo that covered the left side of her temple and forehead. It ended just below her cheekbone in a beautiful intricate knot. In the middle of the design, a clear diamond-shaped crystal rested snugly within her skin at the temple.

D'zia frowned as he narrowed his eyes at Sherri.

When it looked like he would argue with her, Lora gave his biceps an open slap. "Oh, leave her alone, you big bully."

D'zia's open mouth cracked Sherri up.

"I didn't say anything!" He whined and rubbed his arm.

"Oh, I didn't hurt you." Lora snorted loudly before she turned to Sherri with a twinkle in her eye. "Holy Shamoka, he's so sensitive."

Lora's mate, D'zia, was a striking, good-looking male. In his formfitting dark-blue pants and shirt, he appeared younger than her impassive companion Ki and his attitude remained open and jocular. He was a half-foot shorter than Ki's seven feet and had light-umber hair intersected with some of Lora's blonde-colored strands. He kept a small, tight braid at his right temple that hung loosely to his waist with a single braid draped behind his pointy ear.

The bright-turquoise colors of his dual irises set him apart from the other Zerins she'd seen. The inner color was a deep blue-green while the outer ring was a shade or two lighter, a perfect contrast to his hunter-green pupils. Their colors contrasted nicely with the iridescent sheen of his dark tan skin.

Fascinating. He had the same intricate tattoo on his face that Lora did, except his was on the right. The marks were an exact mirror image of each other, right down to the clear crystal nestled in the middle of their temples.

Ki returned Lora's snort with manly gusto. "Can we focus here, people?"

"Ki...dog. How's it hangin'?"

The deep, baritone voice that came out of the small, spider-shaped Spybot named JR10 was always a surprise.

He currently perched on D'zia's shoulder, his twelve, spindly legs curled beneath his two-pronged tagmata silver body.

Thankfully, the AI lacked the chelicerae fangs of a normal Earth spider that would have had her skin crawling. The little bot was actually a study in technological wonder even if his personality bordered on the annoying extreme. Which almost made her feel sorry for the younger Zerin.

"It's chillin'." Ki drawled the surprising answer in his slight, accented tone.

Sherri mirrored D'zia's and Lora's open mouths.

JR10, the idiot, laughed so hard he fell off his perch and ended on a table with twitching legs as he snickered.

Jeez, the answer wasn't that funny, just surprising since it came from the stoic Ki. Who knew he had a sense of humor, much less understood what that Earth slang meant and used it as an answer.

"Yo, dude! Yous so crazy!" JR10 straightened and turned his large, multi-faceted eyes to D'zia. "Why do you always insist he has no sense of humor? Bro, there is seriously something wrong with you." He scolded the male with a shake of his bulbous head.

D'zia opened and closed his mouth a couple of times as if he couldn't decide what to say. His wide, dual-colored teal eyes pleaded with Lora.

Fortunately for him, the other Spybot, JR11, spoke up. "JR10! That wasn't nice. You apologize right this instant!" The anthropoid bot in feminine form was a delicate, deep-violet version of JR10 with a soft, breathless voice. While D'zia always had JR10 with him, Lora, in turn, carried JR11 around.

JR10 looked up at D'zia before his bottom abdomen wiggled as he shook his head. "Nah, we're good." A bulbous eye winked at him. "Aren't we, bro?"

D'zia watched the bot going over the hills and valleys of his arm before settling on his shoulder. After a pinch to the bridge of his nose, D'zia turned to Ki with a grimace.

"As I was saying," Ki continued.

Sherri snickered as she took a sip of coffee as he ignored the exchange.

"Elemi has connected with the Armada's main ship and can now transmit..."

CHAPTER TWO

Ki blathered on and on about "wormholes" and "systems" as he laid out their plans for getting to Earth. Then he covered how they would infiltrate the Chancellor's armada, in excruciating detail. Blah, blah, blah...time for Sherri to zone out.

Weariness pulled her down. Why was she so tired all the time? Once her head hit the soft pillow the previous night, she didn't wake until long past the morning schedule. Sherri studied the chronological calculator on the 3D floating computer screen Ki used and subtracted the number of hours she had slept. She chewed her bottom lip. Over nine hours?

She'd never slept more than six hours at a time in her life. That could be the reason why her responses were sluggish. Her brain might as well be stuffed with cotton for all the good it did her. She inhaled the smoky scent of her hot, nutty beverage and sipped. Maybe its tart taste would help since it was hard to concentrate on the conversation between Ki and the holograms of D'zia and Lora.

"So, how long will it take for you to reach Earth once Elemi creates the safest wormhole?" D'zia asked with his arm around Lora's shoulder. The two of them were on their way to Zerin while Sherri and Ki sped to prevent Chancellor U'unk from reaching Earth.

Sherri's face heated at the sight of Lora and D'zia in a relaxed snuggle. While she was secretly obsessed with Ki, she had a hard time envisioning actually going beyond the friend stage. He was so far out of her league she wouldn't know where to begin to make romantic moves on him.

That made her chuckle in her cup. As the hot liquid passed her lips, the jolt of caffeine made her hum in pleasure and gave her the courage to be honest with herself. For the first time in her life, she was insecure around a man who appealed to her. With her looks, intelligence and accumulated wealth, she'd never had to work hard to attract a man. Normally, she had to fight them off. Another chuckle. Some would say it served her right.

"The trip will be instantaneous," Ki replied to D'zia's question. "Once we're in orbit around Jupiter's largest moon, Ganymede, we'll do some reconnaissance on Earth. Just to make sure none of the Chancellor's forces have made contact."

Yum, the way his fabulous chest rose and fell with each breath. And, *ooh*, the way his body responded; from those full lips rolling around accented words to the controlled tension of his compact body. The more she observed, the more heated she got until her core melted in yearning.

Hoo-boy, knock it off and get hold of yourself.

A pinching, nagging sensation started at the base of her neck. Immediately she unfocused her eyes and went internal to confront her unwanted passenger. That irritating alien was struggling to get free from the constraints she'd put him in.

Oh, no, you don't, buddy! She visualized plunging his outline into a crystalized prison, trapping him inside before throwing it into a vat of thick tar. With smug satisfaction, she watched as the sparkling prison sank out of sight with Maynwaring in it.

There, that should hold him for a while.

It took a few moments to realize the dead silence in the room was because of her. Her face heated as she sheepishly returned their gazes. She shrugged. "What? Asshole was trying to get out."

Ki's face darkened.

Hopefully his anger was for the pirate and not directed at her.

Ki

Every muscle in Ki's body stilled when he watched Sherri struggle with that damn parasite inside of her. As a male of action it was hard to sit back and not be able to help her. What if there wasn't a *Goddess-damned* thing he *could* do to help her?

"Anyway." D'zia's voice brought him back to the conversation. "If the Chancellor hasn't approached Earth yet, what do you plan to do?"

"I've done some research on the planet and have decided it would be best to contact the heads of the major countries covertly. We will stress to them the danger their planet is in and I'm sure they'll welcome our help." Ki nodded, pleased with his logical approach.

Lora and Sherri snorted simultaneously.

Paxt! What was that for? Not only the mirrored effect but also the sincere, flat sound that came from such delicate females.

D'zia stared at Lora with his mouth open. "Why'd you do that?"

Lora's bark of laughter was as deep as her snort. "You've got to be kidding. Right?"

Sherri nodded with a smirk on her luscious mouth. "Have you met any humans besides those who agreed to attend your Exchange?"

Ki shook his head at the same time D'zia did.

"No." D'zia spoke first. "Why would we?"

Ki clarified what his friend said. "Earth has been classified as a sacred preserve and contact with the indigenous species had been strictly monitored." He sat back and crossed his leg over the opposite thigh. "It's only since your population has tripled that we can offer the human females a chance to join the Exchange." He raised an eyebrow. "Now those females have a chance at a better life within the nine systems of the Federation Consortium."

"Wow, that's awfully big of you." Lora crossed her arms over her chest. "Let's discuss how well that's turned out for me, Sherri, Aimee, and some of our friends from the *StarChance*. I sure hope being kidnapped and auctioned off at the pleasure markets didn't fit into your misguided notion, did it?"

Ki's lips thinned as a flush crossed D'zia's cheeks. "Probably not. But even so, I don't understand your reaction to my statement of contacting the Earth's governments to warn them about the coming invasion."

Sherri sighed. "Obviously you've never had to deal with a xenophobic species like humans."

Ki frowned and scratched his beard. What was she trying to tell them? His plan was logical and well-planned. There wasn't any reason for it not to work.

"Look," Lora chimed in. "The human race is barely evolved compared to your advanced systems. The people currently in charge of our major governments are greedy, corrupt, and prejudiced to the extreme. They can't work together, much less be receptive to having some alien come in and tell them what to do."

"We're not going to tell them what to do." D'zia shifted with a frown.

"Right." Sherri came back with a sarcastic retort.

When she sat up, her booted foot accidentally touched his. At least Ki assumed it was an accident. Even with the layers of covering over their skin, her nearness sent his body into lust drive. He took in a deep breath and enjoyed her unique citrus sweetness that settled low in his groin.

She is so delicious. Grirryrth, his symbiont dragon crooned. *We must mate with her soon and start the TrueBond process.*

Sherri is not my TrueBond. Ki internally argued with a dry mouth. *We have to focus on the problem at hand and not worry about some female.*

Hatchling, you have a lot to learn. Grirryrth chuckled as his presence faded into the background.

"It's going to be hard to save humans from themselves."

Sherri's words interrupted his continuing argument with Grirryrth.

"It'd be a lot like expecting toddlers to behave like adults. Not going to happen."

Ki frowned. This information was hard to believe. "And just how do you propose it should be handled?"

Sherri opened her mouth but Lora spoke first with her nose in the air. "First of all, let's get that little bit of bass out of your tone, mister." She wagged at forefinger at him to emphasize her point.

"You go, girl!" JR10 jumped up and down as if to encourage Lora's statement. "Let these arrogant Zerins know who is who."

Ki wanted to defend himself but Lora continued.

"Probably the same way the Chancellor plans to." Lora folded her fingers together. "Come in with a show of force and don't give them an option."

Confused, Ki looked at Sherri for confirmation.

She nodded sharply, as her short, auburn hair swayed across her jaw.

"I don't understand." D'zia scrunched up his face. "How can a people as volatile as you describe be running a planet?"

Both females laughed in unison.

"Earth is under the thumb of an extreme patriarchal society and has been for thousands of years." Sherri raised her palms and nodded. "Why do you think so many human women are eager to leave and join your Exchange? Many of us suffered oppression but also abuse and neglect. Plus, we grow up believing we are inferior to our male counterparts in every way."

Ki blinked in shock. How could any advanced society treat their citizens that way? He must have asked that question aloud because Sherri answered.

"That's why Lora said what she did. The current heads of government will never willingly give up any power base they have, not even to save themselves."

Ki raised his brows at D'zia whose eyes widened. Obviously he wasn't the only one shocked at what the females said. After a few moments of consideration, Ki made a proposal. "How about we go into a closed session of your United Nations and lay out the situation to them?" He ignored the disbelieving grunts from the females and continued. "And see how they react when we prove to them the danger they're facing. We'll outline a way to protect the planet from the oncoming invasion and open lines of trade between us."

"You mean women?" A knowing smile creased Lora's lips.

D'zia rubbed the end of his warrior braid as he answered. "Among other things."

"How will that affect the protected status of Earth?" Sherri asked a pointed question. "Will that change?"

"Normally it would take a vote among the nine systems to change the status on any preserve like Earth. Unfortunately, we don't have the luxury of time before the invasion happens. We have to enact desperate measures to save your planet." Ki kept his tone even and factual.

D'zia picked up the narrative. "However, my cousin Prince Qay has provided the Zerin council with the evidence needed on the Chancellor's activities. Once their approval is finalized, a committee will form to investigate all he's been involved in." In a smooth move, he pulled Lora's chair closer to him.

"That'll take years!" Sherri's jaw gaped with raised eyebrows toward Ki.

"Yes, that's possible." Ki dropped his leg to the floor and leaned forward. He clasped his fingers together. "But everything we've done has been recorded and filed with the proper authorities. Including how the Chancellor abducted you, Aimee, and Lora. We also suspect he has ties with the terrorist faction called the 'Warriors of Light'. We believe he's provided them with alien weapons from Earth called guns. The projectiles happen to be poisonous to Zerin physiology." He gave a nod to D'zia. "Add to that, the Erkek scientist you're taking to Zerin to be interrogated. That should give us plenty of evidence for the Council."

It was important he convince the others things were under control. None of them could afford to get discouraged at this late date. The Earth problem had to be handled with a united front before the Chancellor arrived. D'zia's job was to soothe Lora's concerns on their way back to Zerin. In the meantime, he'd work through Sherri's worries on their way to Earth.

A frown pulled his lips down. From what the females were telling him, dealing with Earth people wasn't going to be as easy as he first assumed. Too bad it wasn't an option to leave the humans to their own fate. A quick glance at Sherri reminded him he couldn't let that happen. His gut burned. That decision had nothing to do with the need in the galaxy for human women as much as the female next to him. Ki's jaw clenched at the oncoming headache.

Sherri's plump lips pressed before she answered. "Okay. We'll try it your way first."

She and Lora shared a look that Ki had trouble interpreting.

"But be prepared to change tactics at a moment's notice."

Ki's smile quirked. "If you think it might come to that." He slid a glance at D'zia. "When you contact Qay, give him a copy of this conversation. Make sure he understands we'll need his support if we have to go in a little harder than anticipated."

D'zia tilted his head and opened his mouth but Elemi's shrill scream interrupted.

"EEK! HELP! There's a Disintegration cannon locked on me! They're going to blast my beautiful body!"

Chancellor U'unk

"Our ships are in place and we have the target in sight." The morning after U'unk met with the new Dread Pirate, Counter-Aide Breccan smugly informed him of the status of the Warriors of Light. He boasted how he and his resistance group found the coveted 11-15 ship that the fools on Naraka base lost. Breccan was the aide to Councilman Aine on Zerin, one of the many sycophants U'unk had put in place decades ago.

"Very good." The Chancellor nodded. Nice to know the information Maynwaring had given him about the ship and how to track it was accurate. "Take the ship back to the Naraka base for refurbishing and dispose of those who stole her."

The 3-D virtual image of the subordinate was smug as his leer widened. "Acknowledged. I assure you, we will have it in our possession within the next several clicks. I have our best male taking the lead, and with him in charge, our success is all but assured."

U'unk studied the male as he talked. The Counter-Aide's nondescript appearance had been an asset to U'unk's underground efforts.

The aide gathered sensitive information continually from the head council member, Aine. Breccan, a middle-aged Zerin, who was neither handsome nor homely, a useful tool in his blandness. He was someone easily overlooked by others.

U'unk had been clever enough to recognize the burning ambition of the younger aide at an early stage and covertly helped Breccan gain authority within the Zerin governing body. Once in place, he became a perfect spy on the council. As a reward, U'unk encouraged and funded the underground "resistance" group Breccan founded, the Warriors of Light, better known as "WOL."

Too bad the group's earlier attempt at killing Prince Qay's human True-Bond hadn't succeeded. The idiot prince jumped in the way of the human weapon and took the poisonous alien projectile for himself. Even that only caused the royal brat to be laid up for a few days before he enjoyed a full recovery. Which was annoying. It would have been much easier if both Qay and his father had died.

No matter, plans were in motion and the galaxy would soon be U'unk's.

"Report as soon as it is done." U'unk demanded as he blinked the virtual communication closed.

He sat in his massive chair in his private sanctum, deep within the bowels of the Chancellor's Palace on the space station orbiting the Zerin home-world.

He moved to open another folder within his ocular video display unit. A chime pinged an alert that his equerry, Fritjof, was requesting attention.

"I stated I didn't want to be disturbed." U'unk purposefully kept his tone even and bland. No need to show irritation, best to avoid emotions with those who worked for him.

"Yes, sire," the Erkek's simpering, high-pitched voice, answered. "But the Consortium's special Triad Council is here to see you."

An unfamiliar weight squeezed his chest. Why would the Triad be there without prior communication? Heat crept up his neck. How dare they come without warning?

"Show them to my office and offer them nourishment. Assure them I will join them momentarily." He closed the channel before he heard Fritjof's response.

U'unk settled into the formfitting seat with his fingertips interlaced underneath his chin, lost in thought. The special council only formed in extreme cases. The trio was an investigating committee dedicated to uncovering corruption in the highest levels of the democratic body. *Hmm*, which scheme might have implicated him? Forget it, second-guessing their intent was a waste of time.

With even strides, he entered his official office. The deep burgundy of the heavy robes barely moved as he stalked. "My apologies for keeping you waiting at your unexpected visit." He kept his voice cool as he made his way toward his dark leather chair and sat. He twitched his nose in distaste at the elusive scent of otherworldliness they brought into his chamber. "If I'd known we were meeting today, I would have had everything ready for you."

"No need for the passive-aggressive attitude, Shon," Councilman Aine admonished. The elderly Zerin's dark hair was more yellow with age than the black of his youth. A simple braid trailed down his back. The butterscotch of age in his warrior braid remained tucked behind his ear as was proper. The elder male's light dual-colored moss- and fern-green eyes were alert and piercing, in sharp contrast to his elderly status. His body may have shrunken with advanced years, but he sat with his back ramrod straight in his simple black, council robe over his plain gray tunic and pants.

U'unk gave a nod of acknowledgment while seething inside. Getting rid of the sanctimonious politician would be one of the first things on his agenda when he eliminated the Consortium.

"However, we extend our apologies for showing up unexpectedly." The second member of the Triad spoke in melodious tones. An Onoel female from the planet Vachurn, Kasdeja was a winged humanoid covered in light-blue and orange feathers. Her species was ethereal and beautiful beyond description, even one as old as the female in front of him.

Since he could not see her expansive wingspan, she must have them hidden within the natural pouch at her back.

She wore a diaphanous gown in the sheer colors of her down-covered form. The garment gave the illusion of concealing her feminine parts while allowing an alluring tease of temptation.

"Never mind the *dlofokyo* manners, for Goddess' sake!" The third Triad member grumbled as he folded his massive onyx arms over his dark, naked chest. "We're here to look into the allegations of one of your operatives working with the Friebbigh. It seems they are illegally transporting human women from Earth to the slave outposts on FiPan."

Tuhon was the youngest of the Triad, but still hundreds of years older than U'unk. The male was a Runihura, well over eight feet tall. His muscled physique covered skin so dark, several colors of the spectrum reflected with each movement. The straight, platinum hair reached to the middle of his back and was kept in place with a thin silver circlet around his forehead. Blue neon eyes were without iris or pupils, but the species' eyesight was without equal. Their range of sight remained legendary among the known star systems. The male had his right ankle resting on top of his wide left thigh. The black-clad material of his thick leather boots reached above his knees.

U'unk sat back and made sure he displayed an indifferent appearance. "Please elaborate." A twitch of his lips covered the hard swallow he used to slow his heart and even out his erratic breathing. It was imperative to show a calm he was far from feeling. With a light touch, he rested the tips of his fingers under his chin—just to show he was thoughtful and contemplative.

Aine cleared his throat, seemingly aware of the tension climbing in the room. With a steady stare, he pulled a holosphere crystal out of the depths of his robe and activated the vid.

The image of the Erkek scientist, Dr. Knum'Nz appeared.

"Do you have knowledge of this individual?" The leader of the Triad asked in a reasonable tone.

U'unk frowned as he pretended to study the visual. His heart gave a loud thump before he regained control. How did these buffoons get a holovid of the Erkek? He'd eliminated every mention of the corrupt scientist, visual or otherwise, within the Consortium records. With deliberate movements, he took his gaze off the picture and considered each Triad member with careful, concise movements. "No, I'm afraid I do not."

Tuhon's snort was rude.

U'unk refused to allow his facial features to show annoyance. "Why do you disbelieve what I say?" He directed the question to the big male with a raised eyebrow.

"In the last known record we have of him, he worked for the Consortium medicinal division, several decades ago. Someone has tampered with his profile, making it look like he never existed. It took expert investigators a painstakingly long time to uncover what little information remains available to us." The Runihura male uncrossed his arms to rest on his thighs.

U'unk tilted his head to show confusion. "I fail to understand why that would bring you to me."

"Those records indicate Dr. Knum'Nz reported directly to you." Kasdeja's delicate hand gestured in waves when she spoke, as was normal for the Onoel. "We are hoping you would be able to tell us what you know about his work."

U'unk raised and lowered his shoulders with a blank stare. "I'm afraid my answer is still the same. I do not know him." How could they possibly get a vid of the Erkek, much less connect U'unk's past dealings with the *gnotdile*?

"What about this female?" Aine shut down the holovid of Knum'Nz. With a flick of a finger, a visual of a Zerin female, Aja, shone in 3D. She had been one of his covert operatives. That is, until he broke her neck with his bare hands. "This is, or rather she claimed to be, Aja-ne L'len R'oxk. Actually, her real name was Al'ura R'oxk Naim. What do you know about her?"

An unexpected chill raced down his spine. Once again, U'unk shook his head in denial. "I'm afraid I'm at a loss. I have no idea who she is." He leveled a steady gaze between the three. "Wait, you said, 'was.' Is she deceased?"

Kasdeja twittered in distress, her fingers waving and weaving as she spoke. "Yes, the poor dear. They found her body abandoned in a most disreputable place. The cause of death has been labeled undetermined."

U'unk gave a convincing frown. "What a shame." Tight muscles relaxed. "She appears to have been a lovely female." The unbidden image of him snapping her neck loosened the tension in his body.

"She was a traitor to the Zerin people." Aine's tone was terse.

"Oh, how so?" U'unk raised the opposite eyebrow and leaned forward to show his eagerness in the conversation.

"This female was instrumental in the kidnapping and selling of human women from the merchant ship, the *StarChance,* to the Friebbigh."

"Really? How unfortunate." U'unk leaned back and twined his fingers together over his flat belly. "And how could she accomplish that? Don't tell me she was able to board the vessel, take any humans she wanted before leaving without anyone being alerted?" He gave a small *tsk* with a shake of his head. "One might logically conclude the security on that ship must have been less than standard."

"Actually, she was one of the crew." Tuhon lowered his leg and leaned forward to rest his forearms on his thighs. His neon-blue eyes blazed. "Apparently she'd been able to confiscate more than one shipment of humans for the slave trade."

"By the Sacred Goddess." U'unk visibly shook to show sympathy. "Those poor females. Is anything being done to recover them?"

"Yes, yes." Kasdeja's hands fluttered. "All is being done to find those poor souls. But what we need to know from you, Chancellor U'unk, is your relationship with the deceased female."

"Me?" U'unk raised both eyebrows. "I assure you, I've never met the female." He tilted his head slightly in the holovid's direction. "Why would you think I have?"

"Right now it is important to delve into this incident from all aspects." Aine's answer was vague. "However, it is our duty to follow any and all leads when treason is involved." The elderly statesman leaned back, his billowing black robe settling around him.

"Quite right," the Chancellor agreed. "It seems you should be investigating the crew of the *StarChance* instead of coming here uninvited to see me." He let anger bleed through his tone. "I assume there is nothing substantial to confront me with, so I believe it is time to end this meeting." He stood.

"Look, U'unk..." Tuhon began before Aine waved a hand in his direction.

The three stood while facing the Chancellor with intense stares of their own.

"We appreciate your time, Chancellor." Aine gave a small bow of respect, which the others echoed.

In unison, they turned to leave.

"Be assured." U'unk cleared his throat. "If there is anything you need from my office, do not hesitate to contact my equerry, Fritjof. He will be more than happy to assist you."

"Thank you, Chancellor," Kasdeja replied in a singsong voice, her waving motions subdued. "We will be in touch as is appropriate."

U'unk stared at the doorway long after the doors closed behind them. He contemplated his next move. The bitter taste of urgency coated his tongue.

After carefully analyzing various scenarios, it became clear it was time for personal action. It seemed it was too late to rely on others to do what was necessary.

"Fritjof," he barked to the room's internal communication. "Ready my personal ship." The doorway to his office opened as the Erkek entered and stopped.

The putrid mixture of his natural body orders added to the clash of colors of his willowy skin in the harsh light of the room. A trace of maliciousness shone out of the small triangles of his orange pupils nestled in a sea of blackness.

The fool at least lowered into a respectable bow.

"Yes, sire." The insubordinate spoke to the floor. "Any other instructions you wish to impart?"

U'unk ignored the simpleton's blatant emotions. He gathered several computer crystals with the vital information he'd need to proceed with his long-term goals. He called up a program in his ODVU and activated the elimination virus he'd created to wipe the computer system clean. A quick glance around the room and he was satisfied he would leave nothing for others to use against him.

However, two problems needed immediate attention. One, he would see to personally, but the other he'd give to the semi-competent equerry. The fool was more than capable of disposing that loose end.

"Yes." He towered in front of the prone Erkek. "Dispose of the Runihura female currently undergoing reconstructive surgery in the medipod." He nudged his employee with a steel-booted toe. "Let no one see you do this. Understand?"

Fritjof nodded his green-and-orange mottled bald head. "Yes sire, I understand perfectly. Your will be done."

Satisfied the Erkek would do as he was told, U'unk left the room without giving the simpering idiot another thought. The Chancellor lengthened his strides to the inner bowels of the space station, down to an area long forgotten except by him. Here the luxurious rooms and hallways gave way to an appearance of a natural planetary cave, complete with dirt, insects, and a stale musty odor. U'unk came to a metallic door at the end of the short corridor that only he used.

His prize captive was inside. His twin, T'terlok.

U'unk had made sure time forgot the male when he'd had him erased from Zerin records. He waved a hand across the scanner on the right side of the heavy door. It opened to let him into the moist, warm air. For the first time in decades, he made sure the doorway stayed open behind him.

"Time to go, Lok." U'unk informed the male lying on the cot with an arm over his eyes and one leg up and bent at the knee.

"Are you going to finally kill me?" Lok's muffled voice rumbled out of a throat rarely used.

"No." U'unk's answer was terse. Maybe later he'd examine why he couldn't bring himself to give them what they both wanted and end his twin's miserable existence. When the time came, he wouldn't hesitate to act. But not until then.

"Get up." U'unk pulled the lean arm away from the dual-emerald eyes he'd coveted his whole life. "We have to leave."

Those green orbs squinted and glared at him. "You're taking me out of here?" Suspicion creased Lok's forehead and tightened his full lips.

"Yes." U'unk let the impatience bleed in his tone as he replied. "We have to go now."

Lok sat up, his long black braid liberally sprinkled with the butterscotch of age pooled on the cot next to him. "And you're not taking me out to kill me?" Those knowing eyes narrowed.

"I already told you, it's not your time to die just yet." The fool had to get up. They had to leave before the Triad learned of his plans. By his calculations, they had a narrow space of time before his activities were either monitored or restricted.

The other male slowly moved his thin frame from the small cot. It was possible he moved thus because of pain or age, or maybe he didn't trust U'unk.

Smart male...his twin wasn't stupid. He used to be a very trusting individual. It had been a flaw U'unk made sure he took care of.

"Where are we going?" Lok stood straight and stared his brother in the eye. "And why the urgency?"

U'unk allowed a small smile as he grabbed his twin's elbow. "Does it really matter?"

Lok stumbled. "I guess not." With a jerk, he pulled his elbow out of U'unk's grip as if he didn't want physical contact between them.

That was appropriate as far as U'unk was concerned. He himself loathed physical contact with others unless he initiated it during sexual activity. Touching his twin was the last thing he wanted to do.

They made it in record time to his waiting vessel. After they entered the small space jumper, U'unk made a split decision. He gestured to the chair next to him. He'd allow his twin to sit in the copilot's seat instead of putting him in the holding cell.

With a disbelieving stare, Lok flopped into the offered seat without a word.

U'unk glanced at his brother after entering the needed coordinates. "Ready for a field trip?" For once, the smile he gave his brother was naturally warm.

Lok continued his silence with a frown and a raised eyebrow.

"Good," U'unk said with his hands on the cold metal of the piloting bar. "Next stop...the barbaric planet Earth. There lies the key I need to destroy the Federation Consortium once and for all."

CHAPTER THREE

Ki

E very nerve in Ki's body stilled before he erupted into motion.

"Elemi, cloaking maneuvers immediately!" he barked. How could anyone catch Elemi off guard?

"Yes, darling!" The breathless voice of Elemi screeched.

The force of the ship as it rolled to the side had Ki gripping the table with tight knuckles. Good to see Sherri did the same.

The cup of dark beverage she'd been drinking flew off and crashed into the nearest wall. It left a starburst of brown liquid with an aromatic, sharp smell.

Sherri squealed and held on.

The holographic images of D'zia and Lora stayed in place as the table appeared to intersect through their torsos. "Get back with us as soon as you can." D'zia waved a hand and their images dissolved.

"Elemi, status report." Ki braced when another quick jerk tried to throw him across the room. "Initiate safety cocoon in the dining prep area for Sherri and me."

Elemi activated transparent safe bubbles that held them in their seats.

He glanced over and made sure Sherri was okay.

With wide eyes, she gave him a curt nod.

"Main engine offline." Elemi's voice regained her normal soft tone. "I have evaded the disintegration array and am currently invisible to them."

"By the father of everything, how did they surprise you?" Ki slammed a fist on the table.

"Unknown." For once, the ship's sultry voice had a pitch of steel. "Running diagnostics as we speak."

As the ship spoke, Ki observed Sherri. He blinked in astonishment.

Instead of the dark brown irises she usually had, her eyes were now white except for the red, thin slit that reached from top to bottom.

The worst was the malicious sneer that crossed her normally plump, tempting lips.

Acting on instinct, he bellowed. "Elemi, contain Sherri until further notice!"

"With pleasure," came the gleeful reply.

"Hey... what do you think you're doing?" Sherri's face became hard as she struggled within the cocoon that held her prisoner. "Let me go!"

"No." He wasn't going to argue with the entity that had taken her over. "Elemi, release me." Now that the ship had stopped its pitch, Ki walked toward the human female. His heart shuddered as her beautiful face twisted into something ugly.

At first, she sneered back before her face relaxed. "Okay, you found me out." A deep voice came out of her delicate mouth. "Now, what?"

"Now, nothing." Ki crossed his arms. "Elemi put her in stasis and restrain her in the lower level." Numb, he watched his female dissolve. He continued to stare at the empty seat long after she was gone. Yes, it was possible Sherri *was* his female. He'd denied that fact for a long time. When he'd first seen her as a captive in Maynwaring's holding cell, he blamed his intense reaction on a long spell of abstinence. It had been an unusual move on the pirate's part, trying to entice him into doing something other than what they initially agreed, using her as bait.

As if a human female could somehow tempt him to go against his moral code.

The slave planet FiPan, three weeks prior

Ki hated FiPan. Just the thought of coming back to this disgusting planet went against every vow he'd ever made to himself. When his friend and prince, Qay, needed his help, he didn't hesitate, even though he had to deal with the lead gangster, Maynwaring. When the negotiations turned sour, the Dread Pirate tried to trap Qay into being indentured to him. Ki would never allow that to happen, so he interceded and took the debt as his own. He'd never let his friend be trapped into doing whatever illegal "task" Maynwaring wanted to be done. Ki had more experience in dealing with the criminal and he had no qualms about doing the pirate's bidding.

Ki concentrated on his surroundings. *Danka shit,* he'd forgotten how depressing this place was. Even so, his recollection didn't come close to the reality surrounding him. The buildings he passed were as gloomy as the heavy air. Most of the structures were only one or two stories high with no visible means of structural support. Broken doors, windows, and roofs did not deter inhabitants from taking possession of the coveted shelters. Eerie eyes stared from the shadows as he strode by.

He kept his pace long and hard, each footfall echoing confidence through the dusky twilight. To avoid the odors that seeped through the cloth mask, Ki breathed through his mouth. A myriad of body orders layered around him...feces and urine mixed with angst and despair. Beneath his feet debris and small pebbles crunched as he walked alongside a shallow ribbon of liquid running down the middle of the cobbled road. Trash and debris swirled around in the rancid air, floating in wispy dust devils.

One hand rested on his blaster while the other was free to grab the laser katana strapped to his back. He scanned back and forth in an automatic reflex, cataloging and analyzing everything around him.

Now that he found himself back on FiPan, he muttered curses under his breath at the pirate with each step. Maynwaring couldn't have picked a worse time to call in his demand, just as he and Qay got Aimee away from the Chancellor's palace. It didn't feel right to abandon Qay and D'zia at this critical time in their efforts to stop Chancellor U'unk. But what choice did he have? Once Ki gave his word, nothing stopped him from completing his promises.

Why did you think you'd never come back here? Haven't you ever heard the wonderful human saying, 'never say never'? Grirryrth gave an unsolicited snarky comment in his normal lazy rhythm as he continued. *Maybe one of these days you'll learn it isn't wise to pigeonhole yourself in absolutes. You and I both know it ends up biting you in the ass in the end.*

Oh, awake, are we? Ki retorted to his longtime companion in an internal dialogue. *I'd begun to think you'd sleep for another couple of decades. Lazy beast.*

Yeah? The humans have another great saying…bite me. The reptilian snort was unmistakable. *If you ever did anything interesting, I might bother to stay awake rather than be bored to death watching you.* The statement ended with a loud yawn.

Ignoring his Solaherra companion, Ki tracked a sudden movement. There, a few measurements to the right, he sighted the creeping of a small, anthropoid as it slithered by. The back legs moved as the front knuckles of his long arms dragged on the ground. Ki kept it in his sights until the creature ambled into a black doorway several feet away. He wasn't familiar with the species, so hard to tell if it was sentient. A long time ago, he'd learned to never assume a species wasn't intelligent unless proven otherwise.

Ki yearned for someone worthy to come out and challenge him. He was carrying around too much pent-up tension, and a knock-down, bloody fight would be just the thing he needed.

Grirryrth was of the same mindset. *Yeah, I dare ya to come and get us...cowards.* Ki had a vision of the Solaherra licking his chops in anticipation, which was a nice trick since Grirryrth wasn't in corporeal form.

Ki bared his teeth under his mask and clenched his fists. There weren't any takers. He had to admit the population of the objectionable slave planet was smarter than their reputations claimed. Everyone they encountered gave him one quick look before running away with fearful, backward glances. Ki had to stop himself from pursuing the fleeing *puntnejis*.

Maybe he shouldn't have dressed to frighten the locals. His all-black, one-piece battlesuit not only housed his Solaherra companion, but it also made them both impervious to any known weapon. Of course, it could be the balaclava covering his head and face, with only his eyes visible. Might be the long, black leather coat he had over his formsuit that scared them off. The material billowed when he walked, displaying his wide variety of deadly weapons.

A fearful Erkek youngling crossed his path before scurrying off into a narrow alley.

As he watched the child, a brief pang squeezed his heart. The twinge of regret of having no offspring came and went. He'd never have a child of his own, one that would repeat the same mistakes he'd made. Besides, even if he wanted to, it's not as if there were any females in his life to make that happen.

It would happen if you'd put some effort into finding your TrueBond. You're not getting any younger, you know.

Grirryrth's unhelpful advice stabbed at the constant guilt Ki carried. When he'd vowed never to have any children, he condemned his dragon counterpart to a premature death. No child meant Grirryrth would die with him and not be passed to the next generation. It was a decision Grirryrth vehemently disagreed with.

With years of ingrained practice, Ki disregarded the symbiont to concentrate on the upcoming encounter with the pirate. With a grunt, he hoped Maynwaring's demand would not take up too much of his time. With stress tight as a vise around his neck and shoulders, it was too bad he and Grirryrth hadn't gotten a chance to bash in some heads before reaching the crime lord's headquarters.

All too soon, he stood at the large, metal entrance to the pirate lair.

The weak light over the door tried to give the impression the area was vulnerable. After a scanner rolled over him, the rusted metal doors creaked open.

Anticipation sizzled down his spine. With hyper-awareness, he walked through the doorway. One of the pirate's sexbots greeted him.

Humanoid female in appearance, this one was a bright metallic-pink with three neon-pink eyes that blinked in unison. Her deep-red areolas poked hard and high on her three breasts through a silky see-through sarong. Her bald head gleamed under the struggling light while her long legs tapered above five-inch stiletto heels.

The aromatic pheromones emanating from her pores stirred nothing inside Ki except irritation. He would rather become a eunuch before he'd have sexual relations with one of the pirate's toys. Besides, the sooner he got off this Goddess-forsaken planet, the better.

The muscles in his jaw tightened as he hardened his facial expression. With arms folded across his chest, he cocked his head in challenge. "Where is your master?"

"Come this way, revered sir." The small bow she performed displayed her perky breasts to perfection.

The sexbot turned and sashayed to lead him to a round reception chamber through a transportation mirror. The next room lacked warmth or comfort. The chill air mixed with the sterile environment and a simple straight-backed chair sat in the middle of the room. The walls were round and pale, a pasty white that matched the concrete floor.

Ki stood next to the chair and crossed his arms. It was an old ploy, show him to an empty room, and make him wait. He refused to let the gangster intimidate him by using an overt manipulation strategy to make him nervous. He'd stand there unmoving for the duration of this game if need be.

The pirate was smart enough not to make him wait long. He rolled in with his usual dramatic flair, surrounded by a trio of sexbots for protection. His glowing orb was clutched in the hands of the humanoid stand he'd made hundreds of years before. The glowing bulb's steady swirl of colors inside displayed Maynwaring's consciousness.

Ki eyed the sexbots and was relieved that they weren't anything out of the ordinary.

One was lime green, another was neon orange, and Maynwaring's favorite, Babette, was the bright-red bitch of terror. The AI was a cross between the pirate's second-in-command and his lead assassin.

He'd always thought she held some level of self-awareness, even though Maynwaring denied it. "All right, tell me what you want." Ki kept his stance rigid and aggressive. He'd give no hint of weakness to the alien.

"Now, M'alalu." The colors in the orb rotated with the words spoken. "Is that any way to greet an old friend?" The statue holding the orb turned toward the chair. "Sit, make yourself comfortable."

Ki barely refrained from snorting. Even if he could fit into that small, spindly contraption, he never trusted appearances.

One of Maynwaring's favorite tricks was to offer a place to sit or food to eat that wasn't all it appeared to be. Like the time a hapless individual sat in a non-threatening recliner only to have the benign piece of furniture turn out to be an alien species. It ate the terrified male the minute his body touched it.

The sound of the male's bones being crunched stayed with Ki for decades.

"Let's just get on with this," he retorted. "Tell me what you want so I can satisfy the arrangement I made on behalf of Prince Qay."

The statue turned to let the orb face him.

All three sexbots kept to the background, but Ki had no doubt they'd get to him long before he tried to harm Maynwaring.

"Very well," the orb continued. "I am not asking for much, and I doubt it will take you long."

Ki narrowed his gaze but remained silent. The hair on the back of his neck raised as his stomach clenched.

We're not going to like this. Grirryrth, the king of understatement.

"Apparently Chancellor U'unk has a new, ah, biological antidote I'd like to relieve him of."

Everything within Ki stilled. What kind of antidote could the pirate possibly want?

Maynwaring went on with his demands. "I am not sure if the design has been completed yet, even so, I want what he has so far."

"Developed what? Is it some sort of weapon?" He refused to participate in any weapons dealing, and the pirate knew that.

"On the contrary, M'alalu!" The orb's colors mixed and rolled in harmony—normally a testimony to his sincerity. "I am well aware that if I sent you on any such errand, you would confiscate the weapon and turn it over to the Zerin High Council." The colors slowed and shifted indiscriminately. "No, no, this serum is made to repair, not destroy." The orb turned stiffly to the red sexbot on Ki's right. "Babette, my pet, please share the file with M'alalu."

The bright metallic android blinked.

A file icon appeared on his personal ODVU. Ki accepted it and went through the readout. After a few moments, he frowned as Grirryrth snorted in disbelief in his head.

"You want me to go to the Chancellor's secret lab? At the palace?" Ki's eyebrows raised as he frowned. "Covertly?" He leaned back and straightened his shoulders. "Even I would have a hard time pulling something like this off."

"Now, now, M'alalu. Why do you think I needed you for this, ah, operation? I knew if anyone could get this for me, it would be you." The milky white orb with its rainbow of colors swirled and spun. "I will, of course, provide you with my best tool to assist you." The colors now solidified into a stream of yellow.

That was a sure sign Ki would not like what the pirate said next.

"Babette will go with you to lend any assistance you might need."

"No." His reply was immediate and insistent.

"Why not? She's the brightest of my ladies and has unlimited talents that will aid in your success."

Yeah, and she'd undermine and discover his secrets and report everything he did to the pirate on a consistent basis. Then she'd stab him in the back. Literally.

"Absolutely not." He was firm. The whole idea was non-negotiable. "It makes no sense for one of your sexbots to accompany me."

Agreed. Grirryrth backed him up.

The colors in the orb brightened and swirled in different hues. "Very well." There was a pause as the rainbow spun faster before the orb spoke. "It's not that I don't trust you, but well, I don't trust you. It's a matter of business, you understand."

Ki maintained his crossed arms while he glared at the orb. "Not my problem."

"Hmm...maybe an incentive is called for," came the enigmatic reply. "Babette, bring in the human."

The graceful bot turned and walked out a transportation mirror.

Human? Why would Maynwaring have a human?

Ki silently agreed with his symbiont as he asked the same question.

The silence was thick in the room while the bot was gone. The colors in Maynwaring's orb remained mute and still.

Ki took the opportunity to concentrate on calming his chaotic thoughts. He wouldn't let being on FiPan and having to deal with the disgusting pirate stop him from maintaining his vigilance against the danger around him.

Humph, you are too calm all the time. I don't know why you're so worried about being distracted. You need someone to get your juices flowing.

Ki ignored his dragon. Grirryrth never let an opportunity pass to harass him about his decision to not seek a TrueBond to carry on the E'eur legacy. Too bad. Nothing would change his mind.

Then *she* came into the room.

At first, the human female wasn't anything out of the ordinary. He'd seen thousands of human women while aboard the *StarChance*, and even had to interact with some. None had stirred his interest—one way or the other.

Her reddish-brown hair was short, cut in the back and falling fuller around her face. Wisps of hair framed long, mink-colored lashes that surrounded the velvet, single-color brown eyes that now blazed in anger at everyone in the room. With her arms bound behind her, her large, round breasts thrust invitingly beneath a loose, soft-yellow tunic.

Ki appreciated her shapely legs encased in snug pants the same color as her tunic. After inspecting her from head to toe, Ki looked back at her face and zeroed in on her luscious... plump...tempting lips. He'd never seen lips on a female so mesmerizing before. They were delicate yet full, in a bow shape made for a male's kiss.

Yessss... beautiful female. Must have.

What was that? Grirryrth had never shown an interest in a female before. That should have tipped Ki off, but he was too busy appreciating her feminine form to pay attention to his dragon's observations.

"Let go, bitch," the female demanded through gritted teeth. She struggled within Babette's hold, but of course, she was no match for the strength of the android. The red fingers of the bot squeezed harder and caused the female to wince in pain.

Rage clouded Ki's vision. It took every ounce of willpower to maintain his calm exterior and not pull her from the bot's excessive hold. He gritted his teeth as he struggled to hold Grirryrth back from reacting the same way. Out of the corner of his eye, the orb's colors stopped in mid-motion. Great, now he'd caught Maynwaring's attention.

"Stop, Babette." The pirate's tone came out smooth with a hint of triumph. "Let's not hurt our guest."

Babette let go of the female's arm, causing the human to stumble.

Ki rushed to catch her and wished he hadn't. When she fell into his arms, they staggered backward. An alluring scent wafted and tantalized. Instinctually he took in a deep breath. A hint of soothing vanilla laced with a citrus sweetness snared him. His heart raced as the mating oils in his palms formed. The human's soft, female body fit—despite their height difference. Her head barely reached the bottom of his pectoral muscles, but she was somehow a missing piece of his personal puzzle. Warmth, calmness, and a heavy dose of protectiveness toward her consumed him.

With another deep breath, the word "TrueBond" slammed him.

YESSSSS...!

Was this human his TrueBond? The mate every Zerin searched for their whole lives to meet? The only female in the galaxy who could ever complete him and present him with offspring.

No! No...it was impossible.

Horror at the implication made him push away to put space between them.

She looked at him in confusion before she nodded as if to thank him for catching her.

He took another step back to put distance between them. He frowned and crossed his arms to glare at the pirate.

The colors were now in a slow spin, the rainbow giving the impression of satisfaction.

Ki refused to take the bait. "I'm not sure how showing me a human female gives me any sort of incentive."

"Ah, M'alalu, playing dense doesn't do you justice," the pirate admonished. "However, I'll play along. Now, I know how fond you are of these creatures and how you enjoy being able to offer them to others in the galaxy." The statue holding the orb rolled closer to the female who stepped away.

She didn't get far when she bumped into the solid form of Babette.

"Through no fault of my own, I found myself saddled with this alien." The orb continued as the colors resumed their normal swirl. "And the Friebbigh have offered me a fortune for her." The colors stopped. "So, here I have a decision to make. Shall I exploit a fortune offered by them or give her to you for free as an incentive to complete your assignment?" The rainbow hues began a slow dance. "Your choice."

By the father of all! A muscle ticked over his eye. How could Ki leave a defenseless human with Maynwaring? Whether she was his TrueBond or not, he'd never leave her there.

Just kill him and take the female, the Solaherra dragon growled.

That's not very helpful, Grirryrth. Ki retorted. *Keep quiet so I can take care of this. I have to make him think she doesn't interest me.*

"I repeat, I don't understand why you've brought this female to me," Ki deadpanned. "As if a lone human would mean more to me than my word to work for you on behalf of my prince."

The colors kept their momentum and did not deviate from their mesmerizing swirl. "While I admit you are an honorable individual...your background as a mercenary notwithstanding."

The fake sigh coming from the orb grated on Ki's nerves.

"I, for one, do not believe in the good nature of others. An added incentive is always a good business practice. Plus it will give you an extra goal to work for."

With conscious effort, Ki kept his voice and body non-threatening. "All right. Now that you've brought her into this equation, let's come to an agreement. State your proposal." He glanced over at the female.

With a stoic expression, she glared with narrow eyes.

He admired her intelligence, watching and learning in what had to be an alien environment for her. The only sign she knew she was in danger was the quick rise and fall of her chest. Good thing she had no idea he suspected she was his TrueBond. Or even what a TrueBond was, for that matter.

Grab her and let's go, the Solaherra once again demanded. *We don't have time for this* puntneji *and his nonsense.*

Patience, Ki admonished.

"Bring me the antidote and any research that goes along with it. The female will be kept in a holding cell to await your successful return. You have thirty solar days."

Ki's left eyebrow raised in surprise. "Don't want much, do you?" He clenched fists on his hips. "I will do it, but when I come back, the human comes with me. There will be no further amendments or changes to the agreement."

The colors swirled and eddied in a fast pace before the gangster answered. "Agreed."

Babette came over and extended her palm toward him.

What an odd thing for the android to do, wanting to shake hands in the human tradition. He glanced at the orb before catching the reaction of the exotic human female. When her eyebrows raised with a derisive twist to her luscious lips, he smiled at her strong will.

What a female! The calm demeanor from her almost made him wish he could pursue her. *Damn...* he didn't even know her name. More than likely, he was mistaken about her being his TrueBond, anyway. Yes, that was it. It had been a long time since he'd been with a female and he probably reacted to an attractive one as any normal male would. However, getting her away from the pirate would be the right thing to do. Then he'd drop her off at the Exchange. No reason to see her again. The alluring female would be safe, and he'd keep his vow of remaining unmated.

Goddess save us from idiots who do not understand what's right in front of them. Grirryrth closed with a snort of disgust.

In return, Ki disregarded Grirryrth. Everything would turn out the way he wanted. No need to make things complicated.

Sherri

Aboard Elemi, present day

Sherri floated in a thick sludge of darkness, a tiny spark of light confined in a sea of nothingness. A muffled sound like a voice talking underwater caught her attention. She strained to listen, but only caught bits and pieces of garbled conversation. At least she assumed it was a conversation between two people.

"Let... go!"

Ah, wait...was that her voice? It was...but that didn't sound like her.

"No."

Okay, that deep baritone belonged to Ki. She shivered whenever he spoke.

"...you...found...out."

It sounded like she spoke again. Now Sherri became desperate. Where was she and how was she talking without initiating the conversation?

"... nothing." Ki's response. "... her in stasis...lower level."

The "air" around Sherri thickened before it expanded and the light disappeared. She swam in a black void so deep she might not exist anymore. She had to hide...or get out...she had to...do...something...

Sssssstop ssssquirming sssso much!

Wait, what was that? It took a while for her to calm down enough to figure things out. A different voice floated in the vacuum. The slimy, slithering inflection in the speech made it hard to grasp.

"Who's there?" Sherri hated the quiver in her voice. Voice? Wait, was she talking or thinking?

You very well know who I am. The disgust in the reply was unmistakable. *Shhhhut up and ssssstay back there where you belong.*

Oh, really? Who did this asshole think he was dealing with? "Look, bub." Oh, now she got it. Her unwanted passenger held her consciousness hostage as he tried to take her body and mind over. She wasn't an avid paranormal romance reader for nothing. "This is my body and there's not enough room for the both of us. If you think I'm going to lie down and whimper in fear over you, you have another think coming."

Too late for you, female. I'm in control now.

What an enigmatic response. The smug inflection laced with each word made her more determined than ever to exorcise the jerk. "Hardly." She'd win this battle of wills... one way or the other.

Before Maynwaring responded, Sherri envisioned the lessons Ki taught her to keep control. She changed it somewhat, considering she was not the one operating her body. She stilled her essence as she blocked out the hissing protests of the pirate. She concentrated on creating a tornado powerful enough to rush around while she kept safe in an impenetrable bubble. Faster and faster, the winds blew. She cleared out the dark environment until she "saw" an outline of four clawed arms, four legs, a short, powerful tail, and a single horn in the middle of its forehead.

Ah...that had to be Maynwaring. Perfect. Time to sweep him away with the rest of the "trash" in her head. Old memories and embarrassments she didn't need. She forced her will harder, creating a firestorm to go with the gale-force winds. Powerful gusts and bellowing licks of flame surrounded her as it burned and swept the area in a blanket of pungent ozone. The light from the fire coalesced and illuminated a black hole. Yes, that's what she needed, a place to put his happy ass.

Nooo...I am in charge here! The pirate wailed through the blustery winds. *You will not banish me...you will...* THUNK!

With all her mental might, she threw him into the gaping maw as the wind and fire sucked in behind him. Mile-thick steel walls slammed over the hole with a resounding boom. The following quiet was a shock at first. Then a calm washed over her while a wavering, small beacon of light bloomed.

Sherri focused on that light, a lifeline her soul needed. She trusted her instincts to enfold who she was within its embrace...and let go.

The rush of warm breath entering her lungs made her lightheaded. The clean scent was sheer pleasure as it flowed inside her body. With great care, she tested her eyelids to see if she could open them. After two unsuccessful attempts, she pushed them up and closed them against the bright light. It was frustrating not to be able to put her arms over her eyes, but they refused to move. The orange light behind her closed lids was sharp and painful, but hey, it meant she was in control. Taking in another deep breath, she lifted her heavy lids. Slowly...ever so slowly, she acclimated to the change in vision. Images blurred, her eyes watered, and tears rolled down to pool at the outer shell of her ears. Her tongue was thick and dry.

"Sherri?" Ki's deep voice was a low whisper. "Are you all right?"

"Ki?" A dark outline moved into her line of sight. Her head rolled at the sound of the masculine voice and she blinked to focus. As his face became clearer, her tears washed away. Mesmerizing dual colored irises were thin lines of blue and green around the widened iridescent dark-green of his pupils.

"How do you feel?" The lush lips thinned under his close-cropped beard as he leaned closer.

"How do you know it's me?" She choked in gratitude that he seemed to recognize her. Tension squeezed at the base of her neck as she clenched her knuckles hard enough her hands numbed. What if he doubted who she was?

Ki gave a winsome smile, the tips of his sharp fangs peeking between full lips. "When Maynwaring is in charge, your eyes change."

He reached over and pushed away a stray bang that was getting into her eyes. A soft scent of sea breeze drifted from him.

With a jerk, he pulled back.

Sherri blinked. "Oh, okay." Was there a problem touching her? She watched his tightened fist as he placed it on his lap before glancing at his stony expression. "Has that happened before?"

"I don't know. I only became aware he'd taken over this time, but it's possible."

Well crap, she didn't like that idea. She also didn't like how his brow and face creased into a frown. The stern expression frankly scared the shit out of her. A shiver slithered down her spine.

"Last thing I remember was talking to D'zia and Lora when Elemi's alarms went off." Her teeth worried her lower lip. "Then I woke up in a really dark place, trapped with something evil."

"How did you get out?"

Heat crept up her neck. "I created a safe bubble and started a fiery tornado to whip around me. When the winds caught him, I threw his happy ass into a black hole." She jutted her jaw. "Let's just hope he stays there until I can figure out how to get rid of him."

"Had you any indication he'd gotten out before?"

"To be honest, I have no idea."

Ki rubbed the side of his bearded jaw and sat back. "Elemi, disengage the stasis field around Sherri."

A short snort came from the ship. "Do I have to?"

Ki's mouth twitched before they pressed together. "Yes, and thank you."

A light tingling pinched before her muscles relaxed in response to Elemi turning off the stasis field. Sherri flexed her fingers and wiggled her toes, delighting in the simple movement of basic motor skills.

Running her trembling fingers through her snarled hair, she gave him a wide smile and pushed upright on the thin cot in the small room. Good thing she'd worn a sweater. The air was nippy, and she rubbed her arms in reaction.

Sherri swung her legs to the side and faced the large Zerin sitting on a chair next to her. "How long was I out and where are we?" She looked around. Uh-oh, she couldn't hear the hum of Elemi's engines.

It was easy to tell they were still in the sentient ship. The black walls had minimum lighting, and the air retained that recycled smell she'd noticed with any space-going vessel she'd been in. The cot might be comfortable enough, even with its narrow width and short length. Nothing else to see but the small chair Ki had squeezed his massive body into.

"We've had to make a forced landing on an ice asteroid. We were under attack and Elemi brought us here to avoid detection."

"Under attack? How is that possible?" Wasn't this "special" ship all but undetectable to outside forces? She might be petty, but a snarky comment was needed. "If I remember correctly, isn't Elemi infallible? I thought no one could find her."

"I am quite convinced it's all your fault." Elemi's superior tone answered. "You must have given them the information not only where to find me but how to detect my beautiful self."

Sherri's mouth opened in shock. "Hey, wait a minute, you bitch..."

"Now, Sherri." Ki patted her hand as he spoke in a quiet, rumbling voice. "Let's take a moment to examine where we are. No need to get into an altercation with the ship."

Not get in *an altercation*... Sherri seethed. He was taking this nasty little ship's side? The middle of her chest squeezed.

Something in her expression must have alarmed him. Dual-colored eyes widened as he leaned closer. "No, don't get the wrong idea." With a glare at the ceiling, he addressed Elemi. "No one is blaming you for anything."

Elemi snorted.

"What I'm trying to say is." He enfolded her clenched fists. "Maynwaring could have circumvented you and alerted someone to find us."

Sherri snapped her jaw closed. Did the pirate take over without her knowing? "Do you think that's what happened?" At his nod, her stomach dropped. No reason to feel responsible, but still... "Do you know who chased us?"

"Of course. I've run a complete analysis on the invaders," Elemi huffed. "The data you've requested is ready, Ki dearest."

Ki closed his eyes.

Sherri pressed her lips so she wouldn't laugh at his pained expression.

"Thank you, Elemi. Sherri and I will join you in the cockpit momentarily. Please disengage and allow us some privacy."

"That is an unwise request, dearest," Elemi protested. "Why, she might be possessed at any time and..."

"Elemi, disengage." The sharp tone didn't encourage arguing.

"Anything for you, Ki, dearest." There was a watery sniff before a ping sounded.

Sherri wasn't sure if the ship left or just tried to make them think she had. Since they couldn't go anywhere that Elemi didn't have access to, worrying about privacy was a moot point.

So, why did Ki say he wanted to talk to her in private? Looking into his grim, unsmiling face, she pulled the bottom lip between her teeth and gnawed on the sensitive skin. Last time she was this nervous, she had been waiting to see if she passed her doctorate program. It didn't help he directed that disappointed scowl at her, either.

CHAPTER **FOUR**

Ki

S herri was trying to kill him. She should just take out a disintegration blaster and be done with it. And if she chewed on that plump lower lip any harder, he'd have to oothe that offended skin with his tongue—just before he plunged into her hot mouth. *By the father of everything*, he was falling fast for this tempting human.

About time you realized it.

Ki mentally shook his head to disagree with Grirryrth. Even if he wanted to make his interest known to her, he wouldn't. Especially since he halfway suspected she might be his TrueBond...

She is.

... the whole concept was too dangerous, especially with Maynwaring in the picture.

That female is only dangerous to your own stubborn, stupid ideas. Once we mate, your preconceived concepts will change.

Ki ground his back molars. He refused to have this conversation with the dragon.

"Sherri, here's where we are." Ki waited until he had her full attention. "We are being chased by a terrorist faction called the 'Warriors of Light.' Their only goal is to cause chaos in the established galactic government and eliminate those who don't believe in their extremist views."

If her twisted expression was anything to go by, he'd confused her. He released her clenched hands and sat back. "While I can't be sure, I assume they're here at Maynwaring's request to rescue him."

"That doesn't make any sense." Her hand waved to encompass herself. "He can't go anywhere without me..." She stopped and her eyes widened. "Wait, he wants to leave in my body?" With her deep breath her full breasts heaved up and down.

Make her do that again.

Ki ignored the dragon's statement. "Right now he wouldn't have any other option." The thought of the extremists being anywhere near Sherri had his shoulders tense. "Since we're aware of what he's done, we can prevent that from happening."

A cynical mink eyebrow rose. "Oh yeah? And just how are we going to do that?"

"We'll just have Elemi..."

"Help! Enemy troops are circling around me!" The panic is Elemi's voice was unmistakable. "Ki, they've got another disintegration cannon! Ack!"

Oh, for the love of the Goddess... "Activate complete visual!" Ki jumped out of the chair and it toppled to the floor with a loud thud.

At his command, the walls disappeared, and he had an unobstructed view of a ragged troop that surrounded the ship. The sound outside was muted, but it was easy to see the piercing icicles as a harsh wind whipped around the figures. The blinding mix of the white and gray atmosphere blurred the dark outlines scattered on the snow-strewn ground. Even so, the visual was sharp enough to confirm each troop carried a bevy of assorted weapons. The disintegration cannon aimed at them made Ki tighten his jaw in determination.

"Holy shit! That doesn't look good."

No point in commenting on Sherri's statement of the obvious. "Elemi, status and analysis." He went to the console and blinked open a program.

"Analyzing," came the terse reply.

While the ship was processing his request, he opened a communication channel with D'zia. Zerin was too far away for real-time conversations, so no chance of alerting his friend Qay.

"D'zia here." His young friend appeared in a holographic image with a frown. "What happened? You and Sherri all right?"

"No," Ki answered. "The WOL attacked, and we had to force land on a rogue asteroid."

"Attacked? *Danka* shit! I thought you lost them."

A deep voice interrupted. "Someone hurt my glorious Elemi?" JR10's silver body rested on D'zia's shoulder and gave a light hop as he spoke. "Elemi, baby... are you okay, my dove?"

The ship's watery sniffle caused Ki to pinch the bridge of his nose.

"Oh, JR10, you have no idea of the horrors I've been through..."

They didn't have time for theatrics. "Enough, Elemi. Report on our current status."

"Fine." Another sniff. "A troop of the Warriors of Light, consisting of approximately 250 soldiers, surrounds us. Each one is armed with varying degrees of personal weapons along with that horrible disintegration cannon. It can completely eliminate our existence."

The theatrical watery tone gave him a headache.

"Not only that, they've put a restraining net over my glorious body and I can't *move*!" The last word ended in a loud wail.

Ki winced at the noise and agreed with D'zia's frown as he asked, "How did they find you?"

"It's all my fault," Sherri whispered.

She stated it loud enough for D'zia to hear. "What? Why would you say that?"

Ki reached over and placed a light hand on her shoulder to make her face him. "It's Maynwaring's fault, not yours." He let go and turned back to D'zia before she could argue the point. "Right now we have to figure a way out of this mess." Ki gave his friend a hard stare. "D'zia, it's imperative you get word to Qay and the Imperial Forces immediately. Even though we might not make it to Earth before the Chancellor's armada does, they have to be involved quicker than we thought."

D'zia blinked for a moment as JR10 crawled up to whisper something in his ear. "I don't know, JR10. I don't think that's a good idea. We're already deep in debt with them..."

Ki's expression hardened at the furtive discussion D'zia and his bot were having without him. "What's going on?"

"Oh, I..." He stopped as JR10's forelegs waved and he continued to speak into D'zia's ear.

Movement caught Ki's attention.

The troops split and a lone figure walked with an arrogant stride down the open corridor they made as they stepped back. Slow, casual as if he hadn't a care in the galaxy, the male made it to the front of the battle line. He was clad completely in black, including a cloak and a helmet covering his head with a vertical slit for his eyes and an opening to reveal his thin mouth.

The icy winds of the asteroid didn't appear to faze the leader or his troops. The subzero temperature had to be grueling.

Ki looked closer at the male, not able to determine what species he was, but suspected he observed a fellow Zerin. The build and height was typical for a male in his prime. It went well with the arrogance and display of confidence. Something about him bothered Ki. *Do we know him?* Ki asked Grirryrth.

The symbiont dragon stretched his senses. *Hard to tell while I'm on the ship.* The dragon paused. *However, I too, suspect we know who he is. I will remain vigilant.*

Ki nodded while he gave Sherri a sharp glance. With a whiter-than-normal face, she wound her fingers around his forearm. He doubted she was aware what she was doing. A deep breath brought in her subtle scent of spicy sweetness. It calmed his tense nerves.

Not that he'd admit the implications of how her touch soothed him.

"We demand your surrender, M'alalu Ki E'eur." The leader boomed his demand across the icy landscape outside.

With Elemi's abilities, it wasn't hard to hear what the male said.

"Bring the human woman out and abandon the 11-15 ship you stole."

Ki snorted in disgust. Just who did this *puntneji* think he was talking to?

"Ki," Elemi whispered.

The tone took Ki aback. Why was she whispering?

"Not now, Elemi." Ki's attention was consumed by the troop movements as they closed the ranks behind the leader.

"Ki," her tone came out louder this time. "We're in trouble."

He took his eyes away from the scene in front of him and glanced at the ceiling in exasperation before his attention jerked by the scream of D'zia's Spybot.

"Elemi!" JR10 shouted in the communication vid. "Transfer now!"

The lights, vid, and outside projection went out, leaving the room in the dark. A sharp pain pinched the back of Ki's neck before his mind shut down.

Sherri

The rat-bastard did it to Sherri again. Damn slimy alien took over her body and held her prisoner in a clear bubble. God, what she wouldn't give to wring his skinny, worthless piece-of-shit neck. Her primal scream of frustration didn't change anything.

Hey, wait a minute...she could see and hear what was going on. Well, at least, she thought she could. There were shadowy movements inside a gray rectangle, like a movie screen with the surrounding sound muffled. It reminded her of the old time stereo one of her foster parents had.

It was, safe to say, an improvement over the last time he'd taken over. Whereas before she had no idea he took her over, now she'd be awake for the horror show Maynwaring was creating. *Ha!* Just watch her get control again.

All she had to do was figure out how.

A dim light caught her attention. She couldn't be squinting with her eyes since she wasn't in physical form, but it was what she imagined doing. Slowly, the picture became clearer. It took a moment before she recognized Ki's prone figure lying on the floor. His massive chest rose up and down and his fingers twitched. Thank God, he was alive!

"NO!"

Was that her voice? It was throwing a hissy fit worthy of any preteen denied the latest smart phone.

An empty hypodermic flew across the room.

"I want that ship back! Bring her back!" Her foot swung back and kicked the limp Zerin.

Sherri watched in horror as her foot pulled back and forth to give Ki a couple more hard kicks. *Oh, no you don't!* Determined, Sherri concentrated on pulling the foot back and gave a whoop of joy when she caused the limb to shudder and falter.

"Let me go! Let me go!"

For once, her screeching voice was music to her ears. She'd made a break-through! Yeah, and bonus for pissing the pirate off. It was now one of her new favorite things.

"Bitch!" Her voice wailed as the pirate warned Sherri. "I've got control and there's nothing you can do about it."

Oh, yeah? That's it genius, taunt the jerk and make him mad. *I don't think so. This is my body and I want it back!*

"Denied," the pirate replied with a sneer, still using her voice.

Wow, she'd never heard that level of contempt roll off her tongue before.

"No matter. I have more important things to do besides talking to an insignificant *hysta.*"

Asshole did not just call her a whore. *Look, buddy, I...*

"Rux, get your ass in here." Maynwaring ignored her as he used her voice to speak into the communication vid he'd been working on. Instead of showing an image of D'zia, a black-clad thug took up the screen.

Sherri couldn't remember when the switch went from Ki's friend to an unknown Zerin.

Helmet held under his arm, the male Zerin had a callous, unyielding appearance. A life lived hard was stamped on his face—furrowed forehead and hard-lipped mouth. His dual colored frog- and spinach-green eyes might have been attractive if they weren't set in a block of ice. His black hair was sweat-slicked against his forehead, the traditional warrior braid absent at his right temple. "Just how do you propose I get in?" The man growled. "Open the *Goddess-damn door* and I'd be happy to oblige."

"I can't!" Maynwaring screamed and stomped Sherri's foot. "The sentient ship escaped somehow and I have no way to regain control."

"What is wrong with you?" The male's face twisted into an unattractive sneer.

"I don't know!" Another ear-splitting wail rang out. "I can't seem to control this stupid female body!"

Sherri snickered to herself. Yep, she always suspected men (or males) couldn't handle the things a woman had to. Her period was supposed to come in another week and her nerves always got tight around that time. Served the rat-bastard right for taking something that didn't belong to him.

"Well, get control and let us in."

Ha! No sympathy there.

Sherri felt her body heaving in exertion. Hey, another sign of progress. Before, there wasn't any sensation, just floating around in a blank sea of nothing. Maybe she was gaining enough strength to build on expanding her awareness to help take herself back.

Which was a weird thing to say.

Maynwaring roared a frustrated yell as he stood in front of the control panel and stared at it.

While Sherri couldn't hear what he was thinking, she got an impression he was analyzing the console to try to find a way to control the ship. After a few moments, she watched her fingers fly across the panel, flip, and twirl impressions. Lights came on and a doorway appeared.

"About time." The lead Zerin stomped in front of Maynwaring and glared at him...er, her.

The minute Sherri thought to glare back, her face tightened with that emotion without any effort on her part. Wow, she wasn't sure if she liked that she and Maynwaring shared the same reaction. Okay, time to take a back seat, listen to the conversation, and figure a way out of this mess.

"Shut the *fruk* up and get me out of here," Maynwaring demanded. "I need to get to Earth before the Chancellor has a chance to deploy that weapon."

"Not so fast." The Zerin held his hand up to stop Sherri's body from moving forward. "You promised me M'alalu E'eur, and I'm not moving until I have him."

"He's right there." Sherri's body went to the prone Ki and gestured for the newcomer to see.

Maynwaring made a motion to kick him again, but Sherri immobilized his foot so it couldn't move.

"Damn it, let go!" Maynwaring stomped her foot on the soft floor. Good thing the surface was forgiving or Sherri's ankles might have buckled under the strain. "*Fruking hysta!* Get me out out of this body. Where's Babette? I need Babette right now!"

Responding to her master's call, the red sexbot pushed her way through the throng of Zerins outside the open doorway to stand before Sherri. "I am here, my master." The bright-red android intoned as she dropped to the floor with her palms flat while she prostrated herself at Sherri's feet. "How may I serve thee?"

Ugh!

The sexbot's rump was high in the air with her face planted on the floor.

Even though the sexbot wasn't a living, organic being, Sherri hated the subservient female display, especially at her feet.

"Did you bring my new orb?"

The demand in Sherri's voice made her cringe.

"I have to get out of this disgusting body as soon as possible."

"Yes, I have brought it, my master." Babette crooned as she stood, her three eyes with their red irises blinking in unison across the arc in her forehead. The wispy, see-through short dress she wore displayed an unshaven mound. Her three full breasts heaved and quivered with each breath and her brick-red nipples hardened into sharp buttons.

The sexbot seemed different from the others in Maynwaring's prison. Those sexbots had the feminine proportions of an overgrown, bald, neon-colored Barbie doll. But this one sported full head of thick, black hair that fell to her tiny waist. The gleam of malevolent intelligence made Sherri uneasy. She poked through the pirate's memories to try to find out what it was about the sexbot that bothered her so much.

Sherri pushed her consciousness forward to sift through some of his recent memories. Instead of finding anything about Babette, she found his intention to kill Sherri once his essence escaped into the orb.

She stopped in shock then seethed in anger.

Hah! Seethe...a word she never thought to use in real life. She'd always considered it an overblown word a writer used. However...seethed was the only word that adequately described her reaction to Maynwaring's plan. She was "seething" so hard she wanted to punch something. Too bad for her the person she desperately wanted to knock out was using her body. *Ugh,* talk about a no-win scenario. All she could do was suffer in literal silence.

"Let go, you piece of *eztli* shit! I'm in control of your body, not you!" The screech from her mouth echoed in the silent ship chamber as her body squirmed and thrashed.

If Sherri hadn't been trying to wrestle control away, she'd have laughed at the shocked expressions on Rux's face and the guards next to him. She must look like an idiot screaming and wrestling with herself.

"Maynwaring, get hold of yourself." Rux slapped her across the face with an open palm.

The contact wasn't painful, but it was enough of a shock to make the out-of-control pirate stop. Sherri's eyelids blinked as she felt her invader glare back. "I will allow that infraction to pass with no repercussion this one time." Maynwaring lowered her voice to come out low and threatening. "But I can assure you it will never happen again. Am I clear?"

The pirate's threats didn't appear to bother the male. Rux's hard dual-green eyes remained steadfast in his glare. "I couldn't care less. I have a mission to accomplish and I can't do it without that Zerin. We have to leave and we're running out of time."

Sherri's chest rose and fell as the pirate took in a deep breath. "Agreed." Her arm raised and pointed a finger at Ki lying behind her. "The *puntneji* you're looking for is over there. Now get us out of here." She turned her back on the Zerin and walked out of the now-dead ship.

The bite of the frozen landscape shocked Sherri as it chilled her to the bone. The stupid pirate didn't have enough sense to take care of her body.

"Babette, my pet." Sherri cringed at the sickly sweet tones coming out of her mouth. "Where is my new orb?"

Babette's bright-red arm wrapped around Sherri's shoulders and squeezed close. With that movement, the sexbot transferred an enveloping warmth so Sherri's body wouldn't freeze. "I have placed it aboard your lead ship, my master." The android's silky voice soothed as her fingers massaged the top of Sherri's shoulders.

Even as a disembodied spirit, she experienced the cold, inhuman feel of Babette's touch. She gave an internal shiver of disgust at the malodorous smell coming from the sexbot.

"Good...good."

Maynwaring answered using Sherri's voice, which was still creepy.

"I want to..."

As Maynwaring gave instructions, several screams and shouts sounded behind them. Sherri's body turned, with Babette keeping a close hold on her. The sight not only startled her, but it caught Maynwaring completely by surprise.

"By the Goddess's titties... what's going on?"

She screamed as Maynwaring tried to run into the fray.

Babette kept hold of her master to ensure Sherri's body didn't escape into the subzero temperature.

There he was! Ki had emerged from the ship like some warrior god of old. He battled Rux and his gathered guards for all he was worth.

A profound sense of smug joy lifted Sherri's spirits. With fascination she watched as he spun into action.

The large and dangerous male in his prime wove through the throng of bad guys with ease, his face set in stone. With sharp kicks, his arms thrusting and parrying, he disabled all ten Zerins in less time than Sherri's body took in one breath from the next.

"You *fruking* asshole!" Rux yelled as he pulled out a small, silver cylinder wand and waved it in front of Ki's glowering face. "I've called off the rest of my troops. And do you know why, you *puntneji* unclean half-breed?" A sneer pulled his craggy face into something repulsive.

Ki's own smile was chilling. "Ah, now I know who you are—Drirux the Coward."

The other Zerin's face blanched before it turned a bright shade of purple on his dark, iridescent skin. "I am no coward." He stepped back and stood with his legs apart in a wide stance. "I want that suit and you're going to give it to me."

Ki crossed his large arms and widened his own position. "Now, why would I want to do that?" He nodded at the slender wand in Rux's hand. "That will have no effect on me."

"Maybe not, but it will on her," Rux nodded toward Sherri enfolded in the bot's arms. "And we both know how soft you are on the humans. You won't let anything happen to her, even if she's a bit defective, what with Maynwaring inside calling the shots."

Ki's body language didn't change, but something told Sherri he wasn't as casual as he seemed.

"You'll die in the blast as well. How will your death help your cause?"

The condescending sneer was back in full force. "My death will cause me to be hailed as a martyr. My name will be a rallying cry for the Warriors of Light so they can lead others into the sacred ways of our ancestors. To cleanse the Zerin people of inferior outside influences!"

Ki gave a loud snort. "You always were a prissy little two-tailed *burhe furbutton*. No one cares who you are or what you think. They didn't when we were young and they don't now. So put your toy away like a good little youngling and I just might let you live."

Rux's knuckles turned white as he gripped the silver wand. "You are not the one in charge here."

Ki chuckled as he let his arms drop. "Well, as we both know, neither are you." He put his hands on the handle of the blasters he had strapped to his hips. "Take your hand off the detonator for the disintegration cannon and place it carefully on the ground."

The other male's face turned a deeper shade of purple as he gave Ki an icy stare before he complied.

"NO! Stop you fool!" Sherri's voice screamed at Rux. "What are you doing?" Sherri's body jerked to move before she could stop it.

Rux's eyes darted toward her and a snide smile creased his lips. His other hand had been holding a hidden knife he flicked in her direction. Between her and Maynwaring trying to control her body to duck out of the way, they weren't fast enough. The weapon struck. The sharp tip penetrated her upper chest.

Pain, bright and sharp. A widening red blossomed from the wound in her chest and soaked her sweater as the bitter metallic taste of blood filled her mouth. For the first time in her life, overwhelming fear made her body run cold. Death stalked.

Maynwaring screamed something in the background, but he was the last thing she cared about. Through a haze of pain, Ki's magnificent face filled her vision, causing her eyes to fill with grateful tears. He would be the last thing she'd ever see. Navy/hunter eyes narrowed and his mouth twisted in rage. He bellowed out a roar that couldn't possibly have come from him. Between one blink and the next, his face morphed. No, not only his face, but his body became larger and changed shape.

At first, Sherri didn't understand what was in front of her. Not because she didn't recognize the species, but because she had a hard time believing what it was. A dragon. She loved dragons. She'd read every romance story she could get her hands on about dragon shapeshifters and their mates. To see one before she died was everything she'd ever dreamed of.

Holy God, this one was beautiful. Opulent, navy-blue eyes at the sides of the creature's thorny, scaled skull blazed with iridescent oval pupils. Several small central horns sat atop his head, just above thin, cat-like ears. Rows of small thorns ran down the side of each jawline. His nose was small and had two wide, elongated nostrils. Sparkling crystal growths gathered along the chin. Rows of sharp teeth poked out from the inside of that impressive mouth.

A broad, long neck tapered into a bulky body, with the back covered in navy-blue scales and a row of small fan-like growths on his spine. The creature's large belly boasted crystal-like skin in a much darker, eggplant color. Four muscular limbs carried his body and allowed the dragon to stand towering and dignified, even when he sat on his haunches. Each limb's four digits ended in strong claws made of what looked like amethyst crystal.

Enormous dark-purple wings grew from his shoulders and ended at his hips. The wings were thick, bladed skin with curved talons growing from each ending like giant scythes.

Sherri studied the end of his graceful tail, topped in a mace-like ball made of the same crystal scales as his claws.

She sighed in pleasure as her awareness dimmed. Thank God Maynwaring's voice faded into the background. Before the abyss claimed her, the dragon's massive head leaned toward her, his huge eye filling her vision. She had to touch him, just this once. She reached up with a bloody hand to brush across a velvet muzzle.

Calm resolution covered her as the tension she'd been holding released. The cold breath of death overpowered her. She gave a small smile as Maynwaring's scream of terror faded into the background. How appropriate the coward relinquished control at the moment of her death. She closed her eyes as wariness pulled. There was enough presence of mind to experience the slightly rough tip of the dragon's tongue as it swiped across her throat. Once.... twice... before a sharp sting punctured her jugular. A firestorm swarmed through and caused her to arch.

She screeched in agony.

Silence. Blackness. Neither hot nor cold permeated the barren landscape.

Sherri stood in unfamiliar surroundings, not sure if she was in open terrain or a large, enclosed room. While the light might be bright enough, the only thing to look at was the nondescript ground and a ring of darkness off in the distance.

Except, of course, for the two critters... ah, aliens... creatures? Who faced each other several feet apart. One was recognizable, one...not so much.

The first one was another dragon, but a definite female a little smaller than the one Ki turned into. This one was elegant and beautiful, in a terrifying predator kind of way.

Small, light-silver eyes lay in her rounded, horned skull. Varying shades of dark metallic silver crystals sat atop her head, just above her enormous, round ears. Several rows of small clear thorns ran along the side of her jawline. Her feminine, thin nose had two enormous, rounded nostrils and there was a trio of small crystal horns on her chin. Several rows of large teeth were visible inside her mouth.

Her elegant neck ran from her head into a massive, rounded body. Her top was covered in small black scales with rows of fan-like growths down her spine. Her curved bottom also had dark silver scales in a deeper hue. Four slim limbs were strong enough to carry her body and allowed her to move with dignity and grace. Each limb bore three digits that ended in huge, diamond nails.

Sherri guessed they had to be made of crystalized bone.

The dragon's enormous wings grew from her shoulders and ended at her delicate pelvis—angel-like wings in silver feathers with a curved talon at the tip. Her flat tail ended in a sharp point with the same shimmery, silver scales as her body.

Sherri sighed as she clasped her fists across her heart in giddiness. Damn, she was worse than a fan going spastic over a movie star. What she wouldn't give to stroke the legendary creature. Were her scales as soft as their downy appearance suggested or hard as burnished steel?

Tendrils of steam wove out of the dragon's nostrils as she aimed an evil grin at the nasty-looking creature in front of her.

The repulsive being had a three-part body like an ant, covered lightly in tiny dark gold hairs. The alien balanced on four clawed arms and four legs along with its tapered short tail. It had a prominent horn on its head over three rows of six burnt-orange eyes in sunken sockets. The mouth took up the majority of the face under an enormous, wide nose with rounded nostrils now flared in exertion. Long pointed ears stood straight up like a bat.

"Leave thissss place." The ugly thing demanded to the female dragon. A forked tongue flicked in and out of its large maw. "There is not enough room for all of ussss." It swiveled its bulky head in Sherri's direction. "You both will be eliminated."

Holy shit, that's Maynwaring! Sherri gaped at the gangster's true form. Where in the hell were they, anyway?

The feral smile the female dragon gave the pirate was chilling. "Oh no, little male. You are quite mistaken. It is you who will finally be eliminated from this galaxy."

Between one step and the next, the large dragon swooped down with her mouth wide open and gulped the hapless alien between her sharp teeth. One crunch...two...and a high-pitched scream from Maynwaring was cut off in mid-breath.

The female swallowed as the large bulge that was once the terror of the Milky Way Galaxy found its way into her massive belly. She gave a delicate burp as wisps of smoke drifted out of one nostril and the edges of her mouth. "Oh, pardon me." The dragon crooned with a sheepish smile.

Sherri smiled back. For some reason, the large female didn't scare her. In fact, she was lighter than air, giddy with relief. "Is he gone for good?"

The graceful dragon's massive head nodded. "Oh, yes." The reply was in a slightly accented voice. "He will never bother us again." Another delicate burp.

Sherri raised an eyebrow. "Us? I'm afraid I don't understand. In fact"—she looked around at the cool air swirling in a misty fog—"where are we and how do we get out of here?"

"This is the in-between times, the only place where I could get rid of that pest." The dragon folded her legs and rested. With a rumbling sigh, she settled her jaw on bent forelegs. "Come here, child, so I may look at my new companion."

"Companion?" Sherri went to the enormous creature, more enthralled the closer she got. The dragon's silver scales had a fine down covering she itched to touch. The warmth coming off the dragon was welcome, especially since until that moment she hadn't realized how cold she was. "What do you mean by 'companion'?"

"Come, sit. Let me tell you a story about how we are bound together." The massive head nodded to the crook of her leg.

Sherri didn't hesitate to accept the invitation and nestled against the downy softness. Once she was snuggled in the warm cocoon, she scrutinized the dragon's immense face. "You're not going to eat me, are you?" She doubted that would happen, but hey, she had to ask.

The dragon gave a slight snort. "Of course not. You are me and I am you. My name is Cheithe and I am now a part of you. My mate, Grirryrth, injected his essence into your unconscious form to release me. That allowed us to bond and prevent your death."

"Your mate?" An image flooded of the humongous purple-and-blue dragon she saw before she passed out. Oh, so that's what that blinding pain was.

"Yes, since your mate—or I guess you call him your TrueBond—is Grirryrth's host, it only made sense for me to merge with you."

"Huh?" That was a weird word. "What or who is a TrueBond?"

Cheithe cocked her head. A silver eye the size of a dinner platter filled Sherri's vision. "You do not know the male, Ki, is your TrueBond?" She drew her head back and shook it, then wrinkled her snout as if she smelled something sour. "Males!" The exasperation was clear. "Why do they have to make things so complicated? I will have a firm discussion with Grirryrth at the earliest opportunity, believe you me." A disgruntled humph. "Little female, your TrueBond is the Zerin male named M'alalu Ki E'eur, the current host of the Crart dragon named Grirryrth. Grirryrth had been last of our kind until he was strong enough to release me inside of his host's mate." Cheithe lifted her head back in a proud stance, her graceful neck elongated with pride. "He has had to suffer being alone for thousands of millennia. No more. Once

I am strong enough, we will bond as mates should. I am eager for the new generation of Crart warriors to again be the caretakers the galaxy needs. Our children will work together against the darkness and not allow it to take hold as it is trying to do now."

Sherri wasn't sure where to start, so she grabbed on a small part of what Cheithe told her. "Ki is thousands of years old?" Talk about a December-May romance...

The dragon shook her head. "No, my mate is that age. Through careful planning on our ancestor's part, Grirryrth's consciousness is in the warrior suit your mate wears. As for your mate, he is very young, only around one-hundred-twenty standard solar years."

Wow, that stunning man had to be three times her age. What she wouldn't give to peel the form-fitting black suit apart and reveal his tight, iridescent skin. She was dying to see how good the "old man" looked without it.

"Child, now is not the time to think of your mate," Cheithe chided. "You must awaken to complete the bond between us."

"Awaken? What do you mean?" Sherri looked around. The darkness was encroaching, with the wispy fog becoming thicker. "Aren't I awake now?"

"No, you were near death and are still unconscious. That is why you and I could meet face-to-face in this place at the in-between." Cheithe nuzzled the tip of her nose against Sherri's cheek. "But our time has run out and you must awaken before it's too late."

"But I still have questions..." Sherri protested as the female dragon gently pushed away from her and stood to her massive height a few feet away.

"All will be well, child," Cheithe promised. "I am ever with you." She opened her jaw wide and blew a string of red, hot fire.

Sherri instinctively knew this was the final step to bind them together.

Instead of experiencing a fiery death, Sherri jerked awake. Startled, she looked around until she caught the steady gaze of Ki's dual-colored eyes.

The inner navy ring of his irises expanded and eclipsed the outer dark hunter green.

His iridescent green pupil widened as she drowned in his intense emotion. Worry... desire... possessiveness. Hard to tell which emotion was the strongest, but whichever one it was, he made her smile.

Then Sherri did something she'd wanted to do the first time she saw him. She reached up, slipped her arm around his neck, pulled him down, and touched her lips to his. The scruff of his full beard was soft and prickly at the same time.

Ki's response was more than she hoped for. Strong arms embraced her as his masterful mouth claimed what she offered. Firm, masculine lips demanded entrance, which she gladly complied with. A masculine flavor joined hers—a tang of sea breeze laced with a sharp bite of brine along with a heightened burst of addicting passion. A moan rolled free from her tight throat.

More...had to have more. With deliberate movements, Sherri pulled him closer. The man must have read her mind, his solid body covered hers on the soft pad. Dual sighs of pleasure filled their mouths as their groins meshed and rubbed. A vibrating groan of male pleasure joined hers as her womb zinged and tightened.

Ki's low growl filled her mouth, and she basked in feminine power. With deliberate movements, she rubbed against the ridged length that strained the front of his formsuit.

His hold tightened as his hips stroked back. He lifted his head and stared at her with slightly narrowed eyes before he lowered it again. Traitorous lips found the sensitive hollow between her neck and shoulder. Sharp teeth nipped as he suckled the receptive skin.

"TrueBond." Sherri breathed into the shell of his ear. The strange word startled her. Why in the world would she say something like that? Who cared? While she had no idea what it meant, she just wanted more. *Ahh*... yes, there he was. His clever hands found the rounded globes of her breasts. *Yes*... fingers massaged as she thrashed, wanting the extra friction. She shivered and broke out in a nervous sweat under the welcome weight.

It took a moment for her lust-filled brain to recognize his still body. The sudden immobility caught Sherri off guard. Reluctantly, she let go of the luscious ass she had no memory of grabbing. Just as she feared, he pushed away and their eyes met. A hard knot lodged in her throat.

"This isn't right." The raspy voice matched the grim look in his dual-colored eyes. "I shouldn't have done this."

He made a move to lift off but she grabbed his forearms.

He stopped with a puzzled frown. "I need to get up."

"No," Sherri shook her head. "Oh no, you're not going anywhere until you tell me what 'this isn't right' means." She firmly stroked his engorged member.

He closed his eyes in reaction and his mouth tightened. "I mean"—he spoke through gritted teeth—"for me to take advantage of you after what you've been through is unacceptable." He pulled away.

She let go and dropped her hands. With the warmth of his body gone, the cold and nerves caused a shiver.

"Besides." He continued to back away. "It's important for us to get out of here as soon as possible." The stark words didn't match the pained expression as the distance widened between them. "Drirux's friends could come back any minute, and we've got to be long gone before then." He inspected her with a bland expression. "How do you feel?"

Feel? Aroused, horny...ready to tangle between the sheets. Dense man...how did he *think* she felt? Not that he need to know. She wasn't going let on how his rejection hurt. So, time for some good old-fashioned sarcasm. "Oh, just peachy. Never better." With slow movements, she sat up from the narrow bed and swung her feet to touch the ground as she glanced around.

"No"—Ki stepped back into her personal space—"how do you *feel*?"

His intense focus made her blink. "Okay, I guess. Why are you acting so weird?"

Ki crossed his massive arms while giving a disgruntled snort. "Look inside. What do you find?" He leaned in and placed fists on his lean hips. "Or better yet, what don't you find?"

"I don't..." Sherri looked away with unfocused eyes. Searching...*ahh-* ...no...it was gone! The heavy burden of the nasty pirate was gone. She probed further and rubbed an open palm over her heart. *Yeah*, he was gone.

But, something else was there. Where the pirate had been before, now a warm ethereal light made up of pastel colors swirled in a cohesive circle. A joyous welcome confused her as much as it centered her and gave her purpose. She gave a metaphorical poke to see what happened.

"Hello, child." The singsong voice of the female dragon, Cheithe responded. *"I told you I'd ever be with you."*

CHAPTER FIVE

Ki

Ki's vision narrowed when Drirux's dagger pierced Sherri. To watch her crumple with a bright red blossom spreading across her soft, autumn-colored shirt had been the hardest thing he'd ever lived through. Wild emotions flared, and he lost control and transformed into an enraged dragon.

Once in corporeal form, Grirryrth did something unexpected. He wrapped a claw around Sherri's torso, lifted her up to lick, and then bit her neck...hard enough to break the skin. The action was gentle and didn't cause a massive wound, but it was hard enough to coat his tongue with hot blood.

What are you doing? Ki internally yelled at the dragon. *She needs medical attention, not you snacking on her!* He was ignored as the dragon blew a puff of internal fire into her.

With gentle claws, he set her back on the frozen ground.

By the father of everything! Terror seized Ki's throat...had Grirryrth lost his mind? For the first time in decades, he was at a loss for what to do.

Grirryrth continued to ignore Ki and gave Sherri another lick, this time across her cheek. With a satisfied whistle through his sharp teeth, he turned his attention to the sexbot standing next to her prone body. With a flick of his massive tail, he swatted the red android thousands of meters away. Satisfied he'd taken care of that problem, he lowered his left eye to focus on the shocked Zerin, Drirux.

Drirux did the same thing he'd done all those years ago when Ki had first taken Grirryrth out to impress the bully. The ammonia scent of piss became heavy in the cold air as the terrified Zerin turned to run.

Even without Ki's encouragement, Grirryrth wouldn't allow the male to leave. With little effort, Grirryrth scooped up the terrified Zerin in his front claws. A high-pitched scream pierced the air and caused the large creature to wince.

Grirryrth brought the captive to the front of his snout and blew out a tendril of flame, causing Drirux to cower and whimper. The dragon gave a low-pitched growl in a warning for the male to shut up.

At least the Zerin was smart enough to obey as he folded himself into a small fetal shape. Not that it would protect him from the enormous beast threatening him.

Satisfied the little male was under control, Grirryrth turned his attention to the two hundred-plus troops of the Warriors of Light. He leaned his massive head to peer through one eye at the trembling figures before him. The group moved back as one before they turned and ran away.

A chuckle rumbled out of the dragon's massive chest as tendrils of smoke wafted out of both nostrils.

Will you quit playing around so we can take care of Sherri? Ki was desperate to see how the female was doing. *She's probably bleeding to death from you biting her!*

Oh, by The-One-Who-is-All. I would let nothing *happen to our mates.* Grirryrth responded by scooping Sherri's prone body up in his free paw to walk over toward the waiting Elemi.

If your bite didn't kill her, she's probably frozen to death by now, you over-grown lizard! Ki's anger was palatable as he struggled to overcome his symbiont for control.

She did no such thing. His dragon reassured him. *She has Cheithe to keep her warm and to heal her.*

That statement made Ki pause. *What or who is Cheithe?*

Cheithe is my mate and your TrueBond's female dragon.

Female dragon? What in the nine systems was the crazy dragon saying? Ki thought back to several lectures his father had given about the Crart dragon, but nothing came to mind.

What do you mean, "your mate"? I thought you were the last of your kind! Ki watched in amazement as Grirryrth reached Elemi and trilled a vibrant song at the ship.

A responding sound reverberated from the ship's hull and the side dissolved to create a doorway. Out of the opening, robotic arms produced a small cage with the top open. Grirryrth opened his other paw and let the screaming Zerin drop. Robotic arms slammed the lid shut before the cell vanished.

Only now could I call Cheithe into being. I've transferred her essence into your TrueBond where she will continue to grow. The dragon brought a paw up to examine the sleeping woman. The large beast inhaled and exhaled with a low rumble of pleasure. *She is in there! She is finally here!*

Grirryrth lowered the unconscience female and placed her with great care within the open doorway. *Hurry, you must bring her back into the ship and get her comfortable.*

Before Ki responded, the dragon let go, and he was once again back in his normal body. With a scramble, he grabbed Sherri off the frozen ground and ran into the ship. Once inside the snug personal quarters, he laid her with extra care on the narrow cot. With shaking hands, he pulled her blood-soaked shirt off, exposing her bound breasts and smooth skin. Her mortal wound was gone. Instead, her breath was steady and deep, her skin a multilayered golden color, flushed with health as she slept. He moved her head to the side to check out the wound where Grirryrth had bitten her. There was nothing. The skin was smooth and unlined. It was as if she'd never been bitten.

Ki pulled over a nearby chair and dropped into it. With a careful touch, he brought Sherri's limp hand to his lips and placed a light kiss on it. What was he doing? He had no business touching her like that. Squirming, he returned her hand on top of her stomach as her taste lingered on his lips. He frowned and sat back to observe her and continued his discussion with Grirryrth.

Obviously, I've missed quite a few things about you. Fill me in on what's happening here. Ki sighed and pinched the bridge of his nose.

Status update, it is. The dragon gave a slight chuckle. *The ship's sentient identity is back from JR10. The Warriors of Light ran off like the cowards they are. That is their leader in Elemi's detention area. He's a present from me to you.* Smug inflection. *And best of all, my mate, Cheithe is bonding with your TrueBond. She'll emerge formed at an appropriate time and the Crart species will once again be born.*

She's not my TrueBond. Ki automatically argued against that assumption. *Even if she was, you know I'll not allow myself one because TrueBond relationships result in offspring. Which I can't afford to have.* He straightened when another thought occurred to him. *If what you say is true about your own mate, your continued existence doesn't rely on me having any children. Therefore, there isn't any need for me to have a TrueBond.*

The dragon snorted within Ki's mind. *We'll have that conversation once my female is strong enough. For now, since Cheithe doesn't have a battlesuit, she relies on my essence and strength to grow. My mate has begun her transformation within yours and will eventually come into corporeal form on her own.* A dragon sigh. *A couple more generations, and I, too, will not need to rely on the suit for existence.*

Ki grunted. Old arguments died hard. He refused to rehash the same old conversation.

"Elemi?" he asked aloud. "Are you back with us?"

"Yes, Ki dearest," Elemi answered with a happy lilt to her voice. "I am so glad to be back! While JR10 is wonderful, it was so cramped being stuck inside his small parameters."

To avoid a painful headache, he refused to think about the implications of that last statement. "I'm happy to have you back," he reassured the sentient ship. "Is your medical probe in working order?"

"Yes, my love. All of my systems are in perfect working order." Elemi's sultry tenor matched the sweet words.

"That's good, Elemi." He relaxed and closed his eyes. With a deep breath, he calmed his racing heart and focused. "Please run a comprehensive medical diagnostic on Sherri and relay the results to me once you're finished."

"If you insist, Ki dear."

The petulant tone made him grimace. While the ship was a coveted system, her inclination to fall in love with whichever male commanded the vessel annoyed him. "Thank you." He answered her absently, already planning his next move. "Do we have liftoff capabilities to continue our journey to Earth?"

A light glow encompassed Sherri's comatose body.

"Of course. Would you like us to resume?"

"Yes. Cruise at a maximum speed until you reach the appropriate coordinates to create the wormhole to Earth."

"Yes, Ki dear," Elemi crooned. "We should obtain neutral space within the next six cycles of the ship's measurements."

He'd stay there until that time. Even though he denied she was his True-Bond, there wasn't any reason he should let her wake up alone and frightened.

Sherri

"How do you *feel*?" The baritone voice of her fantasies jerked Sherri back to the conversation. Ki's body heat warmed her side. His luscious, fresh scent teased her. He'd put a calloused palm over her hand and she grasped it in reflex.

She blinked and glanced at their clasped hands. "Okay, I guess."

He tugged his hand away as his handsome face smoothed into a bland expression.

Damn it! Stop considering the man handsome! It was past time to get over this stupid infatuation. It wasn't as if he encouraged any sort of personal relationship between them. The squeeze in her chest hurt. Fine, two could play this game of pretend. Forget that soul-shattering kiss they shared before.

He cleared his throat. "Good." His sexy eyes glanced away as he leaned back and rubbed the close-cropped beard along his chin.

Whatever he wanted to say, he evidently wasn't comfortable bringing it up.

"Um...is Maynwaring contained for now?"

"No... yes?" Was the pirate gone? "I...I..." She sucked her bottom lip between her teeth. Was it all a dream that a female dragon gulped down the pirate?

No, child. A soothing feminine sound floated from the back of her mind. *I am here... I assure you that male is no longer with us.* The soft voice whispered and then trailed away.

Sherri stilled and swallowed with a dry throat. God, she hopened she wasn't losing her mind. "I...I think he's really *gone*."

"Why do you say that?" Ki's eyes narrowed. Those mesmerizing irises deepened their dual color. He twitched as if to cover her hand again, but pulled back with a frown.

"I... A..." How in the world could she confess what really happened? If she told him a female dragon appeared in a dream and ate the pirate, he'd think she'd gone crazy. At best, their relationship was tenuous, and it wouldn't take much for him to decide not to take her to Earth. No way would she let the Zerins go there on their own. As far as she was concerned, their record in dealing with humans was crappy. Besides, human women had a right to say what happened to them. When she and Lora talked about it, they'd agreed the male leaders of Earth wouldn't hesitate to take advantage and sell women off to the slave planets. Her lips pinched. They probably ask for sexbots in their place.

It was her responsibility to keep an eye on things.

"Not sure," Sherri gave an unblinking stare. "But I know the asshole is gone."

Masculine lips thinned as his head cocked.

She doubted he believed her, but she'd be damned if she'd get dumped somewhere and be left behind.

Ki folded massive arms across his wide chest.

For the first time, she noticed the black leather suit he wore—it was smooth and buttery soft, fitting his masculine body like a second skin. A nagging memory from Cheithe told her the outfit housed the male dragon, Grirryrth. Did she have to have a suit like that?

Scooting back to rest against the wall, Sherri kept her palms flat on the cot to stop from trembling in weakness. With a glare, she dared Ki to argue. His slight frown told her he didn't take the bait.

"I hope you're right." Ki uncrossed his arms and rested his hands on muscled thighs. "How do you feel otherwise? Any physical anomalies?"

Anomalies? What did that mean?

"No..." Sherri drew the word out while she did an internal check. Odd, she remembered getting stabbed, but maybe it didn't happen...maybe the whole thing had been some sort of bad dream. "I'm okay. Just a little weak, I guess."

Ki gave a sharp nod with a frown. "Ready to continue?"

Finally, a change of subject. "Of course." She jumped off the bed but misjudged how weak she was. The sudden movement made her dizzy and she almost planted face-first on the floor.

Ki caught her before disaster struck.

Her gaze flew to his and held as they stared at each other. Time slowed as Sherri sought to see if he was as affected by her as she was by him. Masculine warmth wrapped around her as she wet dry lips.

Instead of the expected kiss, he lowered her and backed away.

Her heart shrank with disappointment as heat crept up her face and neck. "Sorry. I'm not usually so clumsy." She glanced away and ignored the wave of regret.

He stepped back farther, lips tight. "That's understandable, given everything you've been through."

She nodded and looked around. Where were they? It looked like a bland, small room furnished with a chair and the cot she'd been lying on and nothing else. The round walls were a matte-black metallic substance. She couldn't tell if it was actual metal since it surrounded them in one solid piece with no seams or breaks in the construction. "Are we back on Elemi?" The last place she remembered was the frozen atmosphere of the asteroid.

"Yes, you're back in the bosom of my loving care."

The sickening, condescending croon of Elemi echoed around her. Sherri tried to hide her wince but obviously hadn't succeeded since Ki frowned.

"I've also provided you with appropriate attire," Elemi continued. "You're welcome."

Wow, she wasn't wearing a pullover sweater and skinny jeans. Now she had on the basic Zerin attire of a long tunic split at the sides over wide pantaloons and soft slipper shoes. Nice, the almond-crème color complemented her skin tone and hair. *But, Lord...* no mystery on how, or rather who, changed her clothes. Maybe she had been wearing blood-soaked garments, it sure wasn't something she wanted to do, but...*damn,* the thought of Ki undressing her made her mouth go even drier. Clenching her jaw, she vowed that first chance she got, she'd put her own clothes back on.

"Elemi, how far are we from reaching the coordinates to generate the wormhole to Ganymede?" Ki turned and walked out the narrow doorway.

With a sigh and a shake of her head, Sherri followed.

"We are almost there, Ki dear." Elemi's voice at least had a more reasonable tone than the one she used with Sherri. "I am analyzing the correct parameters and should be able to access the wormhole tunnel within the next several clicks."

"Acknowledged." Ki's wide frame strode with purposeful steps through the dim interior before entering another open doorway. He had to stoop to avoid bashing his head before going into the other room.

Sherri didn't have that problem and passed without ducking. *Why didn't Elemi adjust her interior to accommodate Ki's bulk?* She smiled. *Stupid ship wasn't perfect.*

"You can sit there." Ki pointed at one of two black bucket seats in the small cockpit.

Sherri swallowed a retort at his commanding tone and sat where he'd gestured. The minute her butt hit the chair, safety straps crossed her chest and lap. Startled, she gripped the side rests until her knuckles turned white.

Ki took the opposite seat. As his large body lowered onto the soft cushions, it adjusted to his size and strapped him in as he barked last-minute orders at Elemi.

Before the last word left his lips, the ship gave a sharp lurch that pushed Sherri back into her seat.

The 3-D display in front changed and expanded. Instead of the typical stars whizzing by on a wall-sized screen, the surrounding walls disappeared as a swirl of colors in the shape of a funnel whirled around them.

The dizzying sight terrified yet filled her with awe. She glanced out of the corner of her eye toward Ki, just to make sure it was normal. His nonchalant attitude calmed her tight nerves. With concentrated effort, she lifted each finger from the tight grip she had on the edge of the seat. When nothing happened, and she stayed comfortably in place, her breath came out in a whoosh. She was free and flying through space. *Oh, yeah!*

Much too soon, Elemi restored the original vid screen.

With a wide smile, Sherri snuck another peek at the Zerin man on her left.

His large body was a dance of pure grace as he faced forward. Ki checked the gauges and readouts, lips compressed and eyes narrowed. He appeared consumed by what he was doing.

She took the opportunity to study him as his attention remained focused elsewhere.

Those three-fingered hands were dexterous as they navigated across the console. A firm line compressed his lips as his eyes narrowed on the various computer displays in front and to his left. With each breath, his large torso went in and out, showcasing the muscled bulk within the black suit to perfection.

Then there was his lap. The roped muscles of his thighs clenched and unclenched as his body shifted back and forth as he worked.

The sight of his fluid control had Sherri's chest squeezing and her sex pulling in appreciation. She snorted. It certainly didn't take her long to become aroused just sitting there watching him. *Wow,* that had never happened to her before. Even that delicious granite expression as his brow furrowed while he worked was appealing. Why was she attracted to someone who had a huge neon sign blinking on his forehead saying, *No Trespassing*? Funny, that sign was in the "off" position when she kissed him. *Ack!* What was she? A preteen daydreaming about a crush on some boy? Time to suck it up, remain professional, and move on.

Lost in her thoughts, it startled her when she got caught in his sharp gaze. Sweat beaded between her breasts and along her hairline. *Great, now she'd be as shiny as cheap lip-gloss.* It took everything not to glance away. Instead, she raised her chin and returned his powerful stare with one of her own. "Something wrong?" She crossed her arms. He must have caught her staring at him. Her face heated.

A mahogany eyebrow lifted. "I am not certain." He gave her his complete attention. "Is there?"

Elemi disrupted their conversation with a flat tone. "Coming out of the wormhole and approaching Jupiter's moon, Ganymede."

The heat in Sherri's face traveled down her neck. Did Elemi know what she'd been thinking about? *Wait, why did she care what some ship thought? Damn*, now she'd lost it... worrying about what a ship thought.

Ki opened his mouth but Elemi spoke first.

"I have the lead scientist on Ganymede, Researcher Wapho, available for your communication." The feminine voice snapped on the last word.

Oh, for God's sake. Would someone please save her from this jealous ship?

"Thank you, Elemi."

Ki's strangled tone caused Sherri to give him a narrow glare.

"Patch him through." He cleared his throat and stared ahead.

On the 3D vid screen, an image of an upper torso and a head appeared. He seemed humanoid.

Kinda, sort of.

Thick, rubbery, skin with short, light-blue hair covered his head. He sported four eyes, two on the right, and two on the left. They were set at an angle... two eyes were toward the center of his forehead, while the other two nestled over the outer cheekbones. His pupils were elliptical—black slats ending in a dumbbell. The irises were a sea of light blue that matched his fur. Where a human nose normally was, narrow, vertical slits vibrated above a round, open hole for a mouth.

"Researcher Wapho, my name is M'alalu Ki E'eur and I am a representative of his majesty, Prince Qay of Zerin. I respectfully request an audience with you at your earliest convenience." Ki tilted in a bow of respect.

Wapho's mouth opened and a thin tongue vibrated as he spoke. "This is highly irregular, Master E'eur." The mouth smacked before it opened again. "For what reason do you violate the non-contact agreement between the Geidonn research team here and the Zerin monarchy?"

"I'm afraid there is some disturbing news, Researcher." Ki stroked the side of his bearded jaw. "I have it on good authority your base is in danger. I wish to meet and discuss how we may help."

The round mouth flattened before it smacked open. "Will you be coming alone?"

"No." Ki gestured toward Sherri.

Hopefully, the blue alien could see her.

"I will bring my companion, Sherrilyn Cantor of Earth."

The four eyes on the Geidonn widened. "That is a human!" The eyes blinked at various rates while his round mouth made smacking sounds. The light-blue fur across his plump cheekbones darkened.

Asshole. What did he have against humans?

The alien turned those eyes toward Ki, the top orbs narrowed while the bottom ones stayed wide.

Okay, that was all kinds of freaky.

"Humans taken off planet for the Exchange are not allowed back on Earth!" His voice raised with each word as his pinky finger pointed.

Sherri hid a smile as Ki's mouth tightened.

"I will explain the circumstances once we meet."

A huff of air. "Yes...yes. A satisfactory explanation is needed." The lipless mouth smacked. "I will send the appropriate coordinates to the display."

"Coordinates received," Elemi confirmed.

"I appreciate that, Elemi." Ki got up and motioned for Sherri to join him. "Let's go."

"Wait!" Dare she ask for a favor? She had to. "Can I see what we're orbiting?" She stepped back and tilted to avoid talking to his wide chest. "Is Jupiter visible from here?" She rubbed damp palms across the top of her pants waiting for the answer. How embarrassing...her nerd was showing.

Ki's warm, knowing grin made her mouth drop. *Holy God,* that was one killer smile. Good thing he didn't aim that deadly weapon too often, or she'd have to do something drastic. Like cover it with...say...her lips.

Damn, how bonkers was that? Sherri twined her fingers together behind her back. Slow down, missy. Leave the luscious alien alone. He's made it clear he wants nothing to do with you. No need to feed his ego.

He is your TrueBond. Of course, he wishes to do something *with you.* A soft voice chided.

Did her conscience now have a strange accent? *No, he doesn't.* Sherri huffed. *Oh, child, he can't help himself—after all, he's only male.*

Well, she wasn't going to stand here and argue with herself. Before she had a chance to reply, Ki spoke to the annoying ship.

"Elemi, please expose our current position." His smile widened as everything around them disappeared. The walls, the floor, and even the ceiling.

One minute she was standing in the dark interior of the 11-15 ship, and the next she floated free in space. She lost her balance at the abrupt change. With a squeal of alarm, her arms pinwheeled. Before she fell, Ki's strong arms enfolded her. Masculine warmth and strength steadied her as nothing else could. With her nose nestled against his rock-hard chest, a breath whooshed out before she breathed in. The now familiar aroma of male musk layered with his unique sea breeze scent made her heart beat a strong rhythm.

"You okay?" The tone came out lighter than his normal, deep bass.

He'd better not be laughing at her.

With a snort, she pushed away. "Yeah, I'm fine. Just startled." She stepped back but kept a grip on his forearms and peeked around his massive body. Yep, the only thing to hold onto was the large Zerin as the huge land mass of Jupiter appeared behind him. It was easy to recognize the planet due to the churning cloud of brown-and-white strips that intersected with the violent, swirling red storm. The closer they got, the bigger the dusty-looking ball became, until it blocked the vastness of space. The speed at which they approached the largest moon around Jupiter was dizzying. The tight grip she had on Ki's arm wasn't going anywhere.

"Do you want me to maintain acceptable orbiting parameters, Ki dear?"

Great, the femme fatale ship just had to crash the party.

"Yes." His voice lowered.

Sherri stopped gawking at the image of space long enough to be captured by his unbroken attention. Sparkling navy-blue and hunter-green eyes dominated her vision. With a shuddering breath, she leaned closer.

His body bent, dual-colored irises partially covered under heavy lids.

She watched his full lips and her heart thundered at the tempting prospect of them covering hers.

"Ki, Researcher Wapho is awaiting your arrival."

Sherri jerked in surprise at Elemi's smug tone. She closed her eyes and ground her teeth in exasperation. *Damn ship.* One day...

"Shall I transport you to the coordinates?"

Annnnd... the interruptions continued.

With a frown, Ki drew back from Sherri.

Interesting, maybe he'd been acting on instinct and hadn't known what he was doing.

His beard-covered jaw clenched. "Yes." His fingers released. "Once we are there, I will contact you to let you know our plans. Thank you, Elemi."

"Anything for you, Ki dearest," the ship crooned. "Transporting now."

A good thing Sherri hadn't wasted her breath commenting about the ship's syrupy tone of voice. She'd spend all day explaining her choice words to her alien companion.

The blackness of the star-strung space changed to near pitch-black.

What? Where did the stars go?

"Here, put these on." Ki placed a lightweight pair of glasses in her hand. "The Geidonns are photo sensitive and cannot have bright light in their living quarters. These will help you see while you're here."

Heh... reverse sunglasses. It took a moment to blink and adjust to the change. Well, at least she didn't have to fumble around in the dark. A quick check around the area showed a hollow room, empty except for the raised platform where she and Ki waited.

"Good, you are here." A deep, masculine voice boomed. "Please explain yourself."

Sherri twitched, and tried not to jump off the platform. *What the hell?* She glanced around and couldn't find the speaker. Just as she opened her mouth to ask where the sound came from, Ki bowed with his right arm crossing his massive chest.

"Thank you for receiving us, Researcher Wapho." Ki's tone remained respectful as he straightened.

It took a minute before it dawned on Sherri that Ki was looking down—way down—as he spoke.

She jumped when the small, three-foot-tall person, er, alien, moved in front of him.

An alien who glared at her much larger companion, arms crossed over his narrow chest. He wore billowy brown trousers encased in dark-taupe boots with a nondescript tan pullover shirt left untucked.

Holy shit, he was the four-eyed alien who spoke on the vid. Funny, she'd imagined him much bigger.

While small in stature, his body was in perfect proportion for his size.

"Yes, well, this is highly irregular and unprecedented." The little being huffed and smacked his lips, standing with knuckled fists on narrow hips. "But, no matter." He turned to leave the box-shaped room through an open arched doorway. "Now that you're here, let's find out what you think is so urgent."

The tiny male swiveled his head at Sherri as his eyes independently examined her. The top eyes rolled toward the corners while the lower two went cross-eyed.

Wow, that was bizarre on so many levels. Ki had reached over and grasped her elbow while they walked. Good thing he saved her the embarrassment of staring back.

"I assure you"—Ki's gentle grip on her arm kept her focused on where they walked—"not only are we here to warn you, but we have put measures in place to protect what scientific information you and your colleagues are working on."

With steady steps, they went through a sharp-edged corridor the color of milk. Various aliens of the same race as their reluctant host filled the hallway. None were taller than three-and-a-half feet, but the thin hairs on their bodies ranged from light blue to gray to pale silver. Some fur colors appeared dimmer than their counterparts' did. Maybe that was a sign of advanced age.

With a hard right into another boxy room, her gawking got interrupted. The room around them was a matte off-white color, like a place made of plastic.

Great, she was in a milk jug.

The room boasted a square table with four stools. The Geidonn anthropologist sat at the one farthest from the door and waved his hand for them to choose the remaining chairs.

Ki led her to a chair to the right of Wapho while claiming the one next to her across from the alien, probably choosing that place so he could face the exit.

At first when she looked at the tiny seat, she didn't get how she (much less the ginormous Ki) would fit. Soon it was clear she didn't have anything to worry about. The chairs were made like the ones she'd used on the *StarChance*. The seat rose and formed itself to the contours of the person using it. She sat back and got comfortable.

No sooner had they settled in than a female Geidonn entered with crystal tumblers filled with a brown liquid.

A fragrant scent of coconut perfumed the air as Sherri was served. The beverage reminded her of hot cocoa with whipped cream.

"Thank you, Nuepua." Wapho's lipless round mouth smacked and he frowned.

Was he mad at the little female?

Nuepua returned a slight frown with fluttering four eyes.

Oh... The charmed expression told a different story.

Nuepua couldn't have been over two-and-a-half feet tall, with fine silver hairs over thin skin instead of the light blue of their host. Her eyes were silver, but with pale metallic lashes and a thin eyebrow crossing her forehead. The compact body was feminine in design, with only one perky breast in the middle of her chest. The female rounded her mouth and twittered in answer, her head swiveling from side-to-side. All four eyes blinked independently as she left the room on quiet feet.

"Now, Zerin." The anger in the Geidonn's tone was unmistakable. "I must address a most important matter." He took a sip of the drink before his head tilted in Sherri's direction. "Why did you bring *that* here? As I said before, humans taken off planet to attend the Exchange are not allowed to come back anywhere near Earth."

Sherri's face flushed. "Hey, just who do you think you're calling a 'that'?" She rose and smacked her palms on the table. "I'll..."

"Sherri." Ki put a restraining hand on her arm and held her in place. His dual-colored eyes implored while the stern slash of lips said he wasn't happy with the conversation. "Please, let me take care of this."

With a narrow glare and pressed lips, Sherri plopped in the chair. Fine. She'd keep quiet and observe. For the moment.

"Researcher Wapho, I'm afraid I am confused." Ki took his hand away, leaned back, and folded his fingers to rest on his flat belly. He ignored the glass and its contents that the female had placed in front of him.

Sherri decided not to touch hers either. Maybe he wasn't thirsty or maybe he didn't trust the Geidonn. Best to play it safe and mimic his lead.

"Why are you so hostile toward Sherri?" With a nod of his head, he indicated Sherri. "I thought your life's work is studying the humans and the evolutionary path they are on."

The snort the small alien gave was humanlike. "Humans are vile, confusing creatures."

Sherri's face heated and clenched her fists on the tabletop. "Why you sanctimonious son-of-a-bitch..." She rose but Ki's firm grip pulled her back down.

"Look." The little dweeb smacked his mouth before continuing.

"No personal disrespect to your human here, but as a whole, they are a violent, self-destructing species. They have no honor, especially when it comes to their females."

His two right eyes glanced in her direction while the left set kept a steady gaze on Ki.

The light blue alien's round mouth smacked before and after he took a sip of his beverage. "It doesn't matter, anyway." Regret crossed his face and laced his tone. "They're at a dangerous precipice in their development. They'll either overcome extreme adversity within their own society...or they'll blow themselves up along with that glorious, unique planet." He gave another smack of his lips. "Such a waste. All those magnificent species ceasing to exist because of one selfish, sentient race."

Now Sherri's face heated for another reason. Maybe the annoying scientist had a point, but he didn't have to be so condescending about it. It was possible humans could pull their heads out of their ass long enough to survive. Too bad human history didn't support her wish.

"While I would love nothing better than continue to debate the merits of human development with you, there are more pressing matters to discuss." Ki draped an ankle across a firm thigh.

He didn't fool Sherri for a moment. A body that tense had a tendency to explode in action at any time.

The dim lighting went out. A pulsating rhythm resounded as a booming voice announced, "ALERT! Hostile forces imminent! Report to your stations!"

Wapho jumped and raced to the wall nearest the doorway. He waved a hand in front of the brown panel as a vid came into view.

The upper body of a male Geidonn, this one with light-gray eyes, was on the screen.

"Taoll, report!"

The frantic gestures of Taoll's rolling eyes alarmed Sherri. The panic on the Geidonn's face was hard to watch. She stood next to Ki, who had joined Wapho at the display.

"It's the Friebbigh!" screeched the other male. "They've breached our defenses and are now swarming through the halls. What are we going to do?"

The Friebbigh. The Gray aliens so prevelant in modern human mythology. Something she'd learned from Maynwaring's memories. Talk about vile creatures. They were an outlaw race in the Federation Consortium for a good reason. Not only that, but they were responsible for the human female slave trade in the galaxy. Boy, what she wouldn't give to have a real dragon inside to deal with the little vermin.

Oh, child. I am here. I would never let them harm you.

Sherri blinked in confusion before the surrounding chaos grabbed her attention.

The outside corridor filled with the screams and shouts of running Geidonns.

Meanwhile, Wapho tried to calm the male on the vid who was having a meltdown. "Focus, Taoll!" commanded the elder alien. "Release the evacuation protocols and get everyone to the escape pods immediately." With a wave, he ended the communication. He turned to Ki. "Follow me. I'll lead you to an escape pod."

"We'll just transport to our ship…" Ki started.

Wapho interrupted him with a shake of his head. "No, the only place you'd be able to contact your ship is the transportation room. The outer shields are now in place." Wapho grabbed the sleeve of Sherri's tunic and pulled her behind him.

Startled, Sherri glanced at Ki following them, matching his long strides with the shorter ones of the Geidonn.

"Once you're in the pod and it's ejected into space, you'll be able to contact your ship." The smaller male raised his voice against the klaxon alarm. The screeching, scared voices of the other Geidonns added to the bedlam in the corridor.

They pushed their way through the sea of miniature bodies. Sherri had to laugh at the panicked look on Ki's face as he avoided stepping on several of the short bodies milling around.

Wapho yanked on her sleeve to get Sherri's attention. Damn, he was strong for such a little guy.

The Geidonn leader took them toward a dark doorway that turned out to be the front panel of an escape pod.

A small...tiny...itsy-bitsy escape pod with barely enough room for her, much less the gigantic frame of her Zerin companion. She gulped. Boy, that was gonna be a tight fit. The image of her and Ki smooshed together made her girly parts wake up. Too bad her fears overrode anything else. Enclosed spaces made her heart pound and break out in a nervous sweat.

Swallowing past her dry throat, she tore her stare away from the sardine can to listen to the instructions the Geidonn gave Ki. The technical blah-blah-blah went over her head. She watched the dark hatch instead. When the coffin-like contraption slid open, it seemed the confined space beckoned with an evil leer. No way. That stupid thing was smaller than she first imagined, and tight spaces were not her friend. Even the tantalizing image of cuddling with her Zerin obsession couldn't tempt her to think about going inside.

"Let's go." Ki gripped her elbow and led her to the death trap.

"Oh hell, no!" She dug in her heels. She'd rather face the slimy Friebbigh than take her chances in the dark hole. Okay, so it wasn't really a hole—small lights and blips had activated once Wapho opened the pod. But still, it reminded her of an enclosed coffin.

Ki didn't argue. Without breaking his stride, he lifted her and stepped in. Once seated, he rested her between his steel-rod thighs. The smoky glass door closed.

The last thing she saw of the interior of the Geidonn base was the back of its leader hightailing away as fast as his little legs carried him. She leaned against the safety of Ki's wide chest.

The speed of the escape pod was impressive. They zoomed into space like a fastball at the World Series.

The vessel spun and swirled around the image of the moon, and Sherri squeezed her eyes shut against the threatening nausea.

Flush against his broad chest, Sherri was covered in a blanket of his signature scent. Warm breath fanned her neck as her skin pebbled in reaction. A strong surge of adrenaline blazed, and she scuttled into the juncture of his rock-hard lap.

Hot damn! Her eyes opened wide as the crease of her ass encountered the rigid line of a solid erection. She couldn't help squirming.

His hold tightened as his warm breath bathed the back of her neck.

Yum. His length was in direct proportion to his body size. And boy howdy—was he ever happy to see her.

CHAPTER SIX

Sherri

T he thud of Sherri's heart pounded in her ears. Thrown into the throes of sexual anticipation, she wiggled her butt in appreciation.

"Don't do that."

The masculine whisper feathered against her neck. His massive arms tightened around her. Wisps of warm breath fanned her sensitive skin. The clean musk of his mesmerizing scent sent a thrill down her spine. In reaction, she grasped a steel forearm, not sure if she wanted to get loose or pull them closer.

"Do what?" A scratchy rasp came out before she cleared the lump from her throat. But really, her nightly fantasy personified held her close, how could she not move? Her stomach tensed as a large palm encircled her waist while the other hand rubbed the top of her thigh. She shivered, eager for more. Maybe being stuck in the small space was a good thing.

"Stop moving." His wicked whisper accompanied his tightened grip. "It's hard for me to think when you do that."

"Is that so?" She ran a tongue across dry lips before giving him a coy smile over her shoulder. Yeah, something was *hard,* all right. She turned around to hide her smirk. Mr. Prickly might not like being seduced. What? Since when did she want to pursue the attraction between them? But then again why not? He triggered something inside. Everytime she came near him a jolt zaps her hands and feet straight to her gut. Then her stomach drops like she's in a car going over a hill quickly. Yeah, the tension between them was hot.

Hot enough to for her to go up in flames and take him with her. Definantely time to get the man on board with the program. She slid backward to rub against his erect cock. The movement sent a sizzle of lust down her spine. *Damn,* she liked being a girl.

His nose caressed the sensitive area behind her ear.

"Naughty girl."

A rough, slick tongue suckled her lobe.

"It's like that, is it?"

A sharp nip of his teeth startled her before he licked away the sting. Eager for his kiss, she turned.

He had other ideas. His large palm glided up the sensitive skin of her inner thigh until it reached the crease between her torso and leg—and stopped there, fingers folding and unfolding as he massaged her plumped sexual lips.

Sherri squirmed. Desperate, she wanted him at the center of her body. With a wiggle, she opened her legs a smidge, inviting him to explore.

Which was ignored.

Her alien tormentor continued to rub the outer junction between her legs while the other hand tugged her head back and exposed her vulnerable throat. It was hard to breathe, not knowing if he would use those pointed teeth on her or not. A mixture of panic and arousal thundered through her. Ki inhaled and her skin pebbled. When the expected sharp pinch didn't happen, her tight nerves relaxed. One lick, two...then gentle lips suckled as the soft hairs of his beard caressed.

Son of a bitch! A jolt of passion squeezed her lower body. Sherri reached behind her to grab a fistful of mahogany hair.

His devastating play resumed before he settled on the side of her mouth. With a small swipe, he demanded entrance.

She didn't hesitate...she opened so they could join.

At first the moment was soft, two people learning the texture and taste of each other. Slow, gliding skin against skin. Their combined breaths mingled and mixed into something unique. The memory of their previous embrace didn't come close to reality as they physically connected.

Then the soft moment turned into one of intense awakening. From one swipe to the next, his tongue took control.

She drowned in his heady flavors...a fresh sea breeze that swirled and combined with the enhancement of an aroused male. A low moan escaped from deep within as she relished the masterful way he took over.

While she concentrated on the pleasure their combined mouths brought, it took her by surprise when his hand wandered upward to brush against the underside of her breasts. She trembled as her body flushed with internal heat. Wide fingers from his other hand brushed the sensitive juncture between her legs, causing her clit to swell.

Her sex quivered in reaction.

"Ah...so responsive."

His throaty growl in her ear made her quake.

He eased back from their kiss. "Yes, you delicious female...right there." With deft hands, he encompassed her right breast and gently squeezed the hard nipple in sync with a dive between her intimate folds with the other hand.

While he didn't caress her naked skin, the dexterity and pressure he used were stimulation enough. Twisting nerves stretched in her lower stomach. *Oh, Holy God.* She braced for the oncoming orgasm.

"Yes, fly for me, *yofie-na.*" Ki jerked as if whatever he'd said startled him.

She couldn't care less what he said. He could spout nonsense at her whenever he wanted. As long as he kept strumming and crooning in that wicked whisper, she'd go from zero to orgasm in no time.

Ki delved deeper into the crease and moved across her clit.

Her core tightened, the pending release out of reach. She moaned and looped an arm around the back of his neck. Squirming over the hard ridge under her bottom, she made a futile attempt to direct him where she wanted him to go. Desire rose in response to his sensual campaign.

"Sherrilyn, I'm going to give you so much pleasure."

The exotic accent caused her adrenaline to soar. His ribbed tongue licked the shell of her ear even as his lowered voice seduced.

"Do you give permission for me to do this?"

Coherent words died in a dry throat. With wide, unseeing eyes, she managed a nod.

"Exquisite female." Lips suckled along the pebbled skin at her neck. He tugged her head toward his mouth. "Time to worship you." His palm slid lower until he grabbed the edge of the tunic and pulled it up. He bunched the soft fabric to burrow under the waistband, slow enough to make a grown woman cry.

With a light touch, he skimmed over her stomach and made it quiver. Breath held, she waited on the edge. *Ack... too slow!* Sherri squirmed, trying to force him where she wanted. It was useless. He wasn't going to do something he wasn't ready for. Her breath shuddered. In a sensual daze, she gripped the hair at the nape of his neck tighter. There...now he'd get to the tip of her curls saturated with arousal.

A rumbling growl of approval reverberated from deep in his chest.

Thoughts scattered as he parted her folds and stroked the length of the hidden plump flesh. He had an unerring ability to rub the sensitive skin that made her eyes close in ecstasy. Never...never had anyone played her with such skill.

"Ah...there you are, my lovely. Do you enjoy my touch?"

Ki's rich baritone added to her bliss and that commanding purr inflamed her reaction. He gave another stroke before heading to her trembling entrance. A large finger slowly encircled the opening and entered with careful ease. A gasp and moan rolled out of her throat as he pumped and stretched the inner channel. Sherri grabbed his thick wrist to hold onto. He'd better not stop; on the contrary, he'd better go deeper. The sheer magnitude of her response caused her to shake. Her fingers became numb from her tight grip.

"I...you...yes...ah..." *Great, impressive, Sherri.* The deep pumping motion against sensitive walls made her moan.

He chuckled. "Hmm...you like this, yes?"

Dry. There was no moisture in her mouth to form any sort of answer. It was impossible to swallow so she nodded instead. Her core tightened when his finger, damp with her juices, came out to fondle the swollen clit. *"Ahhh..."*

He massaged the hardened flesh with painstaking skill.

If he kept that up, she'd detonate in no time. She sucked in a bliss-filled breath as the tension pitched to a higher level. *Yeah*...just one more flick... He complied...she exploded.

A loud, undignified wail escaped her as tension released and toes curled. As she inhaled, her body collapsed, liquid and limp. Boneless in her alien lover's cocoon, she was surrounded by the warm scent of her sexual musk mixed with his unique tangy blend. So what if her yowl was embarrassing? Dignity was overrated.

Ki caressed her stomach with lazy strokes while nuzzling the back of her neck.

Sherri had never responded to anyone as she did to this enigmatic man. How she let things go so far was beyond her, but right now, all she wanted to do was bask in the warm-and-fuzzy afterglow, secure in his arms.

Yes! He will make an excellent TrueBond. That accented voice purred.

Sherri agreed with the sentiment, even if she had no idea what the voice meant.

His hot breath departed as the restraining straps popped. In a quick move, Ki shifted her until they faced each other.

She gazed into dilated eyes before their mouths joined. Closing her eyes, she savored his taste. She moaned and straddled him, flush against his narrow hips. Cradled by his wide palm, her head stayed in place while Ki burrowed deeper into the recesses of her mouth. Desire rose, sharp and insistent, as if she hadn't just experienced fulfilling pleasure. She wanted him again. She plunged her fingers into the thick hair at the back of his head as she ground her groin into his. A small portion of his mahogany hair tightened around her fingers and held her immobile. Startled, she whimpered.

He eased off their kiss as his eyes narrowed.

It was tough to read his expression because his green and blue irises were dilated to such a degree the iridescent green pupils overtook them.

His face was darker than usual, and deep breaths made his solid chest rise and fall.

Clasping fingers pulled her closer.

"You..." His lips were set in a grim line.

A shiver slithered across her spine. She refused to let him belittle what just happened between them. Taking the coward's way out, she captured his full lips to stop him from saying something she didn't want to hear.

He was stiff at first before massive arms roped around her and returned her embrace. After a few, brief heated moments, he broke away. "Female, you and I..."

"Ki, sweetheart! Oh, thank the Goddess I've finally found you!" Elemi's voice quivered between the exclamations.

The big man shut his eyes and hugged her close.

A surge of satisfaction went through Sherri. Yeah, good to see he wasn't as unaffected by their passion as he might pretend.

"Yes, Elemi." Those sexy orbs opened and placed a steady gaze on her. The blue and green rings of his irises contracted. "Please transport Sherri and me to your coordinates."

"Oh, right away, darling!"

Sherri didn't get a chance to roll her eyes at the ship's endearment before they were pulled through the ship's transportation. Never mind. There'd be plenty of opportunities later.

Ki

No doubt in Ki's mind, he was the biggest idiot in the galaxy. One whiff of her alluring, citrus scent and all higher brain functions ceased. The supple sensation of her body combined with her complete abandon swept him away. The irresistible taste of her exotic response was burned forever into his memory.

TrueBond... yess... Grirryrth was smug.

He wasn't going to dignify that statement with a response. Even if it was true, he did not intend to pursue a personal relationship with her. Determined to keep an iron control on his careening emotions, he ignored the painful squeeze in his chest.

Ah, my little hatchling...

Great. Just what he needed, a condescending badass dragon treating him like a child. Hard to believe the twenty-foot reign-of-terror was a romantic softy at heart. It was enough to make any sane Zerin grit his teeth in exasperation.

You cannot deny the whims of fate, my young one. My mate is growing and becoming. She will soon need her mate to complete her. The dragon's deep voice took on a sharp edge never used against Ki before. *And I intend to be there when she is ready. So, either Cheithe and I will finish the TrueBond or you and your female will before that happens. Know this, you will not jeopardize my female's life due to your stubborn belief you are flawed and cannot have offspring.*

For the first time since bonding with his Solaherra dragon, Ki *felt* his friend and mentor withdraw from his conscious mind. It was as if a heavy door slammed between them. At a loss, he blinked.

Once again they were seated in Elemi's control room. A movement to the side caught his attention.

With a trembling hand, Sherri attempted to straighten her bunched tunic to tame the wrinkles he'd made.

As her hands pressed and stroked her lush body, Ki's dick swelled. When she brushed something off the shelf of her generous breasts, it caused the orbs to bounce with those nipples poking in hard points. At the same time, her aroused musk filled his sense. His breath lurched. *Fruk!* The way her supple body moved caused him to spill in his suit like an untried youth. *By the father of everything.* His teeth and fists clenched in reaction. Sweat beaded along the side of his face. Good thing Grirryrth's bio-suit took care of the mess without a thought. Ki refused to go forward with a large, wet stain on his lap.

At least Sherri didn't know how she affected him. The problem was, her scent covered him. The strongest came from the hand he'd used to bring her pleasure. It was a struggle not to bring his fingers close to inhale her heady aroma. Better yet, reach out with his tongue to lick the taste clean. Instead, he made a fist and dug his nails into the flesh of his palm.

"Ki, are you alright?" Thank the nine systems for Elemi's interruption. "When I saw the huge Friebbigh armada approaching Ganymede. I feared the worse!"

"Your concern is appreciated, Elemi." Ki turned his attention to the front panel of the cockpit.

The black obsidian console flickered readouts in the Zerin language along with multiple vids showing the exterior of the ship. His heart raced at the sight of more than twenty vessels surrounding Ganymede.

They were in the "M" shape of the sleek 10-15s, a new type of fighting ships for warriors. Each was capable of intergalactic missions, not needing a mothership to house and maintain them. The ships boasted a construction of a thin, pliable, material that made them a maneuverable dream. So far, none of the Federation Consortium systems could penetrate their cloaking ability, whether they were in folded or regular space. The firepower they used was one of the best in the civilized galaxy. Impervious to blaster fire, their hulls absorbed the shock and converted the energy into viable fuel for the craft.

Too bad blasting them out of existence wasn't an option.

Good thing Elemi was a step above those vessels. While she had the same basic design of a 10-15, she had all of their benefits plus some unique to her. She had the ability to create her own wormhole to travel faster than any other ship. And, her phasing-out ability kept her from detection. Her hull absorbed outside stimulation and adjusted to any environment to blend in, mimicking other ships. The most impressive thing about Elemi was her sentient status. As an interactive AI, she could integrate into any ship's database without getting caught. A perfect spy.

"What are those?" Sherri's single-colored brown eyes widened as she pointed to the larger main vid. Five of the 10-15s lined up and faced the Jupiter moon.

"Trouble." *Son of a sacrilegious slug.* "Elemi, analyze and report."

"Completed," came the quick answer. "All ships are under the command of the Friebbigh High Council with Erkeks in various positions of authority. They've taken control of the Geidonn research base and they are holding eighty-five percent of the personnel captive."

"Any update on the lead researcher, Wapho?"

"Unknown. Individual identities are not available."

Ki sat back. "Are the scientists in mortal danger?"

"Undetermined."

"Can you determine the intent of the takeover?"

"Yes, they are awaiting further orders from Chancellor U'unk from the Federation Consortium."

Ki blinked. A sudden cold squeezed deep inside. "The Chancellor is on the way to the Geidonn base?"

"Yes, Ki dear. The Friebbigh are in a holding pattern until then."

Ki ignored her dulcet tone and his mind raced. Why would the wily Chancellor leave the comfort of the palatial space station to come to this backward planet at the edge of the galaxy?

"Elemi, is there any way you can put me through on a secure channel to Prince Qay at the royal Zerin headquarters?"

"Easy enough once I infiltrate and use the Friebbigh signals." A disdainful sniff. "I assure you, no one can access my systems until *I* let them."

Ki glanced around after hearing Sherri's feminine chuckle.

The corners of her mouth quirked as her eyes twinkled. "About time this ship turned her snarky comments on you and not me."

She folded her arms under her chest and made her breasts plump in a tempting lift. Mussed from their earlier play, her auburn hair framed her flushed cheeks in wild abandon.

He swallowed dryly and had to tighten his jaw and fists against the urge to haul her to the sleeping area in the back. There he'd make sure her rumpled appearance included more than just hair.

Something in his expression must have alerted her to his thoughts. Her exotic eyes widened as a pink tongue licked those full lips, making them shiny.

That woke his cock up. At an internal snicker from Grirryrth, Ki tore his attention away and concentrated on the floating ships. Watching that deadly threat was safer than concentrating on the tempting female.

"Ki, Prince Qay is available." Elemi's voice broke into his disturbing thoughts.

"Thank you, Elemi."

The 10-15s on the main viewer were replaced by the face of his closest friend, Prince Qayyum E'etu.

By the father of all, Ki was glad to see him again. The first time they'd met, Ki was busy getting his ass handed to him by a horde of Friebbigh determined to separate his head from his body. The slimy little *puntneji* maggots had gotten the best of him, all because he'd disagreed with Grirryrth earlier and left the suit back at his quarters. Fortunately for Ki, Qay plowed right in just as the

Friebbigh started to gain the upper hand. Without Qay's help, he wouldn't have survived.

To be honest, gratitude wasn't the only reason he vowed an allegiance to Qay. A not-so-gentle nudge from Grirryrth convinced him to bind to the wayward prince. And after five solar-years, he'd never regretted that decision. If there were regrets, it was that he'd never shared the truth about his dragon companion with his friend. The need for secrecy about his Crart heritage with the Solaherra dragon had been ingrained into him from birth.

"Okay, tell me everything." Qay's forehead puckered, his eyes narrowed.

Ki raised his eyebrows in return. Why the suspicious expression? He scrutinized his friend for any signs of additional stress.

Qay's black hair was pulled back in its normal braid, prominently displaying his widow's peak. He kept his warrior's braid tightly woven on the right side of his face, exposing the TrueBond mark, the MalDerVon Scroll. The dark green crystal in the intricate scroll announced Qay's son nestled within his pregnant TrueBond. While Ki had always admired the younger male, the level of calm maturity was new. It was rewarding that the weight of a new family and resuming the mantle of the crown prince sat well with Qay.

Here was the male his friend was destined to be. Ki relaxed. The Zerin people were in good hands. He didn't like giving Qay bad news, but there was an upcoming threat to the life of his people and to the foundation of the known galaxy. Now was the time to get the male's advice on what should be done next. Ki gave a quick glance at Sherri.

She leaned toward the vid with her lips pressed together, her full attention on the screen.

Dread knotted his stomach. He'd brought her into this dangerous mess and it was up to him to make sure she stayed safe. "I'm afraid there is an unexpected complication." Ki turned back to the monitor. "Not only is the Geidonn research base overrun by Friebbigh, but they're waiting for the Chancellor to arrive before they move on to Earth. Elemi"—Ki directed the ship—"please display the armada around us for Qay."

Qay's eyes widened before a low growl crawled out of his throat, the tips of his sharp canines exposed. "Goddess damn it! I just knew when the Special Triad Council got involved it would spook that *puntneji* bastard."

Ki tilted his head and gave Qay a blank stare.

Qay sighed and rubbed the bridge of his nose, a sure sign of frustration. "Councilman Aine called the Special Triad Council into session because of rumored allegations against the Chancellor working with the Erkeks and the outlawed Friebbigh." He pulled his hand away while a corner of his mouth lifted. "Complaints have come in across several systems about those aliens selling human women from Earth into slavery. And guess whose name crops up more than once along with those slavers?"

Ki grunted. U'unk had been a careless fool.

Qay continued. "So Aine gets this a brilliant idea to question the Chancellor about his involvement." The snort of disgust was clear. "Instead of gathering needed information beforehand, he and his duo of clowns traipsed over to the Palatial Space Station to talk to him. Idiots. It doesn't surprise me in the least U'unk was smart enough to leave as soon as they left, to speed up his plans concerning Earth."

The Prince of Zerin sat back and tapped a forefinger on the top of his rare, dark wood desk. His gaze unfocused as if he was contemplating what to say.

Ki had been with him long enough to let the silence stretch while his friend formulated his next statement.

The tapping finger stopped. Qay's attention focused on Sherri. "What about the Dread Pirate Maynwaring?"

Ki sat forward with an eyebrow quirked up. "I can assure you, that is one thing we don't have to worry about." He jerked his head toward Sherri. "She got rid of him." At least he hoped so. "That *fruking* piece of *eztli* shit is gone forever."

Out of the corner of his eye he saw Sherri nod and lower her arms. Which made her chest available for his unobstructed view. *Fruk!* When had he become so enamored of a female's form he couldn't concentrate on more important matters? Ki swallowed the urge to watch her.

"Really?" Qay drawled. His left eyebrow rose, mirroring Ki's expression. He leaned back to steeple his fingers. "I'd love to hear how that happened."

Ki focused on his friend. "I'll tell you all about it later." By then he'd have a better idea on how it happened. "There are more important things to discuss."

Qay's face tightened with an emerald stare. He nodded. "Okay, but you and I will have that conversation when this is all over." His jaw clenched. "I warn you, I'm not going to let this and other matters drop." He leaned forward. "Not this time."

Ki sent his friend a sardonic smirk. This wasn't the first time Qay hinted at wanting to know Ki's secrets. Maybe it was time to inform the royal family about his Crart heritage, which included the Solaherra dragon. With Qay's renewed status as the crown prince, his friend would be in the perfect position to help protect Grirryrth if something happened to Ki.

"We'll see." It was the only concession he'd give for the moment. Best to discuss it with Grirryrth first. "How do you want us to proceed?" He nodded toward Sherri, who focused on the conversation.

With clasped hands, she stared at the vid.

Ki couldn't begin to guess what had her complete attention.

"Can you escape your little friends and reach Earth before they do? Undetected?"

"Oh, *please*!" Elemi's exasperated voice interrupted.

Qay's eyebrows rose in surprise. "Can I assume that's a yes?" He cleared his throat. "The Federation Consortium forces are on their way, but we're at least a solar cycle behind him and won't reach Earth before he does."

Ki gave a rare chuckle. "Yes, I assure you getting to Earth without the Friebbigh or the Chancellor detecting us will not be a problem." The chair creaked as he relaxed. It was necessary to maintain the illusion of being relaxed when he was anything but. The deeper they got into this situation, the more he didn't like Sherri being involved. She was an untrained civilian, for Goddess' sake. She had no business being anywhere near this whole mess, especially now that the pirate was gone.

He had every intention to start that conversation but Sherri interrupted.

"Why not start is the United Nations Secretary-General like we discussed before?"

For some reason, it was irritating she focused on Qay and didn't give him a second glance.

"While the UN has no real authority on the planet, it would be better to try there."

"If you're sure..." Ki experienced a strange satisfaction when her intriguing brown eyes glanced at him, no matter how brief.

"Like Lora and I tried to explain, Earth is home to some extreme, xenophobic, patriarchal societies who are fanatical in their own separate superiority."

Her strong snort startled Ki.

"They don't tolerate different humans, so how do you expect they'll react when they take a good look at you?" Sherri pointed a thumb in Ki's direction.

Heat crept up his neck. What was that supposed to mean?

"Not very well, I assure you." She turned back to Qay. "We've had decades of scary movies and bad alien PR to whip the billions of humans in a frenzy of terror if anyone saw one of you. The best way is for me to go to the UN and try to warn them before the Chancellor and his armada arrives." A sheepish smile. "Just let me know how much I can say."

Now the flush crawling up his neck had nothing to do with embarrassment. If she thought she was going by herself, she'd better think again. Especially if the humans were as dangerous as she claimed. He had to be by her side to protect her.

Yes—protect our TrueBond at all costs!

For once, he and Grirryth were in complete agreement about the female.

Qay sat back and covered his lips with a forefinger as he stared at Sherri.

Ki recognized that look. The pit of his stomach rolled. Ki was sure Qay had decided something he wouldn't like.

"Will you be in any danger?" Qay dropped his hand to his lap.

Sherri shrugged and wrinkled her nose. "I don't see why I would be. Unless your guys on the *StarChance* didn't do their jobs and erase my existence from Earth's files."

"Not a chance," Qay piped in before Ki responded. "My people were very thorough with the human women's records."

"Okay, good." She gave a nervous chuckle as she tucked the hair behind her strangely round ear. "I'll need identification restored in the United States system to request an audience with the Secretary-General. You know, something with an official position and title to help get me through the door. Can you pull that off?"

"Oh dear, you are so simple," Elemi responded. "I can make you Queen of the Universe if Ki wants me to." A put-upon sigh filled the cockpit. "There, it's done. You are now a person of Earth with proper credentials."

A panel in the front black console opened. A strange white plastic badge embossed with her picture lay in it. Looped at the top was a metal clip to fasten on her clothing.

Sherri lifted it out to examine. Whatever Elemi made seemed to satisfy her, and she addressed Qay. "This should do." She turned to Ki. "I'll need to change my clothes before I go."

The situation was getting away from him. Time to state the obvious. "Elemi will remain cloaked when *we* transport to the surface."

"You're going with me?" Sherri's eyes widened.

Ki's jaw clenched tightly. Time to end this fantasy she had of leaving without him. What kind of male did she think he was?

"Of course I'm going with you." A tight fist was kept hidden as he leaned into her personal space. "I'm not letting you out of my sight."

Feminine eyebrows rose as she gave him a once-over. "Um, okay?" She leaned away in her seat.

"Good!" Qay slapped an open palm on his desk. "Glad that's settled. Go to Earth, prepare the humans as best you can until our ships reach you. You'll have to hold out for a few Earth hours until we get there."

"Oh Qay, I almost forgot." Ki snapped his fingers. "I have a present for you."

Qay's mouth twitched. "Really? What is that?"

Ki waved a hand to encompass the ship. "Elemi, would you be so good as to show Qay the guest in stasis?"

"It will be my pleasure."

A holographic image appeared of the captured WOL leader, Drirux, caught in the throes of a stasis field.

"Oh, and who is this?" Qay leaned forward with an eager expression.

"This *puntneji* piece of filth is the head of the Warriors of Light, the one who gave the order to kill your TrueBond, Aimee."

The hard expression that crossed Qay's face was one Ki hadn't seen in a long time. The mantle of royalty slid from his noble features. In its place was a primitive male Zerin focused on protecting his TrueBond.

"I thank you, *mihr*." Qay licked his lips as he glared at the image of the Zerin rebel. "I am ever in your debt."

It had been a long time since Qay used the word for "brother" toward him. While it was an honor to receive such a label from his friend, Ki was uncomfortable when it came from his prince. Some days it was hard to separate the two.

"When we meet again, he is yours." Ki bent toward Qay in a slight bow of respect.

Qay's eyes narrowed as his lips pulled back to expose his long fangs. "I look forward to seeing you both soon." His eyes flicked back and forth between Ki and Sherri. "Have your ship give me updates on a regular basis." The crown prince of Zerin sat back as his face relaxed into a warm smile. "May the Sacred Goddess of All protect and keep you. Good hunting, my friend." He regarded Sherri before he addressed Ki again. "In all things. Qay out."

CHAPTER SEVEN

Sherri

I n Sherri's previous life on Earth, she'd met heads of state, presidents, and those of various remarkable achievements. Even so, it was hard for her to believe she sat there talking with an honest-to-god alien prince. It took everything she had to keep her mouth from hanging open and staring like a lunatic. However, the more the conversation continued, the more she realized she wasn't all that impressed.

While he was one of the best-looking men she'd ever seen, he missed that certain something she craved in the opposite sex. True, Qay's dual-emerald eyes flashed with an exotic flair—the deep verdant inner ring surrounded the lighter and matched the iridescent pupils. Thick, black eyelashes gave him a smoky allure. But, those alien irises were not dark navy-blue circled by a dusky hunter green. Qay's obsidian hair remained in a tight braid away from his striking profile. It wasn't shoulder length in a luxurious dark-mahogany curtain that framed a masculine profile to perfection. Qay bore the unmistakable mark of his noble birth; Ki's blunt features had the hard-won earmark of character and grit.

Ki's scar might cause some women to run in terror, but Sherri shivered in wanton appreciation. Late at night, she had hot fantasies about tracing that scar with her lips and tongue, mapping and claiming the angry skin.

Whoa. Sherri jerked and glanced to make sure Ki hadn't noticed her zoning out. *God!* What if he caught her mooning about him? Their playful activities notwithstanding, he'd never given her any indication he was interested in any personal relationship with her, other than a basic sexual one. *Great...* Earth was on the brink of an alien invasion and all she could think about was the hot guy next to her. Some hero she turned out to be.

It is proper to crave your TrueBond. The soft voice spoke in the back of her mind. *When the time is right, we will mate with our males.*

The image made Sherri shiver. After enduring the psyche violation from the Dread Pirate, she now believed another symbiont lived in her. While it might be awkward having someone sharing her conscience, the female blended with Sherri rather than being something separate.

Maybe she should take the plunge and speak to the dragon. It was a big, final step, acknowledging the dragon was real. Once she did, there'd be no going back. Okay... *I doubt he feels the same way.*

Ah, child.

The smooth reprimand from Cheithe soothed the hurt feelings Ki produced when he'd acted as if she didn't mean anything to him. *Humph*, like the man hadn't been all over her...giving her the best orgasm ever.

The boy is a confused and wounded male. It will take patience and cunning from us to show him what is right.

Sherri smiled. The dragon called that huge man a boy. *Cunning?*

Yes, he is male, after all. A light snort. *I assure you—he wants you more than he admits... even to himself. Therefore, we will allow enough time to pass for him to come to terms on the fitting nature of our TrueBond pairing.*

We will?

Yes.

An image of a smirk on the delicate, silver snout made Sherri give one of her own.

However, not too much time. The soft feminine chuckle faded into the background.

"We should arrive in Earth's orbit in a few clicks. Elemi will put us an appropriate distance away from the United Nations in an unpopulated area to avoid detection. From there, she will arrange a transport to take us into the city." A big hand waved at her body. "If you want to change before we land, you'd better do it now."

It took a few moments before Ki's words penetrated the fog of Sherri's mind due to the conversation between her and Cheithe. She blinked and tried to focus on what Ki had said. Clothes? Oh, yeah...going to Earth. Time to get decent clothes instead of the wrinkled, creme tunic she wore. Her heart thundered when she remembered how it got so rumpled, bunched in one of Ki's large hands while the other played her body like a master.

"Um, okay. I'll be right back." She stood without looking at him. Heat crept along her neck as she headed for the sleeping quarters on the other side of the ship.

Once there, she painstakingly described to Elemi the outfit she wanted the ship to replicate. She envisioned a sleeveless dark peach blouse with folding drapes tucked inside a pencil-thin gray skirt topped with a small belt. A soft white sweater jacket trimmed with delicate dual black strips at the wrists and along the breastplate. A pair of platform stiletto heels in the same color as her blouse to match round, dangling earrings. A single gem drop necklace completed the look as it nestled above her cleavage. A matching single-handle purse in white with peach-and-black trim completed the ensemble.

Feeling like herself for the first time in ages, she was ready to face the UN.

"Did you put me on the schedule for the Secretary-General this afternoon?" Sherri asked Elemi, putting paperwork the ship provided into the handbag. She also had a small tube of lip gloss to go with the mascara and light eye shadow.

After a moment's consideration, she folded up the Zerin slipper shoes into a tight roll and put them into the purse. No telling if there'd come a time when a quick departure was necessary. She'd be damned if she'd run around in platform stilettos.

"You have a 3:45 pm meeting." Elemi's voice lacked sarcasm for once.

Ki walked into the small room reading a hand-held device. "Are you ready to—" His head came up. "—go?" He stumbled with wide eyes and an open mouth.

At first, his inspection made her uncomfortable. She ran a sweaty palm down the skirt and glanced to make sure it was on right with the blouse tucked in. When she peeked at him and his dumbfounded expression, she couldn't help the feminine smile of satisfaction.

His dual-colored eyes narrowed. Between one heartbeat and the next, his dark cheeks bloomed in an interesting shade of mauve. "What the *fruk* do you think you're wearing?" With long strides, he stood before her. Mere inches separated them as a blast of his masculine scent surrounded her. The hand not holding the device fisted on and off as if he had a hard time controlling his emotions.

Sherri's face flushed at the aggressive demand. What in the world crawled up his ass? With a fist on her hip, she gave him her best *don't go there* glare. "Look, buddy." She poked the middle of his solid chest. "I don't know what your problem is, but this is how a professional woman on Earth dresses—ack!"

He cut off her incoherent squawk with his mouth.

The unique tang of his taste made her head spin. Sharp and spicy...sinful temptation that ramped up her response. A large palm at the top of her buttocks squeezed as her core clenched and melted. Automatically her arms wrapped around his neck to pull them closer. Feminine softness meshed with male hardness. She stroked with her lips as they caressed and devoured one another. Her only wish was to hang on and never let go.

With a low moan, Ki dragged away, and they slid apart.

Her eyes closed for a few heartbeats as she savored the lingering sensation he'd caused. When she opened them, the burn of twin iridescent pupils filled her vision. Sherri gulped and shuddered. *Holy Mother of God*, his kisses were everything she'd ever dreamed of.

Ki's firm hold held her in place. Hmm, what happened to the device he'd been holding?

"You..."

"Ki, dearest. We are now in orbit around Earth." Of course, Elemi interrupted.

The grip on her ass tightened as his eyes closed. Now she had a free moment to examine the ruddiness that stained his skin under the short beard. Ki was a force of nature, a mature man in his prime. Overt virility ensnared her befuddled mind as she writhed in feminine appreciation.

A vein at the corner of his neck beat a fast tattoo. A muscle in his jaw twitched.

Ah, good to know he wasn't as unaffected as he liked to claim.

Ki released a breath and opened his eyes.

Damn, caught staring.

His fingers tightened before letting go.

Sherri couldn't wait to see what he'd do next.

"I'm sorry." He took a step back. "I shouldn't have done that." The words came out soft as his gaze fell to the floor and he picked up the device where it lay upside down. By the time he straightened, his face was expressionless and void of the previous heat.

A wave of hurt at his indifference squeezed her chest.

He gripped the device with white-knuckles as the screen unnaturally captured his attention.

Sherri swallowed a smile of satisfaction. *Ha!* Someone was working hard on keeping his emotions in check.

"As Elemi stated." He cleared his throat with a deep rumble.

Her smile widened.

"Now that we are in Earth's orbit, we can transport down whenever you're ready." He gave the appearance of stoic indifference.

"How will we meet up when I'm finished?" Sherri spied the purse sitting on the bed and went over to retrieve it.

A choked sound jerked her around. What in the world was that? It sounded like a cross between a growling tiger and a strangled baboon. A quick glance around the room revealed only her and Ki, and he hadn't moved.

Ki's passive appearance had morphed into one of primitive intent.

She gripped her chest when his eyes narrowed and the skin stretched tightly over his sharp cheekbones. Good Lord, he must have eyeballed her ass when she'd bent over. Sherri bit the inside of her cheek to stop a smirk from showing. Instead, she straightened and made sure her face was expressionless. She held the handle of the handbag with both hands in front of her. *Yeah,* that would protect her.

A heavy-lidded male gaze landed on the swell of her chest.

"My eyes are up here, big guy."

Blue/green eyes snapped away from her chest.

Now her grin came out as she sauntered to him. "As I was saying, how do I get back in touch when I'm done?"

Ki may have heard her, but he took his sweet time answering. A sensual smile curved that full mouth, a sure sign of male appreciation. "You are an extraordinarily beautiful female, Sherri."

The deep baritone sent shivers up and down her spine. Caught in his mesmerizing expression and words, she trembled when he invaded her personal space. No need for his touch, she'd become hyper-aware whenever he was near. The heat and enticing scent seared.

"When we're finished here, you and I are going to spend some time alone." It was a whispered, blatant dare.

Normally, when given such a directive, she'd dismiss the person without another thought. Not this time. This time Sherri was in complete agreement. Hard to say where their involvement would end up, but she was more than willing to find out. She rewarded him with a sultry smile and ignored his last statement.

"Is there some kind of communicator for me to use?" The sooner she left, the sooner she'd be back to indulge in their sensuous play. Okay, time to concentrate on the impending invasion of Earth and stop flirting with the tempting man. Her nails bit into her palms. Maybe the slight pain would keep her focused.

"That is not something you need to worry about." Ki spoke into the shell of her ear. His warm arms wrapped around her and pulled her flush against a wide chest. "I'll be close enough for you to touch the whole time."

Sherri's head jerked back. Her nose scrunched as she tried to figure out what he meant when Elemi's transportation dissolved the room.

Ki

A prickle of unease slithered across the base of Ki's skull. Elemi had put them in an area surrounded by a thicket of tall strange brown and green plants Grirryrth described as "trees." Since meeting the delectable Sherri, the dragon had developed an unusual curiosity about all things Earth. Grirryrth promised to give him pertinent information about the landscape of the foreign planet from time to time as he gained knowledge.

Enough. Time to concentrate on the female who walked in front of him. Speaking of delectable... He admired her spunk and intelligence, wrapped up in a feminine package he'd have to be dead not to notice. He gave an involuntary grunt. When he spied her in those Earth garments, all higher cognitive functions disappeared. He'd reverted to a primitive male ready to claim his female.

Caught up in the way her tight ass swayed in that short covering, he almost stumbled. The back of the soft material of her top stretched across her shoulders and emphasized her supple muscles with each movement. Ki blinked as an image of that shirt draping over full breasts had his fingers itching to caress and delve into the softness underneath. He would love to pull her back against his chest and reach under and push those beauties up to create a deep valley. Once her nipples became puckered and solid, he'd turn her around and dive between those mounds to explore fragrant skin with eager lips.

But it was those ridiculous things on her feet that caused him to swell to the point of pain. His arousal was swift, wild, and hard enough to punch through the impenetrable suit of his Crart ancestors. He'd wrap those long legs with the spike heels around his waist and thrust into her tight, wet sheath. Ki's breath caught. *By the father of all,* he was no better than an *eztli* bull in rut. It took conscious effort to step back. With a clenched jaw, he went into protective mode and scanned the surrounding area with an expanded sense of smell. Nothing to note except the normal scents of nature polluted on an industrial planet.

Elemi had promised them a transport nearby, something called an SUV? It should be two measures to the left. Ki passed Sherri. "Do you know where to go to meet this leader of yours?"

A sharp yelp of laughter came out of her full lips. "Are you asking me to take you to my leader?"

Why was that funny? An image of Grirryrth shrugging his massive shoulders. The dragon didn't understand why she laughed either.

With a wide smile, she wiped a small tear from her left eye. "Anyway, we—I mean, you—can't appear at the UN and not cause a panic."

Sherri's exotic brown eyes caressed him, lingering on his chest, which puffed out in pride under her appreciative glance.

"You don't exactly blend in, you know." She stopped with her hands on her hips while she tapped a foot.

Ah, he loved watching her face flush a darker shade of pink that highlighted those exceptional brown eyes. Before he told her how he would get around his appearance, a loud *clack* echoed in the air followed by several repeating sounds.

Sherri flinched, her gaze darting about the landscape.

"What was that?" He scrambled to cover Sherri's back. Senses heightened and expanded, he drew her close. Taking in a deep, probing breath, he again tried to detect danger. Various natural aromas flooded...musky animal, the astringent plant growth, and the humid air. There was also a scent he had a hard time identifying, a mixture of metal, sour sweat and nervous fear. Grirryrth rumbled a warning for him to remain alert.

He must have made a noise because Sherri's head swiveled to gape at him, her short auburn hair swishing across sharp cheekbones. With a raised eyebrow, he dared her to comment.

With a lopsided grin, she left his arms and resumed her walk. She'd changed her stance to place one foot in front of another in careful steps.

Ki snorted. Walking in those contraptions must take a lot of concentration. "What was that noise?" He repeated his query.

"Gunshot."

Ki frowned. That was the same alien projectile that almost killed King Abzu and had wounded his friend Qay. Its ammunition was a nasty, poisonous weapon to Zerins. The battlesuit would protect him, but that didn't mean Sherri wasn't vulnerable.

"Are you sure?" He rested his hand atop the disintegration blaster strapped to his right hip. He extended his senses. Ah...there, several measures ahead of them through the trees. An altercation between a group of humans.

Ki moved in front of Sherri. When she went to go around him, he pulled her behind him. "Stay there," he commanded.

She stiffened but made no sound or tried to move.

"I'll be right back." With extra care, he navigated through low bushes and tall trees before a clearing opened. He stayed in the shadows to observe. The scene turned out to be universal, with one exception. Ki frowned. Something was off. The group being held was different from the dangerous criminals he'd expect with such a show of force.

Weapons pointed, five uniformed law enforcement agents held a ragged collection of frightened humans. There were two elderly males and one matronly female trying to calm three wailing children.

Ki tensed when a guard pushed the fragile oldsters and caused an elderly male to fall on the rough terrain.

The female gave an anguished cry and tried to reach the fallen male but the guard slapped her across the face and shoved her back.

"Stay on your knees, you fuckin' chili shitter!" An out-of-shape male with an enormous belly draped obscenely over a tightened waistline, threatened the terrified female. In a blatant show of superiority, he raised a solid club over her.

The children screamed, their high pitches cries laced with fear and terror. The female covered the children in her feeble arms with a hunched back.

Ki took a step to interfere when a blur of female rage stormed past him right into the fray. "Sherri, no!" With a hoarse growl, he did his best to stop the streaking woman, but she was too fast. How she maneuvered so quickly on those clunky shoes was beyond him.

Her clenched fists and stomping stride told him what he needed. *By the father of everything that female would be the death of him!* He had to get between Sherri and the possible threat. And he had to that without alerting the humans to the fact he wasn't one of them.

Grirryrth, human image now!

Having a Solaherra infused into the battlesuit had advantages other than housing the dragon. He could transform into whatever form he wanted. It was one of the reasons he'd been a successful mercenary with the Alliance of Assassins. There was no trouble maintaining a near-perfect hologram for several macroclicks until Grirryrth became overwhelmed. But he and the dragon had never tested it long enough to find the breaking point.

When Grirryrth announced the transformation was finished, Ki jumped between Sherri and the volatile situation. With a gentle hold, he pushed her behind him. With her safely out of the way, he confronted the five human males abusing the other humans. He made a move to grab a blaster out of the hidden holster under his jacket when a high-pitched squeak stopped him.

"No, Ki!"

Strong fingers stalled his momentum.

"Don't. You'll only make matters worse!"

Ki considered Sherri's pleading expression before he lowered the weapon.

She sucked in a breath as she examined him with wild eyes.

Looks like she'd noticed his change in appearance.

"Halt! You are interfering in ICE business, people." One of the younger males stepped in their direction and held up a palm as if to ward them off. "Move along or we'll arrest you for obstruction of justice." The fingers on the male trembled as he made a move to grab the projectile weapon holstered in his belt.

Why did they call themselves frozen water? No matter, the humans' confusing terminology wasn't important. What was important was the ramifications if he took action against these males in authority. While it would be easy to take control, it was imperative to meet with this leader Sherri wanted to instead of getting involved with something else.

"Ki?" Sherri tugged his arm.

He wasn't sure if she asked about him looking human or trying to stop him from blasting them all into oblivion.

"Did you hear me, people?" The aggressive demand came from the male as he moved closer. "You need to leave now."

Ki opened his mouth but another other human male ran over and interrupted.

"Hey, Stan!" This one was even younger, his fresh face barely out of the pubescent phase.

The first male didn't take his eyes off them when he answered. "What, Barry?" The projectile weapon never wavered.

"It's that famous lady wanted by the FBI for Internet terrorism, Sherrilyn Cantor!" The youngster's voice hitched with awe. "And we's got her!" Strange single-colored blue eyes narrowed as he pulled out his pistol and leveled it at their direction, the tip weaving and shaking.

A gasp came from Sherri behind him.

By the father of all! He crossed his arms in an attempt to rein in his temper. How did this *puntneji* recognize her? They'd erased her identity when she boarded the *StarChance*. At the earliest opportunity, Ki would verify the records with D'zia. Right now the situation had to be defused.

Sherri's warm hand latched around his waist as she leaned into him. He held her tight, keeping a free hand to grab his weapon if necessary.

Barry's announcement caught the attention of the other three male guards.

One gave a swift kick to the downed elderly male before he barked at him. "Get up an' get goin'!" He waved the weapon to encompass the small, helpless group. The children were still crying as the female held them. The other elder male reached down to his companion before he tugged at the kneeling female to help her up.

"Don' get too far, now," the male continued. "'Cause we'll be back for ya soon enough."

No one had to tell the terrified group twice. The two males each grabbed a hand of a child and ran off into the woods without a backward glance.

A surge of satisfaction filled him as the abused humans left. One less thing to worry about. Now he'd enjoy taking care of the little annoying problem that stood in their way. The only question was, should he do it himself or let Grirryrth come out and play?

Too bad Sherri had other ideas. Somehow, the crazy female thought she could talk herself out of whatever the males intended.

"I'm afraid you have me confused with someone else." She opened the strange contraption she carried and foraged inside it.

Ki had no idea what she was doing, but he noticed the twisted mask of impatience on all five human males.

"Lady, you'd better pull your hand out of that there purse right now."

Ki decided Stan led this group of dishonorable males. The human had the audacity to point his weapon at Sherri. Enough was enough. No one threatened his female... A slight metallic click sounded as the human did something to his weapon to make the noise.

Sherri stopped. With rapt attention, she addressed the male. "No need for that. I'm only trying to get out my ID." Her tone was reasonable and calm. "I am a special attaché to the UN and have an appointment this afternoon with the Secretary-General. I just want to show you..."

"I said, 'don't move!' " Stan's forehead dotted with sweat that ran the length of his temples.

Why was this human getting nervous? Ki didn't want to admit it, but he was having a hard time understanding all the dynamics.

"Okay, okay." Sherri took her hand out of the contraption and put her palms up as the loops of the bag slid to her elbow. "What do you want me to do?"

Everything stopped; the five males facing them became immobile with the same expressions of wide-eyed terror and slacked jaws. It didn't take long for childish squeals to pierce the air as the humans turned and ran, dropping their weapons during their mad dash.

ENEMY! Grirryrth's shout caught him by surprise. He jerked to glance behind him. Coming through the thick grove of Earth trees came the last person Ki expected to see.

Drirux. The male he had locked in a stasis field in Elemi. *How in the blasted nine systems did he get free?* Ki couldn't believe Grirryrth hadn't detected Drirux before this. The weight of Grirryrth's confusion held him in place, but so did another problem.

A platoon of fifty Zerins wearing the emblem of the Warriors of Light followed Drirux. That repulsive WOL emblem bit deep into his Zerin psyche—the royal symbol of the Zerin people with primitive spearheads on the left side and the starburst of the joint nine systems of the consortium on the right housed in a double-sided green field — overshadowed by an outline of a smashed fist obliterating the image.

Through the haze of blinding rage, Ki's lips curled at the smug face of his childhood nemesis. He ignored the disintegration blasters pointed at him and Sherri, his fists rolled into hardened balls. It took every ounce of control to consider the best course of action.

"Well, look who we have here." Drirux sneered as he scrutinized Sherri. "A lovely human female standing next to the inscrutable M'alalu E'eur in human form. What's the matter, half-breed? She not like your Zerin looks?" With head cocked to the side, he folded his arms. "Or was the sight of your disgusting scarred face too much for her to handle?"

Ki grabbed Sherri's upper arm to stop her from approaching the male. Sometimes it was better to stay still and let the opposition talk.

"And just how did you accomplish such a feat, eh, E'eur?" Drirux walked nearer.

Too bad he was smart enough not to get too close.

Four of his guards filed in line behind him.

A quick analysis gave Ki the information he needed on the best way to disable all five. Which left the other forty-five guards as a problem.

A loud dragon snort echoed in his mind. *There is no problem. Leave them to me.*

No, not yet. Ki soothed his friend. *I'm afraid you'll attract unwanted human attention if I let you out. Let's wait and observe what happens.*

Fine. We'll do it your way. A mental nudge told Ki he hadn't heard the last from Grirryrth. *For now.*

"No matter, I don't really care how you did it." The male stood with his legs slightly apart as he leaned back.

Idiot—keeping his arms crossed when they should be loose at his side to grab a handy weapon.

"What I really need is for you to get out of that suit." His crooked nose furrowed in a sneer. "And give it to me."

Ki's left eyebrow rose as the corner of his mouth tipped. "You have a desire to see me naked?"

Sherri gave a light titter and moved closer.

Her soft feminine fragrance teased Ki. Not a good time for distractions or a growing arousal. How he could get sexually stimulated when surrounded by hostiles was anyone's guess.

Drirux's sharp features turned ruddy at Ki's mockery. "While I know I can't harm you while you have it on, it's not going to protect her."

A guard yanked Sherri away from Ki's protection. He grabbed air.

Trapped in a Zerin elbow hold around her throat, her face darkened.

That mulish expression twisted Ki's gut and clogged his throat. He couldn't allow her to do something foolish and get hurt. He'd better get to her before she came up with something crazy on her own. "Let her go." Ki growled. He would not ask again.

In response, the assailant flicked his wrist and released a sharp blade that bore into her tender skin. The razor-thin metal pierced, causing a bubble of red to surface under her jawline.

Pain filled her brown, human eyes.

"I wouldn't get any closer if I were you."

The amusement in Drirux's voice had Ki grinding his back teeth.

"Cueryg is one of the most bloodthirsty individuals I've ever had the pleasure of meeting." Drirux strutted to stand next to the Zerin fanatic holding Sherri in a tight clasp. "And he has a particular loathing for other species, especially those beneath us." He stood well within Sherri's personal space. With a hand under her short, red/brown hair, he lifted the strands and leaned in to take a deep breath.

Sherri shuddered and narrowed her eyes.

Good thing she didn't react. Ki was sure Drirux wouldn't hesitate to retaliate if she did.

"While she is lovely...in a primitive, nasty way." Drirux flicked her hair from his fingers and stepped back. "I wouldn't be caught dead touching her."

"That can be arranged." Ki's razor-sharp incisors were on full display.

Drirux ignored Ki's invitation with a fanatical leer.

Ki stiffened.

"Just to make myself exceedingly clear to you. Cueryg *will* kill her, painfully and slowly if you do not give me that suit *right now!*"

The last word raised in a warble told Ki everything he needed to know about Drirux's unstable mental health. Ki's stomach hardened at Sherri's volatile predicament.

Something must have shown in his face because Sherri jackknifed into action. She yanked the end finger of her assailant's hand around her shoulders while she swung her leg back and kicked him in the groin with the spiky heel of those dangerous shoes. She caught Cueryg by surprise and he let her go as he doubled over in pain.

He dropped the knife and fell backward, landing with both palms clutching between his legs. He folded into a fetal position while he moaned and cried as loud as a youngling.

Sherri spun and raised a leg to stomp on the downed male. That would kill him if she plunged the shoe into his heart.

Drirux grabbed her from behind and swung her away with a violent twist that caused her to arms and legs to fling in separate directions.

Those dangerous shoes flew off her feet, whooshed past Ki's head, and ended up embedded into a tree trunk. The shoe wobbled but held steady in the hard surface. No telling where the other one landed. Good thing it missed him.

While he was focused on Sherri, a powerful hand grabbed his left shoulder and a large palm covered his mouth and nose. He jerked to dislodge the assailant but his body refused to obey. The hand over his mouth held a cloth coated with some sort of astringent. Pain stung his nostrils as a pinch of foulness slithered across the back of his tongue and down his throat.

Before Ki took another breath, cognitive thought scattered into oblivion.

Sherri

When Ki fell to the ground with a loud thunk, his head, arms, and legs flopped in a boneless heap.

A screamed bubbled in Sherri, but a large Zerin palm muffled her wail.

"Hold still, you disgusting *hysta*!" A voice of gravel breathed in her ear while the malodorous smell of ripe socks made her gag. "You'll not catch me by surprise as you did Cueryg!"

Sherri recognized Drirux, the leader of this band of losers who held her. She turned her head as she tried to get away from the foul odor. Hard to move in his punishing grip. Damn asshole was going to leave fingerprint bruises.

Sherri didn't care what he said. It wasn't in her nature not to struggle. The only problem was, her shoes were gone and bare feet wouldn't have the same impact the platform stilettos had. "Let me go, you son of a bitch!" *Yay!* Her mouth was free. For a reward he smacked her upside her head.

"I told you to hold still!" The bully thrust her at a waiting guard. "Here, hold this while I get that suit off him."

If the other Zerin hadn't caught her, she'd have planted facefirst on the forest floor. The back of her head throbbed, but the pain faded when the muzzle of a space gun filled her vision. It took effort, but she wrenched her gaze from the narrow three-barrel weapon to peer around it.

The asshole, Drirux was instructing two of his flunkies to figure out how to get Ki's clothes off him.

What the fuck was up with that? She smirked when they could discover no fastenings or tabs to loosen.

Do not worry, they cannot take Grirryrth off your male. Cheithe whispered with a snicker.

"Goddess damned *fruk-ass*!" Drirux swung a leg and kicked the prone Ki.

Sherri tried to rush toward him, but the guy holding her jerked her backward. He dug into her upper arm with fingers bigger than that asshole Drirux's. Purple bruises were definitely in her future.

It didn't take long for Drirux to stop kicking the unconscious man. Ki's body barely moved with each strike so the sadistic jerk stopped and glared with heavy breaths and closed fists. He pivoted and grabbed a sword from one of the guards. He approached Ki and squatted next to him.

"If I can't get this off of him while alive, I'll just have to kill him." The blade swung upward, getting ready to chop off the prone man's head.

"NO!" An inner strength surged through and she yanked free. Sherri dived toward Ki, oblivious to any danger to herself. She had to get to him...to save him.

The blade came down.

Screaming, she wasn't going to make it in time. Fury, hard and bright, engulfed her as time stilled and reality flipped. An all-encompassing power filled every cell in her body. The universe opened its secrets, giving her the will and the knowledge to save him.

Cheithe was born.

She was female of a species not seen in the galaxy for thousands of millennia who now moved through Sherri and morphed into existence. She'd take care of her mate.

Happy to relinquish control, Sherri let go. Anything to spare Ki. Letting Cheithe take over was different from the forcible grasp of the Dread Pirate. The dragon and she had a genuine partnership...two equal souls in pursuit of one goal. Sherri drifted further into the dragon's mind. Time to enjoy the ride.

Cheithe didn't disappoint. With a thunderous roar, the large beast blew a wall of fire toward Drirux and engulfed his body.

Oh, my God...could Ki be trapped in that raging inferno?

Between one heartbeat and the next, the searing fires folded and popped out of existence.

A silent whimper escaped Sherri as the blaze slowly disappeared. Ki lay untouched; no sign of the firey bath he'd endured. Pain clogged until she noticed his chest moved with each breath, his handsome face relaxed. It seemed like he was okay...

The other scraming Zerins ranning amok grabbed her attention. Her vision clouded before Cheithe spread the flames and caught the rest of them in one sweep.

A light breeze swirled, taking with it the smell of burnt flesh on minute particles of ash from the dead aliens.

Cheithe grunted and sat on her haunches next to Ki. With a gentle nudge of a crystal-gray claw, she pushed Ki's seemingly human body.

It jarred Sherri to see Ki looking so....weird. While his overall features stayed the same, the human differences made her uncomfortable. It was as if a child's scribbles defaced a master's artwork. His iridescent dark skin lay flat, a boring tan color. His shiny, glorious hair now lay dull and muddy, frizzy waves lay on his extensive shoulders in a lackluster line. Where were those sexy pointy ears to tease her? In human form, instead of the brilliant navy/hunter-green iris combination, his eyes had been a dismal brown. They lacked the blanked fire and passion that was all Ki. Sherri chuckled. She even missed the alien three fingers. The whole "looking human" visual wasn't right.

Wake up for me, Grirryrth. I won't be able to retain my form for long and I crave to be with you.

Through Cheithe's vision, Sherri watched Ki disappear in a haze of bright-colored lights. In his place sat an enormous, navy-and-purple dragon. When his magnificent snout swiveled toward them, his bright blue eyes blazed.

Strong claws dug hard into the rich earth, their amethyst-crystal color sparkling with each movement. He sauntered his bulky body toward them.

Cheithe responded with a shiver of anticipation that echoed inside Sherri.

Finally, you are here! Grirryrth's masculine cry reverberated in elation. *I have waited so long for you.*

The hollow ache in his voice had a profound effect on Sherri and melted any resistance in being a part of the reunion. She retreated further into Cheithe's psyche to allow the dragons a moment of privacy.

In response, the female dragon welcomed her mate with a purr as they met halfway. The sounds of dragon trills floated in the warm spring air as they entwined their long necks and rubbed their large heads together. Their snouts touched when they shared fiery breaths and nuzzled each other in joyous abandon.

Sherri connected mentally with Grirryrth as well as Cheithe. What a joy it was to experience the peaceful, soul-bond of the two mythical creatures. Within reach, a tiny spark shone in the background, a flickering light that embodied Ki, asleep and safe within his dragon. While Ki slumbered, Grirryrth told her their story. About a guilt-ridden boy-man who witnessed the death of his family and how he blamed himself. Believing he was a flawed individual, the boy refused to allow his tainted bloodline to continue. He viewed his past actions as those of a coward and refused to allow his heritage to carry on to another generation.

Then the dragon explained how a Zerin male mated for life with his True-Bond, the only female he'd be able to produce children with. In a secret whisper, Grirryrth stated Ki suspected Sherri was his TrueBond.

Really? But, what did that really *mean* she was his TrueBond?

With an impatient snort, Grirryrth gave her a general description. When a male and female found their TrueBond mate, the MalDerVon scroll appeared at the same time on each of them. The scroll proclaimed the pair legally married as it bound them physically and psychologically. When separated for an extended period, the couple experienced separation anxiety that could incapacitate them.

Sherri let the silence stretch. Well, that explained the mark on Lori's face the last time she'd seen her. Sherri assumed it had something to do with her friend turning into an alien.

That aside, Sherri experienced a sense of calm that confirmed the rightness of what Grirryrth suggested. This is what she wanted when she'd left Earth. To find a man meant for her. While running away from the threat of twenty years in prison was incentive enough, the prospect of finding lasting love had made the decision all too clear.

And what a man her alien was. Exceptional intelligence, honorable, mature, and deeply principled. Add to that—tall, muscular, and gorgeous with the most beautiful, exotic eyes she'd ever seen. What more could a girl want? Best of all, Grirryrth assured her Ki returned her feelings, even though he fought the attraction.

Ah, poor baby. Looked like Ki needed someone to guide him through a touch of insecurity. Sherri smiled. And she was just the gal to help him work through that little problem. She snickered, convinced they deserved to be together. No way was she going to let the man's commitment phobia stop her from claiming her mate—er, TrueBond.

Besides, how could she lose? She had two large dragons as backup.

CHAPTER EIGHT

Chancellor U'unk

As his signature ship approached Ganymede, Chancellor U'unk scrutinized his twin sitting in the copilot's seat next to him.

Drawn and thin, Lok sat with an apathetic expression and seemed to ignore everything around him.

Somehow, a slight twinge of guilt crept in. U'unk quashed it. Everything that happened to him when he was younger was Lok's fault. If it weren't for Lok, the family would have accepted him without question. Life should have turned out the correct way sooner, with him on top and in charge.

"Welcome, Chancellor U'unk. All is secured." A tinny voice filtered through the console communication.

U'unk motioned for the vid to open.

A khaki-green head of one of the Erkek lieutenants faded in, the carnelian color of the triangular pupil fixated on a point to the side.

U'unk grunted, appreciative that the underling had the intelligence not to look him in the eye. "Very good, Waesk. Ready my approach."

"At once, Excellency." His caramel pupils moved to the opposite side. "We await your arrival at landing dock K-3. Would you like a tractor beam to guide you in?"

Lok stiffened beside him.

"Yes, proceed."

"Acknowledged. Waesk out."

U'unk sat back and crossed arms over his chest.

"What are you planning on doing with me?" The bass timbre of Lok's voice came out as a thick whisper.

U'unk faced the other male. It was possible taking Lok with him had been an impulsive act he'd soon regret. Common sense told him he should have eliminated his brother decades ago, but where would the fun be in that? Besides, it excited him to make Lok live under his complete control.

However, with the Special Triad Council asking impertinent questions, his time as Chancellor had come to a premature close. Even so, U'unk had one final thing to accomplish. Having Lok as an indisputable sacrifice once everything was in place would solidify his power base. The public execution would be an excellent example to those who refused to grant him an undying loyalty. The resulting legend of holding his twin hostage and then killing him in a public execution would leave no doubt about U'unk's right to rule with an iron control. There'd be no confusion on how he dealt with those he deemed unworthy.

"For now, you will remain at my side and bear witness when I take my rightful place as Emperor." U'unk flashed his sharp incisors in an aggressive Zerin display of dominance.

Lok bowed his head lower and wrapped thin arms around himself.

U'unk savored a surge of satisfaction at seeing his previously arrogant sibling broken. Yes, *by the Goddess*, he'd proven he was the better male.

The ship docked into the research station and interrupted the brief interaction. The sound of the engines died as the hatch dissolved to show an opening. That was their signal to move out.

"Come on, Lok," he sneered. "This won't hurt a bit."

Without another word, U'unk stood and stepped back. With a wave of his hand, he gestured the silent Lok to go ahead as they exited the ship.

Shuffling, Lok's features tightened as he stepped forward.

The landing bay was small, with barely enough room to house his private star jumper.

Standing at attention was Waesk with a contingent of four Erkek guards behind him.

The flat recycled air mixed with the normal foul body odor of the aliens made U'unk's nose twitch. He surveyed the gloomy space. Something was missing. "Where are the Friebbigh?"

After Waesk genuflected a respectable bow, the seven-foot Erkek bent his double elbows and clasped his two-pincer fingers together. His standard military one-piece suit was a murky yellow that highlighted the sickly green of his skin. The insignia of lieutenant was a bold wide stripe with a tint of copper that started at his right shoulder and crossed his skinny body to end at the tip of his bony hip. His knee-high brown boots shone with precision that declared pride in his appearance and rank. It was unfortunate that the normal stench of an Erkek lingered.

U'unk schooled his expression to mask his displeasure.

Lok lacked the discipline to hide his reaction to the rotten egg smell. He coughed and sputtered as he hid his nose behind a palm.

U'unk sneered in his direction before putting his attention back to the Erkek who was speaking.

"They are with the rest of their contingent holding outside Earth's orbit." The monotone voice was muffled in the small room. The thick metal walls were sterile, void of any esthetic characteristics.

U'unk allowed a frown to show his irritation. "I did not give them leave to abandon this base."

"No, sire," Waesk agreed. "It seems they did not heed your command."

U'unk crossed his arms. "What about the Geidonn scientists? Are they secured?"

"Yes, sire." The Erkek gestured with one pincer toward the dual steel doors leading out of the bay. "Will you interrogate them at this time?"

Insubordinate puntneji. U'unk stifled a spurt of irritation and glowered.

Evidently sensing the mistake in his phrasing, the Erkek bowed at the waist and touched his knees with his forehead. "Please accept my apologies, sire." He spoke to those knobby knees. "I meant no disrespect by questioning you." He held that position.

Beside him, Lok stiffened and backed away from the group.

U'unk suspected Lok's actions were natural for someone who'd been by himself for the last fifty years. It appeared his pathetic brother was overwhelmed by so many bodies around, especially with the rank smell overpowering the small space. U'unk dismissed any further thoughts about his twin and allowed a few precious clicks to pass before he spoke. "Have crews see to my ship. I want it refueled and restocked. You will now take me to the lead scientist."

Waesk straightened and clasped his pincers together in submission. "Right away, sire. Please follow me." Orange pupils flicked a glance at Lok, but he didn't make a comment. The Erkek turned toward the two steel doors while the four guards flanked behind U'unk and Lok.

They entered a cramped corridor that was stark and devoid of color, just as the docking bay had been. Its ceiling was low, causing U'unk and his Erkek companion to bend as they walked. Having lost body mass and weight over the years, Lok didn't have the same problem.

Waesk led them to a conference room containing a handful of the Geidonn scientists. The small aliens stood together in a circle, their humanoid bodies intertwined in nervous fear as their stumpy tails wobbled in distress. The group trembled in unison when U'unk and the others entered, and each Geidonn's four eyes twitched and watched with independent actions. Their speech pattern followed a popping sound as their mouths smacked when they moved aside for their leader.

Wapho walked through with a confident waddle.

U'unk allowed a twinge of mild surprise that the scientist hadn't already left. Past experience made him assume the selfish nature of the Geidonn people would have prompted the leader's quick escape.

Wapho smacked his round mouth before he spoke. "What is the meaning of this, Chancellor? Why are you here and holding us hostage?" His lips popped while the small alien thrust a tiny, beefy hand for emphasis. His nose slits vibrated while his dim-blue skin flushed purple in anger. The ears in front of his head twitched, a sure sign of agitation.

U'unk considered the diminutive male from his extensive height. The Geidonn reached the bottom of his waist, yet the elderly alien approached him as if he was an equal.

Pathetic.

"I think you are under a misunderstanding, Researcher Wapho," U'unk crooned. Out of the corner of his eye, he saw Lok slouching. At least his sibling was intelligent enough to know what happened when U'unk used that tone of voice. Blood and pain were usually involved.

U'unk bent at the waist to glare into the horizontal pupils of the Geidonn's blue eyes. "You are not in a position to make demands." He straightened and crossed his arms while opening his legs in an aggressive stance. With a scowl, he fixated on the group of scientists as they shook in a huddle.

They twittered and cried around the smacking sounds.

"Take them somewhere else." U'unk tilted his head in Waesk's direction. His gaze didn't move off the lead researcher. "Wapho and I have plans to discuss that do not involve them."

Wapho's face paled as his lipless round mouth smacked. "Please, don't hurt them." The tone was soft so the others in his group couldn't hear.

U'unk presented a blank stare at Wapho's plea before giving a regal nod.

The smaller alien sighed with a slapping sound. "Thank you." His shoulders slumped as he focused on the metal floor.

"Waesk, make sure they are comfortable and given food and drink."

"Right away, sire." The Erkek pounded a fist across his chest in salute as he bowed. "Is there anything else you desire?"

The four Erkek guards herded the crying and twittering scientists out of the room.

Waesk straightened and awaited orders.

"Yes, find appropriate refreshments for us." Fangs flashed at the shorter Geidonn as his mouth watered at the prospect of enjoying the smaller male's fear.

"I'm afraid we're going to be here for quite a while."

Sherri

Sherri couldn't stop staring as Ki lay motionless on the soft small cot in the safe confines of Elemi's ship.

He'd reverted to his normal Zerin features but remained unconscious.

Damn, those had to be some hefty drugs keeping him down.

She might be exhausted, but didn't trust Elemi enough to fall asleep. The ship probably wouldn't hurt her, but after the harrowing afternoon she'd endured, why take the chance? Besides, she enjoyed seeing the arrogant ship made humble since the Zerin prisoner escaped.

From what little information Sherri pried out of Elemi, allies of Drirux called the Warriors of Light (*what kind of stupid name was that?*) bypassed her security and boarded her to force her to land on Earth. With a disintegration grenade, they threatened to make her dissolve if she didn't let the prisoner go. So, as any intelligent being would do, she gave in. Once she landed and released Drirux, the group left with a remote detonator for the grenade next to her vulnerable engines and promised to use it if she interfered. Why they didn't steal her when they had the chance was anyone's guess.

The only real question was—how did an advanced, sentient ship like Elemi find herself taken by surprise? When Sherri asked, she got a response full of righteous disbelief.

"I was orbiting a primitive planet! Why should I spend any extra energy to be cloaked?"

Sherri smiled at the memory. The damn ship was nothing if not consistent in her arrogance.

While in their dragon form, a weary Cheithe found her way to the invisible ship with Grirryrth's help. But, with each step, the dragon's strength waned, and they almost didn't make it back in time. When they reached the sleek "M" shaped vessel, both dragons morphed into their humanoid hosts so Elemi could transport them inside. Grirryrth's exhaustion was due to healing the posion Ki inhaled and Cheithe barely made it after being forcibly thrust into existence before she was ready.

With a sigh, Sherri brought herself back and ran a soothing palm along Ki's face and bearded jawline. The relaxed expression was a surprise, she didn't realize how tight he'd held his emotions until this moment. Normally, he maintained a steady, unemotional facade. No wonder she believed he was indifferent to her most of the time.

Asleep, his rugged features softened and gave him an almost boyish appearance. The facial scar shone along his iridescent golden skin and reflected in the cool light of the ship. Her fingers caressed the jagged edges across his high cheekbone and wandered over to full lips.

As she touched those plump mounds, his mouth opened and the tips of his pointed canines peeked out. She couldn't help it; she had to lean down to press her mouth against his. Ki's masculine sea-breeze scent enveloped her. The underlying musky smell created an ambrosial mixture and made her heart thump. The sight of the fading pink mark around his neck where the side of the sword had cut him caught her eye. Tears gathered at the pain the injury caused; she pressed her lips against the angry skin to give a gentle kiss before pulling back.

Sherri smiled. Looked like sleeping beauty needed more than a kiss to wake up. A shuddering breath escaped the prone man as if disappointed she had moved away.

She put a hand on top of Ki's clasped fingers that rested on his solid belly. She brushed a wayward strand from his face and glimpsed the tips of his ears peeking out of his rich mahogany hair. The move exposed a thin, tight braid she hadn't noticed before. It started at the right temple and rested behind his head. Here the puckered skin was lighter with age. A pang of sympathy tightened her throat at the pain he must have endured from that wound at such a young age.

With her free hand, she followed the aggravated skin from his forehead, past his left eye, and down his cheek.

His sharp cheekbones and a neatly trimmed beard covered his lower face. The facial hair combined a unique blend of dark brown highlighted with yellow. It was a testament to either his age or a stressful life.

Sherri continued to explore his outstanding features. He had the regal nose of a bygone conqueror, long with a slight break in the middle. Masculine brows full of thick mahogany hair were mixed with a scattering of light butterscotch. Lush dark eyelashes fanned his closed eyes, thick and lengthy. Those were something any woman would pay good money to possess.

Ki twitched and moaned before he settled back into a normal breathing pattern.

Sherri put a hand over her chest, glad Grirryrth reassured her Ki would be all right. The posion in his system had been flushed and the throat wound was superficial. It healed when Ki changed into his dragon form. If that was the case, then why did he still carry that old scar on his face? No matter, better to let him sleep and let the healing process continue. Grirryrth also assured her the man wouldn't have any ill effects from the drug once he woke up.

When he'd moved, his head tilted and exposed his left ear.

A shining glint caught her eye as she bent closer to look.

There, embedded in the folds of the upper shell a small, jewel glittered. The multiple facets of the gem shone deep and clear, winking and teasing in the low light.

Fascinated, she traced the outer shell with the tip of a forefinger.

He moaned.

Wow, what was up with that? Maybe his ear was a personal erogenous zone. Hmm—something to explore. She took a quick peek to make sure he still slept. *Ah,* his face was relaxed and his breathing resumed a normal rhythm. Emboldened, she resumed and traced the tip of his alien ear between two fingers.

He jerked, his hands unclasped as his fingers twitched. A low moan hissed through those tempting lips. After a few breathless seconds, he settled again.

Mouth puckered in triumph, Sherri found it oddly arousing to see him react that way. What would happen if she licked there? With a slight chuckle, she ignored the niggling shame to stop and leaned closer to the exposed ear. With a puff of soft breath, she traced the shell with her tongue.

Whatever reaction she expected, it didn't come close to what he did.

Roaring, his dual-colored eyes popped open and his head snapped toward her with a narrow glare.

Palms up in surrender, she gave an involuntary childish squeal.

The submissive gesture was futile. He jackknifed to a sitting position on the bed, grabbed her upper arms, and pulled her underneath his solid, naked body. The pencil-thin skirt didn't allow room for her legs to part, so his large thighs cradled hers firmly between them. Her head was held captive between massive palms.

The navy/hunter irises disappeared when his viridian iridescent pupils took over.

A manly snarl escaped, and his exposed, overlong teeth captured her attention. She quivered in reaction. Another growl rumbled from deep within Ki's chest and trembled where their bodies touched.

She stilled, trying to figure out what his body language told her. She gulped when the meaning of his tight face finally became obvious. The time for play was over; the male on top of her wouldn't let her go until he was good and ready.

Sherri's heart thudded with impatient joy as she sucked in an excited breath. Yes! Finally they would act on their mutual attraction. Throat tight, his aggressive dominance flat-out did it for her. She, who'd never allowed a man to take control in the bedroom before, found herself docile as her body softened in welcome. In an opposite reaction, her clit filled and poked from between puffed folds, causing a zap of pleasure each time she moved or breathed. Not to be outdone, her nipples creased and her womb tightened. Blatantly she wet her lips in a deliberate invitation.

Navy/hunter-green irises zeroed in on her lips as he held her head before touching his mouth to hers. She half expected to be ravished. Instead, a gentle caress surprised her. His body moved in a sensual dance as old as time and allowed her to indulge in the feel of his warm, hard torso on hers.

Wrapping her arms around his neck, her hands slid into his thick dark hair. Just as before, the strands tightened and twirled around her fingers and held tight. Now was the time to bring their interaction higher. Her mouth parted in invitation.

Ki didn't disappoint. He took up the offer.

Once inside, the small ridges along his tongue brought a unique flavor to Sherri that was all Ki. His tang of spice spilled and ignited her heated blood. She returned the kiss with fervor, stroking and caressing the warm cavern of his mouth as if they'd done this a million times before.

Sherri writhed and moaned under the male weight, the friction making her lightheaded.

Ki pulled away.

The unexpected cool air made her blink before it dawned on her he was talking.

"There is no going back now, Sherri."

The growl of his words made it hard to understand. How did he expect her to be coherent when he ground his groin into hers? She hissed as her toes curled.

Ki reached down, yanked her loose blouse out of the tight skirt, and ripped it in two.

Shocked at the near-violent action, Sherri's breasts heaved in her peach-laced bra. Her body shook under his intense scrutiny.

"Time to finish this, right here and now." Ki's declaration came out muffled as his lips covered the tips of the bra and soaked the material with his tongue. Then he gave a sharp nip on the hardened tip. He lifted the waistband of the skirt and tugged it aside.

Her mouth fell open as the thick cloth split apart with one sweep. The cool air on her lower lady-parts caused her flesh to pebble.

His attention shifted to the juncture of her thighs and the peach-colored boy shorts covering her sex. His mouth hovered over the garment that was soaked with her feminine juices.

Her heart thundered as the hot cavern of his mouth became a notable contrast to the chilly atmosphere.

A low growl vibrated through the wet fabric and made her eyes cross in bliss. *Damn...* she was so close! Just one more pass, and she'd go off like a rocket. What a neat trick since he hadn't even touched her in the flesh yet.

With a firm finger on the sides of her boy shorts, he shredded them. The delicate fabric ripped, pieces flung away with a flick of his thick wrists.

No use searching for those miniscule parts later.

Ki interrupted her musings. A rumbled noise bubbled out of his throat, his attention focused on her exposed pussy.

She experienced a moment of embarrassment as her full bush was uncovered. He didn't appear to mind her being "au naturale" one bit...

With firm lips, he suckled her rock-hard clit between his teeth and tongue.

It only took a split second for her to burst apart. Yelping at the surprising detonation, her eyes rolled while she broke apart. Desperate, she grabbed the top of his head and loose hair. The strands covered her, and she rode the pleasure streaming through her quaking body.

Between one inhalation and the next, Ki's massive frame prowled up as her hands fell away. His smug glance curled her stomach into another bout of anticipation. Here was the male counterpart she'd waited for. When he settled, her legs wrapped around his lean waist.

With relaxed muscles, she welcomed him in. She was slick enough for him to burrow his wide, flared head inside with minimal resistance. Tears welled as she and Ki faced each other at the precipice before they jumped off together. As one, they took in a deep breath, eyes locked as he sank fully into her quivering depths.

Sherri moaned at the fullness. Ki's hard-as-steel member pulsated in time with their combined heartbeats.

Face tight, he raised his head high enough to glance where their bodies joined.

She followed his example and watched as he pulled out, the dark skin slick before plunging back in. The forceful piston pushed her deeper into the soft cot as she absorbed the succulent friction that zinged from her womb to her head. Her sex tightened as her knees gripped his flexing hips.

Ki shook his head with narrow eyes. "Oh no, lovely *yofie-na*. You will not lead this time." Reaching around, he settled her ankles on the top of broad shoulders.

The position may have given her less control, but it allowed his plunging cock to hit every sensitive nerve. She gripped his muscular forearms, her fingers digging into hard skin.

His thick arms circled kept her in place as he thrust his lean hips. Masculine pleasure contorted his face as a vein thundered along his neck with a constant beat.

"Ah... *fruk*... yes. Feel this..." The demand hissed through gritted teeth. "*On'amunt* female, yeah, right there." His hips swirled and plunged while his hands tightened to keep her in place.

"No... that... want..." Panting in reaction, she pumped back.

"Yes...again." Exotic iridescent-green pupils widened as his sharp teeth poked between full lips.

Oh yeah, she'd only be too happy to. With a tight grip on his forearms for leverage, she narrowed her eyes and pursed her lips at the delicious friction.

The abrupt movement must have made her breasts bounce because his eyes jerked toward them. A slow tongue across his lips moistened the slight curve of his mouth. Unwrapping his arms from around her thighs, he rubbed his palms together. He stopped thrusting and placed his palms over her hardened nipples.

Sherri's eyes flickered in confusion as she dropped her hold to grip the linens. What was that? Her skin under his hands became hot and cold before a sharp pang of unbridled lust engorged the sensitive nipples and went straight to her core.

Ki licked the bottom of his full lip as his palms moved in circular motions from her breasts down her torso and stopped at top of her curls.

Sherri blinked at the shining coat he left behind.

With a lusty grin, he caressed the puffed lips of her sex and massaged the exposed nub.

She jumped when the hot sensation of thick oil touched the sensitive nerves. Wait, where did the oil come from? How did he find the time to get some without her noticing? *Argh*...who cared? She squirmed. He had to move. Pushing her hips up, she tried to force the issue.

"Luscious, sensuous female," Ki crooned with a slight swat on an ass cheek. "Stay still. Revel in what I give you."

He swiped his palms across her again as warm oils penetrated her thirsty skin and lit receptive nerves. Her stomach shook as lust rose. Uncontrolled, she grabbed him by the neck to pull him into a frantic open-mouth kiss. She didn't know what kind of oil it was, but it sure was a potent aphrodisiac. In response she nipped, she bit, she ravished.

Not to be outdone, Ki's returned her sexual demands. He shifted until she was on his lap, legs wrapped around his waist. The move didn't dislodge his throbbing cock that remained deep inside.

Strong masculine arms pulled her flush against his solid chest as their kiss continued. Flushed with pleasure, Sherri joined Ki in a collective mating dance.

Without warning, Sherri's orgasm rushed toward completion. With a jerk, she turned her head away and moaned as her back bowed in ecstasy. Her core tightened, desperate to keep his hard cock lodged in place as she chased her pleasure with each strong thrust.

"*Fruk,* yes!" Ki roared with a lurch. He grasped the globes of her ass, pulling her back and forth with each jolt. With a slight stumble he stilled, his hard dick pulsating as a hot stream of release coated her in jarring spasms.

Sherri folded against his chest and wrapped her quivering legs around his waist. He leaned over her without causing his massive weight to crush her. Ragged breath matched the aftershocks rumbling through her. Ki's ribbed tongue leisurely stroked the sensitive skin between her neck and shoulder, giving her a profound sense of calm. She released a self-satisfied moan as she snuggled further into his embrace.

They remained unmoving until his penis softened and slowly slid out.

Gathering her sluggish thoughts, she scooted back and gazed into his exceptional eyes. The iridescent viridian pupils were wide, but his navy-blue/hunter-green irises remained prominent as he regarded her. The blank stare made her nervous. Did he regret what they'd done? Well, she didn't, *damn it*, and he'd better not either. Her chin tilted.

Something must have alerted him to what she was thinking because his demeanor changed. Gone was the unresponsive, unmovable male and in its place a knowing smile transformed those rugged good looks into a unique thing of beauty.

As they tucked their bodies together, the light oils covering his torso bled onto hers. An irresistible masculine scent floated around them. Sherri's nipples tightened while a rising wave of passion began. She pulled back in astonishment and met a masculine expression of self-satisfaction.

"What in the hell *is* that?" A demand. How could his sweat make her squirm in lust all over again?

Ki rubbed his nose against hers. "Do you like it?" The big man all but purred.

She pulled back and frowned. "Um, yes, I do. But where are you getting this massage oil from?" And what a wildly potent massage oil it was. On Earth, she'd make a fortune selling it. She glanced around, trying to see where the container was.

"What are you looking for?"

Ki's rich voice caused her skin to pebble. "The rubbing oil, where is it?" She inhaled. *Double damn*, by itself, that fresh salty scent was dangerous.

Between them his freed cock stiffened. "What massage oil?" Warm breath nuzzled behind her ear while he rubbed circles over her rear.

Her naked skin soaked up the heated oil as her core rippled, bemoaning her emptiness. "Um." Can't breathe. Her body recognized the erotic sensation while her brain checked out. "Ah, the oil you're rubbing into me right now."

He smiled against her neck. "That is the natural secretion a Zerin male shares with a female during a sexual encounter." A leisurely lick followed. "Do you like?" Another rumbling purr. "Want more?"

Sherri jerked in surprise and watched his expression. "That's from you?" Her stare fastened on the glistening planes of the rugged chest filling her vision. The slick oils highlighted his iridescent skin, giving off a warm and welcoming glow. She patted his solid pecs, just above flat, hardened nipples. She couldn't help but rub her hands over the dark hard nubs and coast down the six-pack. With every stroke, her passions climbed higher, escalating and throbbing with need. There wasn't a lot of chest hair, except for a dark line of fine down that rested at the top of his magnificent groin.

As she explored, his breath deepened and he flexed his large torso. What would all that taste like? The idea burned as she leaned forward for a lick.

With one swipe, erotic tension clenched her core with a spastic jolt. Unique flavors burst forth...the normal musk and saltiness of a male, but also with a hint of *other,* an addicting blend of spice and wildness that made her clamor for more.

Scooting closer, she leaned down to place her tongue on his ribbed penis. Strong hands gripped her upper arms and she found herself flat on her back. The aroused male covered her as his hardened cock slipped inside. "How can you be ready so soon?" *Crap! Was that breathless kitten whisper from her?*

His hips rolled as he thrust. "I'm not a human male, remember?"

Thank God, not human!

She must have said that aloud because a wicked laugh rumbled as he pounded into her willing body with hard, steady strokes.

Ki

Ki jerked awake. Something was wrong.

Grirryrth, are we in danger?

Humph? The dragon's sleepy voice reassured Ki that there were no mortal threats close. *You are such a skittish youngling. Go back to sleep or enjoy your female.* A metaphorical yawn had the dragon snapping his jaws. *I can assure you, you'll need your rest when I claim Cheithe.*

Claim. A chilling shiver ran down his spine as he sat up. He took in a deep breath as a sensuous scent of spicy sweetness filled his lungs. Sherri was near.

Not just near, but within reach...naked and sprawled on her stomach on the narrow cot. Plump, full breasts spilled from her sides, visible because her arms rested above her head. The rich globes of her ass topped splayed legs, revealing the tempting lips of her sex peeking from under the soft blue bed coverings. Memories flooded of their decadent time together.

Running a hand down his face and chastising himself, his blood ran cold. How could he let this happen? His libido had never been out of control before. He'd always maintained complete restraint over every aspect of his life. Sherri's throaty moan caught his attention as she rolled over.

Ki swallowed dryly.

She lay partially on her back, her torso twisted at the waist as her legs crossed.

The move put her magnificent breasts on prominent display, the rosy tips hard and begging for his touch. Those full lips remained slightly open and beckoned with another temptation all on its own.

Holy Goddess...wait...no...no! This was wrong. Wrong. Fists tightened, he willed his heart to settle and maintain a constant rhythm. The last thing he needed was to get emotional with this female sprawled next to him.

Ki withdrew from the cot with slow, deliberate motions, moving the tangled sheets away from the warm female. Every instinct screamed for him to stay and wake her up with his throbbing cock tucked into her hot, wet body.

With a sharp shake of his head, he refused to give in. While he enjoyed what they'd experienced, now wasn't the time to indulge in selfish pursuits. Even if by some miracle she turned out to be his TrueBond...

She is.

Ki snorted and ignored the dragon.

... it was time to concentrate on preventing the takeover of Earth. It was imperative they thwart the Chancellor's plans to overthrow the galactic government. Ki nodded to himself. Yes, that's where his focus should be. He could enjoy the female if the opportunity arose, but that was no reason to give up on his life's vow to avoid a TrueBond. Ki shuddered...and refrain from having children.

To make sure, he touched his right temple and met smooth skin. With a shaky chuckle, he realized the MalDerVon scroll hadn't appeared while he'd been asleep. Usually, after a rousing bout of first TrueBond sex, a destined couple would find the scroll imprinted within hours. Finding nothing different, he rolled the tight muscles of his shoulders and released the tension.

Then Sherri moaned as one of her hands reached up and cupped a full breast as a whisper escaped her plump lips. "Ki."

That's all it took...he was undone.

Every intention he had to avoid Sherri disappeared. Ki became an aroused male seeking his female as he joined her on the cot.

Elemi interrupted. "Ki, I have rescheduled you and that female to meet with the UN Secretary-General within the hour."

Her voice froze Ki in place as he pulled back and stood straight. "What's an hour?"

"Comparable to a click, but with extra sub-clicks added in." Elemi's tone was steady, with no inflection. He suspected she didn't approve of the change in his relationship with Sherri. *By the father of all,* he wasn't sure if he approved of the change himself. Especially since the change eluded him.

Stubborn, blind youngling.

Just what he needed. An infuriating dragon providing a running commentary on his love life.

Stay out of it. Maybe the stern warning in his voice was enough to make the Solaherra dragon know he wouldn't listen to him.

A smoky snort assured him Grirryrth didn't care what Ki meant.

A short feminine laugh caught his attention, and he glanced in Sherri's direction. She was wide-awake, one hand under her head while the other tweaked a tight nipple. She lay on her back, her naked body open with a knee bent. Feminine eyes sparkled with mischief.

A renewed surge of lust filled his cock. With closed eyes, he tensed before he opened them again. Her wide smile filled his vision accompanied by a beckoning crook of her delicate finger. A delicate pink tongue licked full lips as her exotic gaze focused on his groin. With every breath, he wanted to rethink his decision.

With a stiffened spine, it took every ounce of strength not to go and wallow in the pleasures she promised. An involuntary deep breath didn't help as the musky aroma of their mingled scents made things worse. His screaming instincts caused him to cross his arms and assume a wide stance for protection.

No. Shoulders back. Time to leave. They had an appointment to keep. "While I would love nothing better than to join with you again, *yofie-na*—" Ki stepped away. "—there are more important things to do."

A sable eyebrow rose and her full mouth twitched. "Oh, really?" She sat up with a sensuous movement that would tempt any male. When she shrugged, her bountiful breasts bounced. "Okay, if you say so."

Ki swallowed a painful groan. A male could only take so much. In one long stride, he pulled her up and ravished those bewitching lips. Tongues clashed and danced as he absorbed her robust feminine taste.

She jumped into his arms and bound her supple legs around his waist.

Her wet core rubbed, and he was lost. Breaking their kiss, he leaned their foreheads together. "Have mercy, *yofe-na*. I am but a humble male you've ensnared. I beg you, give me the strength to walk away. We must concentrate on saving your planet."

Sherri's head jerked back. The saucy mounds of her lips thinned into a thoughtful pout. "Well, you're right, of course." Her legs dropped, and she stepped away.

The uncomfortably cool air caused him to frown. "Elemi has a new appointment with the Secretary-General in what she called an hour."

A look of horror crossed Sherri's exotic features. "An hour?" Her eyes darted in frantic movements. "You destroyed all my clothes! What am I supposed to wear?"

"Oh, for Goddess' sake, human female. Be calm."

Elemi's condescending tone grated on Ki. When this mission was completed, he'd put in a request for D'zia's AI, JR10, to reprogram the ship to be more responsive to others who weren't the male captain of the vessel.

"Here are some Earth clothes I've remade for your use." Elemi opened part of the wall to display the same alien clothes Sherri had worn before. "I've calculated you both have less than an Earth half hour to complete your dressing process before I can safely transport you to a different area outside the UN building to save time. This will aid you in traversing the varied security protocols the humans have and will ensure you arrive at the meeting room in time."

Sherri's squeal of alarm made Ki smile and shake his head.

Without another word, she scrambled to the refresher room to shower.

It was fascinating to watch her ritual of getting clean and putting clothes on. Ki scrubbed a hand over his close-cropped beard when she came back, her magnificent body now covered with the strange Earth garments. It didn't matter how nicely the formfitting garments enhanced her glorious figure. He didn't like them. He'd rather see her naked.

Ki eyed those ridiculous contraptions she put on her feet. They not only made her taller, but it made her luscious ass curve in prominent display. His mouth dried and his eyes narrowed. Now that she was dressed, he wanted to rip those tight clothes off and bend her over the nearest surface to plunge into her feminine depths.

After putting on those shoes, she stood and faced him. With raised eyebrows, she took in his nude form. "I certainly hope you're not going like that." Sherri laughed while pointing a finger at his nude form.

While he wanted to tease, he'd save that for later. "No, I was too busy watching you." Arms raised, he commanded, "Grirryrth, attend me." In a whirlwind, the Solaherra suit rose from within and covered him in battle armor. The natural process was cleansing as well as refreshing.

"That's not any better." Sherri frowned, one hand on a cocked hip.

By the father of all, was there anyone more adorable than his human lover?

"Will this work?" Ki envisioned his prior human image, complete with a dark Earth formal suit, a white button-down shirt and red tie. What a ridiculous outfit, but it was imperative to dress as a native to the planet.

"No, I mean yes, you look fine." She scowled and muttered. "I like you better as a Zerin."

Sherri probably hadn't wanted him to hear that, but with his exceptional hearing, it was hard to miss. He smiled.

Sherri blinked.

"Ready?" He lifted an elbow for her to grasp. That was an Earth custom he'd once read about. "Let's go and save Earth, shall we?"

Chapter **NINE**

Sherri

No matter how glamorous something appeared, reality had a way of messing it up with a blend of boredom and sameness. Sherri had been so excited at the prospect of seeing the Secretary-General in the famous UN building, only to face disappointment once they arrived (a jarring experience going from the ship to an unused storage closet). Bureaucracy and security protocols were the same everywhere, restrictive and with no purpose. What was worse, they were barred from meeting the man. Instead, their appointment was with an underling who barely had time for them before he dismissed them with a threat to call security.

Walking down the spacious corridors on their way out of the building, Sherri's heels clanked and clicked with each frustrated footstep.

Ki walked beside her, in his quiet and confident manner, with his hands clasped behind his back.

The condescending aide embarrassed her to no end. *Well...crap!* Now what? The Chancellor would take over Earth and sell every woman of child-bearing age to the highest bidder. Humanity was doomed to slavery...

"Where are all the females in charge?" Ki's deep voice interrupted Sherri's contemplation. He slowed his long stride to match her shorter one and appeared to take a leisurely walk.

"Huh?" His random question caught her by surprise. "What are you talking about?"

"The females. Where are all the females in charge?" His large hand waved toward the wall on their right that displayed a list of titles, names, and countries of the delegates to the UN. "Most of those are males, are they not?"

Sherri had no idea where he was going with his questions. She stopped and turned with palms on hips. "Yes, they are. So?"

Clasped hands once again behind his back, he regarded her with a mild stare. The motioned stretched the jacket apart and displayed the white shirt straining at the buttons. His tan skin under the cloth was a pale imitation of his normal glowing color. She frowned. The longer he stayed in his human disguise, the more she didn't like it.

"It is a well-known fact throughout the galaxy that the most productive societies have a blend of male and female leaders. If Earth has a female counterpart to your Secretary-General, we should put our request to her."

Sherri crossed her arms. While she agreed with him wholeheartedly, she defended her society. "If I remember correctly, Zerin only had a king—no queen."

Ki nodded his head, his bland human hair pulled back at the nape of his neck. The round ears looked odd against his skull. Wonder where that jewel in his ear went to. "Yes, you are correct." Massive shoulders shrugged. "It has been that way since Qay's mother, the queen, passed into the universal consciousness when Qay was a young boy. Because she was his father's TrueBond, the king could not unite with another female in this lifetime." He turned to resume their walk out of the building. "Now that Qay has been reinstated and has joined with his own TrueBond, he will ascend to the throne shortly. It is customary for the Zerin people to enjoy a joint rule by both male and female."

Shock caused Sherri to stumble before righting herself. It took a couple long strides to catch up with her larger companion. Lora had told her their mutual friend, Aimee, was Qay's TrueBond. "The Zerins will let a human become a co-ruler?"

"While there have been factions opposed to an alien on the throne, the majority of the Zerin people have not made it an issue." He stopped and turned to her. "Again I ask, where are your female leaders?"

Sherri's neck heated as she contemplated his stern expression. His close-cropped beard and mustache didn't hide the frown that deepened the pull of his full lips.

"Females in charge are a rare thing on Earth," she began. "But over the years we've been making strides..."

He walked again, and she followed. Under the watchful eye of armed guards they exited the building. There they joined hundreds of people milling around.

"No matter," he stopped and observed his surroundings. "Are we in the country called the United States?"

Sherri nodded as she murmured, "Yes." She shivered in the bright sunshine. The sunny day wasn't any help to get rid of the danger everyone faced.

"Let's meet with your President, then." Ki stated in a firm tone.

"I don't think that will work..." She didn't get a chance to finish her sentence before Ki gave Elemi a command. From one blink to the next, she stood with Ki in a famous American room.

The Oval Office.

In the White House.

Holy shit, they were in trouble. She grabbed the crook of Ki's arm when the prominent individuals of the current administration jumped up and shouted.

With an empty feeling in the pit of her stomach, Sherri peeked toward the famous Resolute Desk and the President. The leader gawked in their direction as a shimmering figure solidified behind him.

Sherri blinked. It was the Chancellor she'd seen from Maynwaring's memories, dressed in a merlot-red thick robe. Intricate gold and silver piping adorned the bell sleeves and flowing bottom as well as the frog fasteners on the breastplate. There he stood, in all his seven foot, baldheaded, Fu Manchu, black-eyed glory. He tapped the President on the temple. The septuagenarian slumped back in his chair with eyes closed and mouth wide.

"Greetings, people of Earth." The big alien crooned with a smarmy lift of the corners of his fat lips. "I am here to relieve your extremely heavy burden of ruling this fine planet." Chancellor U'unk kept a large palm on the top of the President's head and gave it a couple pats as if the man was a domesticated animal. An onyx pinkie ring twinkled as he moved.

"Just who do you think you are? I will have you shot for trespassing!" This demand came from another elderly guy, his bald head littered with age spots and tufts of white hair here and there.

He was the National Security Officer, if Sherri remembered right.

He stood with clenched fists on hips and glared at the large alien while the others whimpered and cried.

No such luck for the politician. The Chancellor put his cave-black stare on him briefly. With a wave of his huge three-fingers holding a small copper cylinder, he disintegrated the man into a puff of gray ash.

The sickly odor of burnt flesh had Sherri breathing through her mouth to avoid the stench while an oily coating slid down her throat. With a hand over her mouth, Sherri scooted closer to Ki and seized his upper arm. Wanting an anchor, she clasped his solid muscles with tense fingers.

He hadn't moved; his focus stayed on the surrounding scene.

"Questions?" The Chancellor's hard eyes skimmed the area.

The surviving humans kept their mouths shut except for a whimper and a moan now and then. The scent of someone's bladder releasing scorced the air.

"Good." The enormous alien pulled the President's leather seat back and pointed toward the prone man. "I presume this is your leader?"

No one said a word. They all stood there in a transfixed daze. They acted as if the sight of the large predator mesmerized them and they did their best to avoid individual attention.

No response.

His penetrating stare settled on Ki. "You, human."

The deep, gravelly voice increased the shivers down Sherri's spine. At first, she glanced behind Ki to see who the massive alien talked to. Oh yeah, her companion was in a human disguise. No way could the Chancellor know Ki was in human disguise.

"Is this your leader?"

Ki's back stiffened. "Yes, that is the ruler of this country."

Well, that was interesting. Ki didn't claim the man was his leader. *Hmm,* maybe the Chancellor had the ability to smell a lie. She'd better remember that if, God forbid, his attention came her way.

The Chancellor straightened at Ki's answer, a blank expression on his cold features. His iridescent skin might be lighter than that of the other Zerins she'd seen, but his sharp canines and pointed ears were in line with the species.

Something about him nagged Sherri—he wasn't quite right. She agreed with the others around her and did her best to avoid his attention. Better to stick to Ki and follow his lead.

"That is good." The imposing male stated in a monotone. With a sudden jerk, he tumbled the unconscious man out of the chair to flop to the hard floor in an undignified heap.

Short cries rang from the group when they saw their president treated in such a callous manner.

The Chancellor didn't glance at the unconscious man when he took the seat with a grace not usually seen on such a huge creature. The thick material of his robe swirled as he settled back.

Between one blink and the next, the group was surrounded by a mixture of repulsive little gray Friebbigh and khaki-green Erkek aliens. Each was holding a long stick made of various metallic alloys, all pointed at a specific person.

"Kill them." The Chancellor ordered with a negligent wave of his hand. He sat back and plonked his feet on the top of the sacred desk. The robe split and exposed his calf-high boots with black pant legs tucked inside.

At that declaration, panic raced through the room. People scrambled and screamed, racing around a still Ki.

With calm intent, he pushed through the crowd and stopped in front of the menacing alien. He stood tall and unbending with his hands clasped behind his back. "You are making a mistake." A bland statement.

The Chancellor lifted a thick, black eyebrow. "Oh, how so?" He raised a fist, a signal to halt his last command.

"You'll need some of these people to navigate through the various systems they have in place, if you want to ensure a successful absorption of their culture." Ki shrugged. "If you want to save time and resources, you should revise your assessment of blindly eliminating assets you could otherwise use."

The Chancellor cocked an eyebrow and formed a steeple with his fingers under his chin. A steady gaze pierced Ki.

The surrounding people stopped and quieted at the conversation.

Most shook and whimpered and the astringent smell of urine burned Sherri's nose. A nervous sweat popped between her shoulders as the silence in the room became thick with tension. She shivered.

"Explain."

Ki folded his burly arms over his chest as he returned the Chancellor's icy stare. "You are obviously lacking the appropriate information if you didn't know who the leader of this country was." He nodded toward the now-snoring President who lay at his feet.

A thoughtful frown pulled the smooth skin of the Chancellor's mouth and made his long mustache droop.

Sherri held her breath as she waited to see if Ki's statement made a difference.

The Chancellor narrowed his eyes before giving a slight nod of agreement. "Valid point, human."

A whoosh of relief escaped Sherri's lips.

The mammoth male jerked his head toward the aliens surrounding her and the others. "Secure the rest of this building and lock these humans in a different location."

Accompanied by cries of confusion amid whimpers from everyone around her, Sherri found herself pushed and shoved out of the room with a jumbled knot of humanity.

Except for Ki, who'd been ordered to stay behind.

Sherri and the group were confined in the cramped White House press briefing room. She sat in a typically uncomfortable chair as she watched the slimy little Friebbigh. They were disgusting little things with large bulbous heads and enormous almond-shaped black eyes. Not to mention they were creepy as hell. Their waxy gray skin and lanky arms, legs, and fingers gave her the willies. The Erkeks' stench of rot made her gag whenever they got close.

Around the pressroom was a hodgepodge of personal groups. Various White House staff sat with their friends and colleagues, whispering in frightened tones as they huddled for comfort.

Being there under pretense didn't give Sherri the luxury of friends. She found a seat at the back of the room.

You are never alone, child, whispered Cheithe.

At the calm tone of her dragon, the tense muscles squeezing her neck loosened. She kinda liked having the company. Still, she worried about Ki. Would she even know if something happened to him?

Sherri huddled in the hard, steel chair and wrapped her arms around her waist as she leaned her head down. A shuffling noise caught her attention just before feminine shoes came into her line of sight. They were a pretty pair of gray pumps with kitten heels.

With a nervous glance, she straightened to peer at the middle-aged woman in front of her.

Dark hair with strands of silver and white intertwined in a spiky cut above the famous face of the Secretary of State. The woman's plain features were in a stern line, her gray eyes narrowed while hands rested on skinny hips. "And just who in the hell are you?" The world-famous raspy voice demanded an answer.

Several people around them stopped talking and gave her suspicious glares. Sherri's nerves stretched as some expressions became serious and hostile. "I, ah..." she began.

A loud scream interrupted. "Oh my God! They've got the President!" A woman in the front screeched as the TV screen behind the podium lit up.

At first, it was difficult for Sherri to see the image with a variety of heads blocking her way. The sea of humanity parted, and she got an unobstructed view of the President of the United States next to the Chancellor.

The alien's beefy hand rested on the elderly leader's shoulder. It looked like they were on the front lawn of the White House, standing in the bright sunshine with a light breeze causing the Zerin's burgundy cloak to flap lazily behind him. The President's comb-over flapped in the wind and exposed his age-spotted bare head. The massive height of the Chancellor dwarfed the human man who was cringing and whimpering.

A large palm settled on her shoulder. She jerked as she was pressed into a broad male chest. Ki's sea-breeze scent caused her arms to pebble as her knees buckled in relief.

"We have to get to where they are," Ki's deep voice whispered in her ear. "Before it's too late. Do you know where that is?"

Sherri nodded as her heart thudded. How in the world did he show up there so fast? Thank God he was okay! "Yes, just outside on the front lawn."

"Excellent. Elemi, take us where the Chancellor is." Ki put a warm arm around her. "Hold on."

Before she could say anything, the familiar sensation of Elemi's transport tingled through her. They stood on the lawn of the famous American building, behind the Chancellor and the President.

Sherri's eyes widened as she took in the aliens with their backs to the Chancellor in front of her. The mixture of the little bulbous-headed gray aliens and khaki-green Erkeks in a protective circle around the Chancellor had obvious weapons pointed at the humans standing outside the iron fence.

Cries of fear and shouts of anger filled the air from those humans.

"I have to stop to this." With a gentle push, Ki put Sherri behind him. He hadn't taken two steps before the Chancellor began his tirade.

"Humans of the planet Earth." The deep baritone voice boomed. "Your life is no longer your own. As of this moment, you belong to me to do with as I will." He waved a large three-fingered hand as a huge monitor appeared behind him and split into multiple screens. Even though each visual was small, it wasn't hard to determine the major rulers of Earth found themselves in the same precarious position as the American President. All were being held hostage either by a group of Erkeks or the slimy Friebbighs.

"Know this—there is no hope for you. Your leaders are no longer able to help you." As soon as he spoke the last word, the Chancellor pointed a copper cylinder at the American President, who abruptly burst into a cloud of gray ash...which drifted away on a lazy breeze. At the same time, the other world leaders puffed into clouds of dust. Some had been indoors, where their ashes floated in wispy tendrils to the floor, while others had been outside, and their ashes floated away.

Screams of terror filled the air.

Sherri stood there, frozen in shock. With a hard gulp, she stared at Ki's broad back.

He never got close enough to stop the Chancellor. With a stiff posture, he resumed a purposeful stride toward the other Zerin.

"Humans of Earth, you will now…"

"HOLD!" Ki's thundering bass reverberated without the aid of electronic devices. "I claim my Right of Acquisition for the planet Earth!" He stopped in front of the Chancellor, careful not to step on the small mound that used to be the President.

Sherri warmed at the outward sign of respect for her people. She reached down to tear off the stilettos in order to scramble around to watch what Ki was doing from a better angle. The grass was slick and cold under her feet. *Damn it!* She'd brought those Zerin slippers in her purse for a reason…but God only knew where she'd left the stupid thing.

Stopping at Ki's side, Sherri witnessed the look of savage disgust on the Chancellor's face.

"Human, you have no rights here, much less qualify for a Right of Acquisition." He folded his massive arms and glared.

Even though she couldn't observe Ki's expression, she imagined a stern glower crossing his handsome features since the Chancellor's cold appearance was plain to see.

The obsidian eyes hardened when Ki gave a mirthless chuckle.

"I am not a human, Chancellor U'unk," Ki declared as he raised his arms. The image of a bland, boring human morphed and Ki turned back into his glorious natural state as an iridescent, three-fingered, pointy-eared, fanged Zerin.

Sherri sighed in pleasure. Was any other man in the universe as beautiful as her lover? Her statement caught her by surprise. *Well, hell*…when had she become someone who spouted poetry about a man in her life? Guess the answer was when she fell in love with the man. *Whoa*… Sherri's palm covered her chest as her heart sputtered before it beat a hard rhythm. Her face and neck flushed with heat. With an internal focus, she tested the theory. Yes…yes, she *did* love him. Well, wasn't her timing just perfect.

Ki's deep baritone interrupted her internal reflection. "As the first Zerin to step on this planet, I claim the Right of Acquisition." He mirrored the dominant stance of his adversary.

Chancellor U'unk's face thundered into a dark shade of purple. With thick eyebrows drawn, he glared at Ki. "How dare you?"

The last came out in a whisper Sherri almost didn't catch. She doubted Ki had any trouble hearing what the other man said.

"By the laws and bylaws of the Federation Consortium concerning protected planets, I can claim this right before you do." Ki's stance became loose with a bent head, a laser focus on the other male. "I demand you leave this planet immediately and take your illegal companions with you."

U'unk straightened his impressive height and sneered. "I know you. You are the mercenary M'alalu E'eur, who has followed the shamed Prince Qay around like a good little sycophant." The black hair of his Fu Manchu framed exposed fangs.

Ki threw his head back and gave a hearty laugh. "I am so glad you acknowledge who I am."

Sherri moved to catch Ki's expression.

"It will make things much easier now."

A malicious frown crossed U'unk's face. "Oh no, you traitorous imbecile. Nothing is ever that easy." In one hand, he pointed the small, copper cylinder. Every gray alien and Erkek jerked their attention toward Ki and raised their weapons at him.

A primal scream ripped out of Sherri. She ran, her legs hardened with a strength she never had before. NO! She had to stop them... An Erkek grabbed her arm and threw her to the ground to land with a painful thud on her tailbone. Not waiting for her brain to unscramble, she jumped and raced to Ki.

Lights sparkled and engulfed Ki's body as he changed into the massive Grirryrth.

Sherri had just enough time to stop her momentum before she plowed into the enormous reptile. With an incredulous stare, she watched the stern features of the Chancellor change into one of astonishment.

He took a step back and tilted his head.

Grirryrth's navy-blue scales shimmered and winked in the early afternoon light.

With morbid fascination, Sherri viewed the aliens scattering in every direction with piercing wails and nasal screams.

"Hold, you fools!" U'unk bellowed. His voice was thunderous enough for the panicked horde to hear. He stopped moving backward and aimed the copper cylinder at Ki/Grirryrth. "I will kill it!"

Sherri's vision clouded with black spots. She couldn't breathe. Between one blink and the next, Sherri was once again a traveler in the enormous silver body of a dragon.

Thundering around Ki to confront the Chancellor, Cheithe reached down to grab the now-tiny Zerin within her massive gray claws.

Instead of screaming in terror, the Chancellor roared his anger. He raged and shook his fists with threats and commands toward the other aliens to kill. At least he was smart enough not to discharge his weapon in the dragon's crystal claws.

Sherri stood mesmerized as Cheithe ignored the aliens who ran and bumped into each other in their mad stampede to get out from under her enormous feet. She chucked as they ran as fast as their spindly legs carried them.

Some took aim in her direction, but her dragon had more than brute strength to rely on.

A shimmering wave appeared, covering her large body in a clear bubble.

The beams aimed at them bounced off and struck the individual who shot it, with unerring precision.

Wow, that's a neat trick! Sherri commented to Cheithe.

Thank you, the female dragon replied. *In a previous life, my nickname was Karma. What evil is done returns threefold to the sender.*

That startled Sherri. *Really? I thought Karma was an Earth idea.*

Well, we called it something different in my language, but the concept is universal.

Sherri chuckled. *What are you going to do with him?* To help the dragon figure out who she meant, she envisioned the still-screaming Chancellor.

I do not have enough experience in this reality to make that decision. She shared a vision of clear lavender skies dotted with pink, yellow, and pearl-white clouds. The air was crisp and cool above a blue grassland. *This was my home before it was destroyed a thousand millennia ago.*

The sad tone filled Sherri with a profound sense of sorrow.

Everything here is different. I must rely on my mate to guide me until I can grow in this environment. I will wait and ask him.

Cheithe rested on her haunches, which caused several small aliens to scramble out of the way before they became a dragon pancake.

Their high-pitched squeals made Sherri laugh. With glee, she and Cheithe relaxed as their mates took care of the disgusting aliens.

Instead of blowing fire on the scrambling aliens, Grirryrth dug a deep pit with a hind leg, scooped them up, and dropped them inside. Apparently, he didn't care if any of them got hurt. He must be holding them for the Imperial Forces to deal with.

Cheering and clapping from her fellow humans outside the gates caught Sherri's attention as the aliens went into the dark hole. After a bow with a massive swing of his wide snout, Grirryrth dissolved in a burst of starlight.

Ki stood there dressed in his black battlesuit and faced the large TV screen behind him.

"To every Erkek and Friebbigh remaining on Earth, the Chancellor of the Federation Consortium is under arrest. As a citizen of Zerin, I claim Right of Acquisition of the planet Earth. All species not indigenous to this planet are hereby ordered to vacate immediately or suffer the wrath of the Imperial Forces."

On cue, a boom vibrated in the air. A small triangle-shaped ship lowered on the grass of the lawn inside the famous black iron fence surrounding the White House. It touched ground without a sound, lifting loose debris and dirt. Once settled, one side disappeared as four Zerin guards marched in front of a single figure heading to Ki.

It was the Zerin prince in the flesh. Shorter than Ki's seven feet, he stood about six foot six, with midnight-black hair that reflected blue highlights in the sun. The small braid at his temple was a shocking white that swayed and curled above his crotch as he moved. The rest of his long strands twined in a loose thick ponytail down his back. The bright emerald of his dual-colored eyes twinkled in his iridescent russet-brown skin.

As she shared Cheithe's superior eyesight, it was easy for Sherri to make out minute details of his Zerin appearance. What surprised her was the small gold hoop at the tip of his pointy left ear she hadn't noticed before. That tiny piece of gold came off as a bit of whimsy that didn't match his stern and serious expression.

His physique was slighter than Ki's, but his trim figure was hard-packed with muscles in tight black pants tucked into calf-high dark boots. His tan open-collar shirt had sleeves that reached midway on his forearms.

The younger man went up to Ki and clasped his forearms.

Ki relaxed enough to offer a small smile that his friend mirrored.

"Goddess damn it, Ki!" Qay released his hold, stepped back, and crossed his arms. "You left nothing for us to do."

"Yeah, especially since we had to haul ass to get here and save your cranky carcass."

Sherri's eyes widened when Lora's TrueBond, D'zia, came out of the ship.

He walked over to the duo and clapped a hand on both of their shoulders. A wide smile was bracketed by two magnificent deep dimples. His dual-colored irises were a startling turquoise while his skin tone was a lighter pearlescent tan. He wore a similar outfit to the prince's, except his shirt was a vivid blue/green that matched his eyes. His MalDerVon scroll still had a clear diamond facet that winked in the sunlight.

Sherri glanced at the ship's opening. Was Lora coming out?

"Holy maggoty hell, Ki! What'cha got here?" The younger Zerin turned in her direction and sized her up with a wide stare.

What, he didn't remember her? Oh, wait... she was still in dragon form.

The Chancellor had grown quiet and unmoving within Cheithe's prison. He stood defiantly in her clasped claws, grabbing them like the bars of a cell. His glare dared anyone to approach.

"This is Cheithe." Ki waved at them. "And she has something for you, Qay."

"Oh? She's with you?" One of Qay's dark eyebrows raised as he peered at her. How odd he didn't seem surprised to see a two-ton dragon.

"Yes, I'll tell you about her later." He gave a nod in her direction. "Let him go, Cheithe." The female dragon blew a small breath of smoke in his direction as she loosened her claw and tossed the prisoner out. The motion must have caught him by surprise as he rolled before he stopped facedown with his ass high in the air.

The deliberate action caused Sherri to snicker.

Cheithe joined in the amusement with a dragon chuff.

Ha! The asshole deserved it.

Qay motioned for two of the Zerin guards to grab the downed politician. With quick efficiency, the guards searched the Chancellor and took away the weapon he held.

Once in front of the crown prince, with a narrow-eyed glare the Chancellor jerked out of the hold the guards had on him.

Ki and D'zia moved closer to Qay as the other two guards followed close behind.

Weapons remained steady at the bald Zerin, who dropped his arms with a blank stare. Well, not really. Blazing hatred darkened his already black eyes as he brushed the dirt and grass from his torso and arms. The piercing glare never wavered.

"So, U'unk." Qay inspected the taller Zerin with a smirk. "You've been caught in a treasonous action against the Federation Consortium. By the laws of the constitution of the nine systems, I place you under arrest until you are tried by the judging body."

The full lips of the Chancellor pulled into a responding sneer. "You have no authority to proclaim such a case." The disdainful expression included everyone watching.

Undeterred, the prince of Zerin smiled as he gave an exaggerated blink.

Immediately a 3-D holographic image of three different aliens came into focus for all to see.

Even from Cheithe's advanced height, Sherri could tell one was an elderly Zerin male, one a winged female humanoid covered in light-blue and orange feathers, and the last was another male, this one taller than either Ki or the Chancellor, with skin so dark, several shades of the spectrum reflected with each movement.

The Chancellor maintained his stony expression. The man had nerves of steel or lacked any sort of emotional bone in his body. Hard to tell.

"I'm sure you've met the current Special Triad Council." Qay crooned with obvious pleasure. "They have been with us during this journey and bear witness to the recent proceedings conducted here on Earth."

The elderly Zerin's holographic figure stepped forward. "That is so." A regal nod at Qay. "As the Lead Councilman of this Triad, you...Chancellor Shon T'terlok U'unk...are hereby stripped of your titles and assets and placed in protective custody until a trial by your peers from the nine systems is conducted."

The Chancellor narrowed his eyes and stood straight as he rested his hands on the lapel of his dark merlot-colored cloak. "It is you who is mistaken, Councilman Aine. I am not only taking over this Goddess forsaken planet, but I will completely dissolve the Federation Consortium. Then I will take my rightful place as Emperor of the Milky Way Galaxy."

"Oh dude, you're so high, you're hearing surf music." JR10 made his appearance. His small, metallic spider-like body crawled out of D'zia's light-brown hair and rested on his big shoulder. His shiny silver frame reflected in the sunlight while the bottom was a matte black that matched the tips of the spindly legs. "Or you're just plain stupid." The little guy wiggled his bulbous lower body in a happy dance.

Cheithe cocked her massive head to the side to see the enigma clearer.

Sherri got the impression JR10 amused the dragon.

"And bro...just so ya know...we've got your MindWipe machine in custody." JR10 waved a tiny foreleg in the air for emphasis. "Sheesh, you'd think this was our first rodeo or something."

The Chancellor's face turned an alarming shade of grayish-purple. His thin, black eyebrows narrowed. "*Giasiager* take you all." His voice rattled around the words as if he spat as he spoke.

Ohhh, Cheithe intoned in awe. *That was a death curse.*

Sherri wasn't sure if having Cheithe available to translate was a good or a bad thing. She got the impression Cheithe took cursing as a serious business.

"Alrighty, then. All nice and legal-like." D'zia rubbed his hands together. "Qay, do your high-and-mighty thing and have your troops take him away."

Qay nodded. "Quite right, D'zia." He motioned to the two Zerins who stood behind the Chancellor. One poked the disgraced politician to move toward the triangular ship.

Chancellor U'unk gave one last glare at the group as he tromped away between the armored guards.

Qay turned to the holographic images of the Special Triad. "I thank you, Councilman Aine, Triad Associate Kasdeja, and Triad Associate Tuhon, for your attention at today's event."

All three made a curt nod of acknowledgment.

"We will place ex-chancellor U'unk into stasis and deliver him to the Imperial Forces on Zerin." He gave a regal bow to the trio. "Unless it is your wish that other accommodations are made for him."

The elder Zerin spoke. "No, that is acceptable for now." With a gesture, he included his companions. "A hearing will commence at the earliest possible time, so when you arrive with him we can immediately proceed." A thoughtful frown. "Usually in a situation like this, we'd contact family members to have a say in the process. I've never heard of U'unk having any surviving relatives."

"Bro...no way!" JR10 hopped up and down on D'zia's shoulder. "Hey, D'zia! Guess what?"

The braided tawny hair of the younger Zerin moved to drape over the opposite shoulder as he glanced down. "No, what, JR10?"

"Elemi tells me the Chancellor has a twin brother aboard his ship orbiting Earth right now!"

Confused expressions all around.

Councilman Aine spoke first. "T'terlok is alive?" He wrung his hands together as his face darkened with quick breaths.

Holy crap! If he didn't calm down, he was going to give himself a heart attack.

"Dunno," came the unhelpful answer. "You want Elemi to transport him here?"

"Yes!" Councilman Aine's jaw tightened. He flung his arms wide. "I must make sure it's him."

Within seconds, the shimmering shape of a large Zerin male came into being. While the newcomer was as tall as the Chancellor, the body mass was painfully thin and gaunt. Instead of a bald head, he sported a full head of black hair with yellow strands pulled back into a braid that reached his ankles. Where the Chancellor had black eyes, this male's were a clear jade—the inner iris boasted a rich green surrounded by a lighter shade on the second ring. The opalescent viridian pupil widened, terror clear as he took in his surroundings.

The trembling man wore a dirty white tunic and trousers and hunched into himself, fists clasped in the center of his chest.

The fearful look he darted around broke Sherri's heart. She started toward him but forgot she was still a massive dragon.

When the ground rumbled as Cheithe took her first step, the frightened Zerin gave a cry of fear, crumpled to the ground, and put his hands over his head in defense.

Sherri and Cheithe stopped as one.

The holograph of Councilman Aine rushed over to the downed male. "Lok, is that you?" He squatted as he moved into the other male's eyesight. "It's Aine. Come, look at me."

A low whimper came from the frightened man before he lowered his arms. He took short breaths as he tilted his head and gazed with narrow eyes. "Aine?"

"Yes…it's me! By the Goddess, Lok…you're alive." Aine's voice became firm but gentle. "Don't worry, you're safe now."

"Safe?" The skin around his cheeks and lips tightened. "Where's Shon?"

"U'unk is in custody," Aine reassured him. "Come, sit up." Aine coaxed in a soft tone.

Lok's gaze darted around before he nodded. His body wobbled as his thin frame struggled to stand. "Where am I?"

"You are on a small planet called Earth, on the fringes of the galaxy," Aine replied. "Please follow me into the ship and we'll get you comfortable." He turned his head toward his fellow Special Triad Council members. "I will join you at the meeting room within the next seventy-clicks."

The female winged humanoid and the huge onyx male nodded in agreement before their images disappeared.

The hologram and the broken Zerin vanished into the triangular ship.

"Well, that was fun." D'zia stated with hands on hips. "Are we finally done with this pile of crazy?"

"One can only hope." JR10 piped in.

While Sherri enjoyed this weird episode of her reality show, all she wanted to do was slide back into her own skin.

Cheithe, I think it's safe for me to come back now.

Yes, child. It's time for me to rest, the mammoth dragon agreed. *I've warned Grirryrth I'm leaving so your mate can get you some clothing.*

What! You mean I'll be naked? Holy shit, no way did she want to prance around nude for all to see.

"Cheithe, it's safe for you to go now." Ki stood in front, holding a dark green cloak that billowed in the soft air.

Where he got such a thing, Sherri had no idea.

Between one blink and the next, Sherri experienced the tingle of changing from a large dragon into a small, human female. Landing on a bent knee, she shivered in reaction. Ki placed a warm cloak over her head and around her shoulders. She was glad for the disguise, no need for the onlookers to know she was something other than human. The warmth was a welcome reprieve to the bright sun and cooling breeze. She stood and held the shroud closed in a firm grip.

Sherri peered up at Ki and became lost in his intense scrutiny. Her cheeks burned as his lids drooped over the blaze of navy/hunter-green orbs. At his detached expression, Sherri frowned as her stomach clenched.

"Come on." He held a hand out. "Let's go and join the others."

Sherri glanced at his stretched palm. Taking a deep breath, she plastered a phony smile on her face and placed her hand in his.

Ki

When Sherri appeared, naked after Cheithe relinquished control, it took every ounce of Ki's inner strength not to turn his back on his responsibilities and friends, pick her up, and carry her away. With her head hidden under the curtain of auburn hair and a naked bowed back, he experienced a strong surge of protective lust. Taking a deep breath, his lungs filled with the spicy musk that was all Sherri. Of course, he thickened in reaction.

Grirryth had warned him Cheithe would soon revert back into a naked Sherri. So, if Ki didn't want other males to see his female's nude form, he'd better find something quick.

As if he read his mind, Qay handed him a cloak long enough to cover her.

As the fabric flowed into place, he had a tinge of regret all that succulent skin had to be covered.

She stood and with a tilt of her chin gazed into his eyes.

At first, he scrutinized her like a possessive male. Then he remembered his earlier resolve. His infatuation with her began to override his lifelong intent. He wasn't some child who had to act on his baser instincts. *He* was in command, not his wayward libido. With a firm grip, he clasped her cold hand and walked closer to Qay and D'zia. As they got closer, it was in time to catch the end of their conversation.

"... and go back to Zerin," D'zia finished.

Qay nodded in agreement. "While I'd like nothing better than to stay here and coordinate the next move for this planet, I've got to return to Aimee as soon as possible."

Ki frowned. "Is she not well?" The expression on Qay's face was one he'd never seen before...part fear and part awe.

"Yes, she's fine. But I can't leave her alone for long." Qay scanned the surrounding area. "She is the first human to have a Zerin child. I won't take a chance of anything going wrong while I'm away."

D'zia nodded. JR10 traveled up his shoulder before he nestled within the tawny strands of his friend's hairline. Ki admired the spybot his former commander in the AoA had created. If he wasn't mistaken, D'zia had bonded with the little AI and had no plans of giving him back.

Sherri stepped closer with a white-knuckled fist clasping the cloak together. "What will happen to Earth now?" With a quick glance, she motioned behind him.

For the first time, Ki noticed the throng of humans outside the iron fence who were eerily quiet. Only whispered murmurings floated among them.

Sherri pulled the hood of the garment to cover her face more.

"Qay, maybe you should make some kind of statement before you leave." Ki nodded to the humans peering at them.

Qay's mouth twisted in a familiar frown of disgust. "Yeah, you're probably right." He turned to Sherri before he addressed Ki. "Why don't you take her aboard the ship and get her something to wear." He pinched the bridge of his nose with eyes closed. With a deep breath, his eyes opened and his hand dropped. "Explanations are needed and I'd like to meet with both of you before I leave."

Ki nodded. With a gentle move, he placed an arm across Sherri's shoulders to steer her into Qay's ship. They passed two Imperial Forces guards at the entrance and walked up the smooth metal plank into the cool, dim interior. The gentle hum of the ship's engines gave little comfort. It only meant his time with Sherri was coming to an end.

Shaking the morose thoughts off, Ki examined the inside of the ship. He'd never been in the particular vessel before, but Imperial Star Cruisers all had similar constructions. Unerringly, he headed toward the guest quarters. The markings on the second door to their left showed an unoccupied room, so he waved the door open to allow them entrance.

When the wall solidified, ensuring their privacy, Sherri turned with a half-smile. "What now?"

With a grin, he returned her sheepish expression. "I think first things first. It's time for you to change clothes and to catch your breath." He placed his palms on her shoulders with a quick massage of comfort. The scent of her warm, fragrant skin made his heart race. When she closed her eyes and gave a quiet moan, he jerked and let go. With a swift turn, he went to the replicator and programmed a neutral tunic, pants, and shoes in her size. Gripping the clothes to hide his shaking hands, he let go of a held breath. Shoulders back, he turned and offered them. He cleared his throat before speaking. "Here, something to wear."

With an unfathomable stare, she accepted them with a slight nod.

"When you come out, we'll meet up with the others and discuss what to do next." He tilted his head. The expression on her beautiful face didn't give away any secrets.

Sherri shrugged elegant shoulders and rewarded him with a half-smile. "Okay. Don't mind me, I'm just tired. I'll be right out." The refresher room sealed behind her.

The soft pad of the sleeping cot beckoned, and he shuffled over and sat, with a heavy heart. Eyes closed, his head hung as dread weighed him down. Time to get away before it was too late.

Yes, he'd be able to leave with a clear conscious. No MalDerVon scroll meant no need to worry about passing his defective genes on to another generation. Ki ignored the brackish taste in his mouth.

Unbidden, an image of her passionate response stung. No...he refused to change his mind. Now wasn't the time to be selfish. His family lineage had to die out. Nothing had changed. He was still the same person he'd always been. The threat to her planet as well as to the galaxy was over. The absence of the scroll reinforced his belief she couldn't be his TrueBond.

He pressed a fist over the pain pounding in his chest.

Grirryrth remained silent.

Chapter TEN

Sherri

When the bathroom door closed behind Sherri, an unexpected sob caught in her throat. It was hard to breathe. What was up with the dismissive expression on Ki's face? Had she done something to make him pull away emotionally? His tight frown and rigid body language sent a shiver down her spine. The man had acted as if he couldn't bear to be near her when he'd led her inside the Zerin ship.

Cheithe?

She probed to see if the dragon was awake. After their transformation, Sherri experienced the weight of her companion's weariness. It might have been too soon for her to take form, but if she hadn't, they'd both be dead.

Yes, child? Cheithe's replied in a light but steady voice.

Has Grirryrth told you if there is something wrong with Ki?

What do you mean? Cheithe sounded puzzled. *In what way is something wrong with him?*

Maybe she imagined things and worried for no reason.

Um, never mind. How are you feeling? The dragon was a newborn and shouldn't be exerting herself too much.

I am well, thank you, child. A soft sigh. *I will rest now.* The next words she said in a firmer no-nonsense tone. *However, if you have need of me, do not hesitate to call.*

The maternal statement made Sherri smile. *I won't. Go back to sleep.*

Cheithe gave her a soft mental caress before she pulled away and faded into unconsciousness.

With a shrug of her shoulders to loosen tight muscles, Sherri stepped into the shower. It didn't take long to dress in the light-cream tunic and pants Ki had given her. After a verbal command, a 3-D mirror appeared over a counter that held various grooming utensils. She brushed her hair and teeth while she examined her reflection.

Damn it! Stop being so nervous about going out there. She narrowed her eyes. Since when did she hesitate even when her stomach churned and her throat closed? It had never stopped her before and she sure as hell wouldn't let it stop her now. She'd never been afraid of taking chances and always dealt with conflicts head on. She enjoyed being with Ki and wanted to see where this "relationship" went. Too bad if he didn't want to, he'd just better get with the program.

Sherri pulled her shoulders back and gave herself a stern glare before she exited the small, clamshell-colored bathroom. Okay, where was the big lug? The compact sleeping quarters had only a twin-size cot and no sexy Zerin waiting for her.

At least the doorway was open. She would never admit it out loud, but she kinda missed Elemi's snarky personality. On that ship, all she had to do was ask where Ki was, instead of bumbling around like a clueless tourist. Sherri stepped through and peered up and down the narrow corridor. The light on the ship was at a comfortable level, so she had no trouble seeing to the end of the straight hallway. The sterile steel material of the floor, ceiling, and walls didn't match the warm atmosphere of the ship. Since the cream tunic only boasted a three-quarters sleeve while the pants ended in a slight flare at the ankles, it was a relief the clothes were comfortable enough in the tepid air.

Not sure which way to go, Sherri stopped to listen. Quiet murmurs sounded from the right. *Ah...* that must be where she needed to go. When she approached the open doorway where the sounds came from, she walked through.

It was a rectangle-shaped conference room, complete with an oval table made of the same metallic material as the ship. Sitting around it were the familiar faces of D'zia, Lora, Prince Qay, and of course, the man himself...Ki.

The group stopped talking when she entered.

Lora jumped up with a happy cry and ran to engulf Sherri a fragrant hug of spicy cinnamon.

When they pulled apart, Sherri blinked at the changed features of her friend. While the similarities were still there, it was startling to see an alien Zerin where the human used to be.

"My God, you look great!" Lora held Sherri's upper arms in a firm grip and scrunched up her nose while examining her.

Sherri placed her hands on Lora's forearms and gave a reassuring squeeze. "Thanks. I'm glad you're here."

Lora's dual-colored gray eyes crinkled at the corners while she grinned. "Damn, I wished I could have been there when you tried to warn the President." They dropped their hold as she frowned. "While I didn't vote for him, I didn't wanted anything like that to happen to him." She sighed. "Or to the other world leaders, for that matter." Her quick smile exposed the points of her fangs. "Anyway, let's sit down. We're just discussing what we've got to do next."

As they approached the others, Lora leaned in to whisper, "You're gonna love what they've come up with!" With a wave of her three-fingered hand, she encompassed the Zerins around the table.

Sherri had avoided glancing in Ki's direction. After Lora's prompting, she took a chance and finally peered at him. The profile of his dark, iridescent face was an expressionless mask that gave no hint of what he was thinking, much less feeling. A hollow pit expanded in her stomach at his lack of reaction. *Shit!* By his cool reception you'd never know they'd been intimate.

With a defiant lift of her chin, she sat in the empty seat next to Lora. Right across from him. Now he'd have no choice but to look at her.

Which he did, but his expression remained closed as he crossed his meaty arms over his massive chest, still wearing the black battle suit that held Grir-ryrth. His shoulder-length hair was loose and fell in soft waves around his hard face. The facial scar was in stark contrast to his dark skin, a frown on his full lips under the beard.

When she'd entered, Prince Qay stood to greet her. "Ah, glad you're here, Sherri." He resumed his seat. "We've been discussing the fate of Earth after the devastating events of the day." Leaning back in the chair big enough to hold his powerful frame, he fingered the side of his square jaw. While the prince was nowhere as big as Ki, as a Zerin he was still a formidable male figure.

"Earth is not part of the Federation Consortium and is, in fact, a protected habitat. That's why the Gidennon were there to study the planet. Fortunately, we were able to rescue the whole research team and took them back to their base."

Sherri tapped a finger on the desk. She might not have liked that little dweeb, Wapho, but she was glad he and the other little aliens were okay.

Qay continued. "And because it is a protected habitat, a member species cannot be placed into the leadership of this planet. However, until the Council of the nine systems can meet and decide the ultimate fate, we have to put in place someone from Earth to lead and act as a liaison between Earth and the Federation."

Sherri nodded in agreement and turned toward him. With laced fingers, she sat forward—this way she'd avoid the stony expression on Ki's face. Him, she'd deal with later. Right now, it was imperative to go over the plans Qay and the others had come up with.

"Tell me, Sherri." Qay's voice took on an inflection that was hard to understand. It sounded like a mix of trepidation and caution. "Is it true you started your own successful company on Earth called 'Phoenix Destiny Studios'?"

Lora let out a short gasp.

Sherri could understand Lora's surprise—the name of her company was as well-known as Facebook or Twitter. She contemplated the royal Zerin heir.

His handsome features were serious as his dual-emerald orbs regarded her with a detached coolness.

Out of the corner of her eye, she saw D'zia chuckle at Lora's dumbfounded expression. He picked up her limp hand and gave her a quick kiss on the knuckles before placing it on his thigh.

No reaction out of Ki. He sat there with eyes focused on Qay.

His indifference started a low burn in her gut. "Yes, that's correct." Sherri refused to dwell on the hurt feelings his attitude caused. "It's the reason I left Earth. With false evidence of me illegally performing corporate espionage, they convicted me in an airtight case." She glared at Qay. He'd better figure out she wasn't easily intimidated. "Those charges and the phony proof were deliberately set up by my best friend and partner, Natalie, in a power-hungry grab for full control of the company." Heat flushed her face in renewed anger. It had been a big mistake staying out of the limelight and letting Natalie be the figurehead. Most people had no idea who Sherri was until the charges created a sensational splash of tabloid fodder.

Qay put up a palm in a universal gesture of acceptance. "Actually, we put an expert on the case. All the phony charges have been exposed, and the charges dropped. You are completely exonerated and the guilty party was arrested."

She paused with a creased forehead. "What? How?"

D'zia supplied the answer. "Have you ever heard of the hacker, VØØDØØ?"

Sherri snorted. "Anyone who's anyone in the computer business has heard of VØØDØØ. What does that have to do with anything?"

"Once she was on the case, you were cleared within thirty minutes, Earth time." D'zia supplied with a grin.

"Her?" Lora's mouth puckered. Her Zerin pearlescent skin reflected the soft light in the room.

Sherri admired the intricate scroll that started in the middle of her friend's forehead and covered the right side of her face just below the cheekbone in dark purple ink. In the swirls at the temple, a teardrop crystal, clear and bright, twinkled.

"Yeah, you and Sherri know her better as Chloe." D'zia's grin turned into a smirk. Lora's wide-eyed astonishment made Sherri bark a quick laugh, even though she probably had the same stupid expression. "Chloe? Chloe from the *StarChance?*" Sherri glanced at Lora for confirmation, just as stumped. She shrugged with her palms up.

"People, we're off topic here," Qay interrupted. "Sherri, we have a proposal for you."

His stern face made her mouth go dry. No way was she going to like what he said next.

"We need you to head up the coordination efforts between the Federation Consortium and Earth and become the *de facto* leader of your planet."

Yep, she was right. She didn't like what he had to say. "Um... ah... excuse me?" She hedged. "You want me to do what?" She couldn't help but glance at Ki whose attention remained on Qay. That slow burn deepened. Would it kill him to look at her? A little support from him would go a long way to help calm her frayed nerves. She gripped her hands until her knuckles turned white.

"We have to move as fast as possible before your people create a mass panic after the deaths of their leaders. The void of their departure will cause a vacuum hard to control unless we fill it immediately." Qay's mouth thinned to a stern line.

"But...why me?" She took a quick glance around the table. "I'm sure there are millions more qualified than I am to do this."

"While that may be true—" Ki turned those navy/hunter green eyes her way and his intensity struck her dumb. "—we do not know or trust any of them. And you have proven yourself with your bravery and intelligence in striving for the betterment of your planet. Add to that, you have a better understanding of our galactic government than any of your human peers."

Sherri blinked. Wow, that was some speech.

"Good, it's settled."

Qay didn't give her a chance to respond. It looked like he considered the matter closed.

"Contingents of Federation Consortium advisors are on their way here as we speak. Even though I've made a preliminary announcement to your planet, we'll do a follow-up once the Imperial troops are in place to keep the peace. Gentlemen, time to leave." Qay got up with D'zia and Ki close behind.

Tongue stuck to the roof of her mouth, Sherri sat there, lost. It took a moment before she realized Lora hadn't disappeared with the others. "What the fuck just happened?" she whispered. The back of her neck squeezed in panic.

Lora gave a human shrug in her alien body.

From her pointed ears to her three-fingered hand and opalescent skin, her otherworldliness was secondary to the bombshell that had dropped in Sherri's lap.

"It's a weird-ass universe, that's for sure."

Sherri glanced at the now-alien Lora. *Well, wasn't she the picture of the understatement?*

"All ya gotta do is remember the motto that puts everything into perspective." Lora's mouth quirked.

Sherri raised an eyebrow. "Oh yeah? And what's that?"

"Earth doesn't need a hero, just a professional."

One month later

Sherri stood in the Oval Office of the White House with her hands clasped behind her. She stared with unseeing eyes through the large picture window, her back to an empty room. She wore a silk business suit in a deep cobalt blue, the pants flaring at the top of her bare feet. A contrasting pale-lavender blouse remained untucked, the fabric resting outside her waistline. Designer shoes with sensible three-and-a-half-inch heels were tumbled to the side of the Resolute desk, the famous furniture normally reserved for the President.

Which, of course, she wasn't.

Although the burden she carried was heavier than any president ever had. The last month had passed in a blur of activity no mortal woman should have to endure.

Good thing she was more than human, even if she resembled one on the outside. She'd come to terms about her changed humanity that now included a powerful dragon. On the upside, sharing her life with the Solaherra dragon gave her an abundance of energy and stamina—something she needed on more than one occasion.

Oh well, best to focus on the good and not the bad. The only real downside was Cheithe had to be let out on a regular basis. It took a careful adjustment of her packed schedule to travel to a remote area to let her dragon fly when the pressure became too much. Once a routine was set, living with Cheithe had became easier.

One of the advantages sharing her life with the dragon was an increased need for protein in her diet—up to six times a day. Sherri's appetite doubled, which she did her best to hide from the public. How could she explain eating enough for two grown men at one sitting since her metabolism increased? She ended up hiring a personal chef—after the woman signed a confidentiality agreement. Sherri now ate balanced, nutritious meals (heavy on the meat) every four hours. Best of all, she indulged in any chocolate decadence she wanted. She'd even lost those last five pounds that had plagued her adult life.

The hardest thing to deal with was Cheithe's grief. At odd times Sherri would find herself engulfed with a mourning so deep, she had to excuse herself from others to wade through the pain in private. Every day it became harder and harder to offer reasons blinding misery wouldn't overtake and incapacitate her. Things were getting out of hand and she worried she was losing her mind.

She had to admit the grief wasn't just Cheithe's.

All because Ki left.

An unbidden image of him made her chest crush in pain and her breath shorten. Her heart thundered in her ears, making her deaf to outside noises.

The choking sounds of her silent tears notwithstanding.

Damn it! She had to get a handle on her spiraling emotions. With conscious effort, she unclenched her fingers and forced her arms to hang at her side.

We must fly.

Cheithe spoke the same refrain whenever Sherri found her feelings careening out of control. The memory of soaring through the air unfettered by machines or the presence of others soothed as nothing else could.

Unfortunately, now wasn't the time.

I promise. After this meeting, we'll get away for a couple of days. How do the cold mountains of Canada sound?

I need my mate! Cheithe's petulant cry broke Sherri's heart.

I know, I know. I need mine too. Sorrow weighed her down. *Meanwhile, we can fly.*

Yes. Cheithe sniffed. *We will fly at nightfall.* The Solaherra dragon withdrew, but her presence never went away. Sherri appreciated that. Cheithe's companionship was invaluable and lifesaving. When not bogged down with sadness, her dragon had insights on how to mold the human race into becoming viable citizens of the galaxy. That was something most Earth people weren't equipped to handle.

"Sorry to interrupt, Leader Cantor—" Basimah, her assistant, spoke in a soft voice in the Bluetooth in Sherri's ear. "—but the others are ready to begin."

"Thank you, Basimah. Please tell them I'm on my way." She'd given up trying to get her Muslim-American partner to call her by her first name for weeks now. Basimah's tenacity was one trait Sherri admired most about her, so she shouldn't complain.

Going to where her shoes were, Sherri slipped her bare feet into them. She loved the jaunty spread of small peacock feathers on the face of the dark-blue pumps that gave color without being gaudy. For what they cost, gaudy wouldn't dare show its tawdry face.

As she straightened, Basimah walked in with silent purpose.

With quiet efficiency, she handed Sherri a tall cup filled with her favorite hot latte.

With a deep inhalation of the nutty fragrance, Sherri took a tentative sip. *Sigh* The shot of caffeine was more than welcome. She gripped the warm cardboard container, her lifeline.

Basimah's dark, knowing eyes smiled as she passed Sherri a trim briefcase with the necessary notes. The traditional headscarf of the woman's faith was in a soft dove color as it left her exquisite, bronze features open. Her floor-length black skirt flowed under a long-sleeved blouse in a light shade of gray.

"How are the natives today?" Sherri forced herself to concentrate on the job and not on her ongoing depression. "Anything new on the horizon I need to worry about?" She looped the strap of the leather portfolio over her shoulder as they walked through the busy outer office.

Basimah shrugged her elegant shoulders. "Oh, you know—nothing new. The never-ending death threats coupled with the growing petition from the majority of the men on this planet to remove women from power."

Sherri smiled at a passing male colleague who returned her gesture with a shy one of his own. She took another much-needed sip of her beverage. "Thank God not all men are complete morons. Most of them realize it's their own fault Earth needed a change in leadership that would hopefully make things better for the human race."

She nodded a greeting toward the Zerin guard in front of the double doors leading into the conference room.

He stood at attention and focused his dual-emerald eyes on them as they approached.

"Plus, they're smart enough to realize they aren't the big kahunas on the planet anymore."

When the guard acknowledged her, he reached over and opened the doors. Like most Zerin males, he was well over six feet and built of solid muscle.

Sherri swore every human female on Earth was in lust with every Zerin male on the planet.

Not that she blamed them. They were without a doubt the sexiest things walking on two legs. Too bad the sexy Zerin she wanted most of all was out of reach. With a shake of her head, she refused to relive the hurtful way they'd parted. Her breath came out in a quick rush. Time to focus. She stiffened and pushed her shoulders back and entered the most important room on the planet.

Making sure she had a smile plastered on her face, she greeted the assembly of the Leadership Seven seated at the oval table. "Good morning, ladies." Basimah left her side to take a seat against the wall while Sherri made her way to the leather chair at the other end. Holographic images of the other six world leaders "sat" in the chairs around the table. In reality, each leader was on her respective continent handling the same volatile situations Sherri coped with.

Sherri thought the Federation's idea to replace the executed world leaders with women was a sound one, because of the historical evidence of women being enslaved and brutalized for thousands of millennia, The Federation Consortium "encouraged" Earth to let women lead for the next hundred years. With that contingency met, the Imperial Forces agreed to be at their disposal while the humans prepared to join the civilized galaxy. *Humph.* It served the men of Earth right, having to change their patriarchal society and replace it with something more balanced.

While it was rewarding work, not for the first time Sherri wished the North American continent was someone else's problem. Sitting in her executive chair, she pulled the leather portfolio off her shoulder. With a wave, she opened the computer monitor in the table's middle and populated the screen with the reports scheduled to be voted on.

It wasn't that she couldn't handle the tough assignment, especially since the Special Triad from Zerin was there to guide her through the complicated business of Earth joining the galactic civilization. She had just lost the will to do so. Every day was harder than the day before. Only with the promise of getting away and letting Cheithe fly did Sherri's heart settle and allow her to concentrate on the meeting.

After several grueling hours, the session came to a satisfactory close. It was a juggling act, dealing with the people of Earth who reacted to most of the changes in a violent manner. Good thing the Imperial Forces were stationed throughout the planet. They helped to maintain stability and keep the humans from committing genocide in a frenzy of xenophobic fear and religious fervor.

After relaying her best wishes to the other women leaders, she left as their images vanished.

Basimah joined her as they walked down the crowded corridor.

"I have to get away tonight." Sherri kept her tone low, not wanting others to overhear her plans.

The other woman frowned. "So, you're planning on disappearing again?"

Sherri barked a short laugh.

People and aliens around them stopped and stared as she chortled.

"Ha! I'm never that lucky." Wiping a tear from her eye, they continued walking. "As if you'd let me get away from my communication implant."

"Yeah, but you don't always keep it on." Basimah grumbled as they went into the Oval Office.

It gave Sherri a nervous twitch whenever she entered the room. She hadn't wanted to be anywhere near there for her base of operations, but Councilman Aine from the Special Triad insisted she should use this room as a show of leadership and strength.

God save her from politicians—they were all the same. No matter what planet they came from.

Sherri settled on one of the facing couches in the room; her assistant sat on the one across. After putting the leather portfolio on the walnut tabletop between them, Sherri kicked off her shoes and tucked her bare feet to the side. She rested her head back and closed her eyes as her system tightened and screamed for Ki. *Crap*...that just pissed her off. Once again, she started a cycle of fighting with herself...

No wonder she was tired all the time. What she wouldn't give for a few moments of peace. Not only from external problems but also from the internal struggle to try to soothe the two-ton dragon nestled in her psyche.

"Are you all right?" Basimah asked in a quiet tone.

"No." She wasn't all right. "I mean, yeah, I'm okay. Just tired." She pushed the weariness down before it became apparent in front of the other woman. "Please cancel my appointments for the rest of the day and ready my plane to take me back to the Canadian Boreal Forest cabin." The remote mountainous area was the perfect place to let Cheithe out to fly to her heart's content.

"You're not going to ditch your Imperial guards again, are you?"

Body heavy, Sherri shook her head. "No, but I only want two this time, okay?" The last time she tried to get away, she had ten guards dogging every step.

Basimah frowned but nodded. "All right, everything will be ready within the hour."

"Great." Sherri closed her eyes and rested against the soft back cushion. The refrigerated air wasn't the only thing that made her shiver. "Wake me when it's time to go."

In record time, Sherri was aboard her private plane heading north. She snoozed most of the trip, only waking up when someone gently shook her shoulders.

"Wh'a?" She rubbed bleary eyes as she peered at the figure in front of her. She relaxed at the smirk crossing rubbery features, a sure sign they'd reached their destination.

Striyx, the Nok alien who was one of her trusted guards, didn't appear to be under any duress. Amusement shone out of his two solid-silver eyes nestled in deep sockets. He stepped back as his gaze swept their surroundings. A pug nose rested over wide lips, now enlarged in a sardonic smile that revealed two crooked canines bracketing a flat tongue. His small, square ears sat behind brunet horns rolled like a goat on each side of his large, narrow head. Wavy, white hair fell in a thick curtain to his shoulders.

With a natural slumped pose, he dragged two long arms at his side as his knuckles trailed on the floor. Under normal circumstances, he kept his black, pointy claws curled to avoid scraping as he walked. Today, he had a small blaster clutched in one hand. His legs were gangly and bent, each ending in a broad, flat foot. Striyx's body had a pale, coarse skin that covered a thin layer of white fur matching the hair on his head. His shoulders were broader than his pelvis and Sherri tried not to compare him to a gorilla. But once that image stuck, it was hard to get rid of it. Striyx wore the standard Imperial

Forces uniform—a one-piece loose blue garment, with the pants encased in knee-high black boots.

One thing about the Nok guard, he had a wicked sense of humor to go with his wicked way with weapons.

"Com' on den." He snapped his fingers to produce a popping sound. "We's better go 'afore Shysutá heres starts a-killing fer no reason."

A snort from his female companion let everyone in on what she thought of his opinion. "I *always* kill for a reason, moron." The deep purple orbs narrowed a glare at the Nok. "Even if it's 'just because'."

Shysutá had recently learned the English word "moron" and used it instead of calling Striyx by his given name.

No one could say a member of an almost extinct, bloodthirsty species didn't know how to have fun. Before Sherri's friend Lora left with D'zia to go back to Zerin, she told Sherri all about the purple-skinned mercenary when Shysutá's name came up as one of Sherri's personal guards. Once Sherri met the Merkaba, there wasn't a doubt in her mind the ferocious female would be a great protector.

Shysutá resembled an Anime character, complete with large, pulsating eyes, a tiny waist, and big boobs. The biggest difference was the Merkaba had two sets of arms instead of one. And, as far as Sherri could see, Shysutá was ambidextrous with all four hands.

Shysutá kept her thick lilac tresses clipped close on the back of her head, with long curls framing the side of her face and flowing down to her waist. The last two inches were a deep pool of purple. With a fanciful wisp, her bangs lay across her forehead in varying lengths. They topped her large, expressive pupils in the same mesmerizing color as the bottom of her hair. Her pale, lilac skin was as smooth as porcelain.

Covering her impressive breasts were twin triangles of barely-there blue cloth tied around her neck and back. A usual, she wore a black leather jacket with fingerless gloves on her two sets of hands. A black, tight skirt fell just below her rounded bottom; onyx thigh-high boots with heels to give any reasonable creature a nosebleed completed the badass outfit.

Sherri eyed the long Katana laser sword in its holster at Shysutá's back that solidified the "don't fuck with me" vibe. *Huh*, she couldn't be in better hands. Those two were the best protection on this or any other planet.

The only downside was they'd be hard to ditch.

The fog of her small nap dissipated. Sherri straightened in her seat, stretched her arms above her head, and enjoyed the popping vertebrae on her back. She reached down, grabbed her briefcase, and stood. "Okay." She led the way out of the plane. "Let's get out of this tin can."

She'd bought the remote compound soon after she had her name cleared and her fortune returned. With a rustic appearance on the outside, the gambriel roof, two-story log cabin was state-of-the-art inside, with every luxurious amenity known to mankind. Several yards away from the main house, there was an enormous pole-barn to hold various snow transportation machines on one side and a place for horses on the other. Since Sherri hadn't spent a lot of free time at her new home, horses were the last things she'd purchase.

Besides, if she wanted to go anywhere in the rugged mountain range, all she had to do was ask Cheithe to come out and fly.

After Shysutá and Striyx prowled the premises and the interior of the house and proclaimed everything was "all clear," Sherri went up to her large master bedroom. With a heavy toss, the briefcase landed on her bed. She'd better let Basimah know she'd arrived or her assistant would be likely to call out the National Guard to check up on her.

Less than an hour later, Sherri changed into sweats and Zerin slip-on shoes. Basimah had contacted her (again). After reassurances and further directives, Sherri headed off another emergency and called off the military her assistant had on standby. She was proud she didn't snap at poor Basimah before hanging up. It wasn't the other woman's fault Sherri was on edge.

Now came the hard part, convincing Shysutá and Striyx to let her go alone into the forest.

The three of them stood in a standoff in the middle of the living room. A large picture window framed the thick woods in the late summer afternoon sun. It was a chilly day outside, so a cheery fire blazed in a fireplace big enough to stand in. A plush tan couch with contrasting plump pillows faced the flames, with a colorful Native American blanket thrown across the back. It was hard to ignore the invitation to sit and relax in the soft cushions. Matching sofa chairs paired with a full bookcase along the opposite wall added to the warm atmosphere.

The last thing Sherri wanted to do was relax. The only thing on her mind was to let Cheithe out. Maybe then she could breathe. Sherri was drowning in the thick emotion she and the dragon created. She couldn't handle it anymore.

"I'm sorry you feel that way." Sherri tried for a reasonable tone with uncrossed arms and a hip jutted. "But I'm not changing my mind. I am going alone and neither of you can go with me." She rested her fists on her hips. "Believe me, I don't need your protection. I'll be perfectly fine."

Striyx scanned her with an upper lip curled. "You gots ta be kiddin'. Lil' biddy thing as you ain't goin' nowhere without one of us."

Sherri's face heated at the Nok's derisive tone.

"What the moron is trying to say"—Shysutá interjected—"is that we're here to protect you." Her stance mirrored Sherri's, except with top arms crossed and bottom limbs fisted on slim hips. "Even if it's from yourself."

Sherri contemplated the two and came to the inevitable conclusion. If she somehow escaped them, they'd eventually find her. No matter what form she was in. Plus, what if one of them got hurt when Cheithe appeared? Or, worst case, what if Cheithe got hurt?

"Fine." Sherri threw her hands in the air. "Follow me." With a dry throat, she stomped out the door and headed for the clearing in front of the house. The area had enough room away from the trees to change into dragon form.

Shysutá and Striyx shadowed her and stopped when she did.

"I'll show you why you don't need to come with me, but please understand this is highly classified and cannot be shared with *anyone*." She glared at them. "Ever." She crossed her arms again. "Only a handful of other people in the galaxy know my secret, and I doubt they'll say anything." An image of Ki gave her an unexpected block in her throat. With a hard swallow she kept going. "So if this gets out, I'll know where it came from."

The two aliens gave her their full attention. Shysutá's purple eyes narrowed while Striyx's wide silver ones expanded.

"I demand complete loyalty on this." Sherri glared at them. "Agreed?"

A few heartbeats passed before dual nods of consent were given.

She scrutinized their expressions before her shoulders relaxed. "Okay, then." She stepped back. "Give me some room."

The two guards slid a glance at each other before they stepped back several feet. With identical thin frowns they kept half an eye on her while scanning the area.

"Before I do this, you must agree not to follow me," she insisted. "I'll only be gone for the night. I promise to return in the morning." A sudden wave of grief choked as her sinuses and eyes filled. *Damn it!* Her emotions were out of control. Time to get a handle on things. Yes, that's what she had to do. Make a plan, come to terms with Ki leaving, and find a better way to deal with her violent reaction to his desertion.

Maybe it was past time to *really* trust Cheithe on how to solve their little problem.

Ignoring the heat filling her face and neck, Sherri took off her running suit and folded the clothes on the ground. She stood naked in the cool woodland morning with a stiffened back and spread her arms wide.

Let's go, Cheithe.

No one had to tell her dragon twice. The morphing sensation engulfed Sherri's body with a pinch that left her breathless. Once again, she was a passenger in an immense, silver dragon. With a cocked eye almost the same size as her companions, Sherri smiled at their dumbfounded expressions.

Shysutá was the first to recover. "You are a Solaherra dragon?" Awe made her mouth and eyes wide on her lilac features. She took small steps to Cheithe who sat on her haunches. The Merkaba raised one of her top hands as if to touch a silver scale. She checked for permission before a nod came from the dragon.

"But your kind is extinct." She spoke in a soft whisper. With a light touch, she petted the scales until she reached lower to a deep-silver one.

Cheithe lifted her snout in a rumbling pleasure-purr.

Shysutá's head jerked. "You were there the day the Chancellor was arrested! But...you are human! How can this be?"

"We's gonna have a lon' talk when she gets back tomorra." Striyx stopped behind the Merkaba and crossed his arms. It didn't look like he wanted to touch the dragon.

"Yes." Shysutá's mauve lips widened in a grin. "You obviously can take care of yourself. We will discuss this when you return." With a tilt of her head to examine Cheithe, her eyes pulsated with a twinkle. "Until then, little human." With one last glance, she turned toward the house.

Striyx gave his own narrow-eyed glare before he followed the swaying hips of his lilac companion.

Freedom! Blessed freedom! The joy of flight was theirs! Cheithe lifted her imposing, angel-like wings with their translucent white feathers to lift her heavy body into the multi-colored sky beginning its twilight.

With each flap of the dragon's wings, more of Sherri's tension released. She'd already gone over how dangerous humans could be and directed Cheithe to the sparsely populated areas of the mountain range.

Sherri floated in a hazy sea of subconsciousness until Cheithe set down on a ledge above the tree line on a cold mountaintop. The blistering wind blew and whipped around the dragon's steady body. Encased in the solid scales of her dragon, the frigid temperature wasn't a problem as Cheithe surveyed the alien landscape of Earth. She shared pictures of her previous homeland with Sherri—light-purple sky dotted with yellow, white, and pink puffy clouds.

Blue-and-violet grasses were dotted sparingly with massive trees with metallic trunks in silver, gold, and copper and matching blue-and-purple leaves. The timbers were so big and thick, a dragon could land on a limb and rest after a long flight.

The extinct horizon shone with the brilliance of the twin colors of the sun—yellow interior with a bright orange ring. Cheithe basked in its warmth as the fragrance from a myriad of intergalactic plants perfumed the air. The memory of her homeland soothed Cheithe's weary soul.

Sherri shared the dragon's pang of homesickness for a world long dead and mourned its loss.

The dragon's contemplation turned to her absent mate. Visions of Grirryrth and his masculine navy-blue dragon evoked a chuffing sound from her lengthy dragon throat. While dragons might not have tear ducts, they sure had powerful vocal cords.

In the tradition of her people, Cheithe bellowed her anguish at losing her mate. With an open mouth shooting flames of grief, she cried, intense and deep, a primal scream that echoed her agony along the unforgiving mountain ravine. The night became bitter and lonely. The repeated dragon cries sounded until dawn before Cheithe collapsed in weary despair.

Sherri admitted her own emotions had evened out throughout the vigil. And one thing became more than clear. Putting up with Ki's bullshit was over. Time to wrap up things on Earth and go after him. Even if he didn't want her, Grirryrth and Cheithe deserved to be together. She'd be damned if her dragon suffered any longer. Nope...not if she could help it.

We'll find my mate? The hopeful tone in Cheithe's voice solidified Sherri's determination.

Damn right, we will. Sherri reassured her as they once again took to the skies. During the flight back, she plotted how to get everything arranged before leaving Earth.

The mood turned buoyant and playful as they reached their destination. By the time Cheithe touched on the grassy lawn at midmorning, Sherri was at peace. What surprised her was neither Shysutá nor Striyx had come out to greet her. You'd think they'd be bugging her with endless questions. The cool breeze shifted the delicate feathers on her wings and brought the scents of the local birds and animals.

Strange. Normally the dragon either heard or was able to smell the body-guards mixed in with the earthly aromas around her.

After she nudged Cheithe to let go, the dragon relinquished her hold and Sherri stood naked in her front lawn. Walking over to where she'd left her running clothes and shoes, she put them on and glanced around. The morning air was cool and clean. It didn't take long to dress before going into the house.

It was eerily quiet in the building.

While neither the Nok nor the Merkaba was clumsy individuals, Sherri should have been able to hear or sense them moving. "Hello!" She called, walking toward the kitchen. She was starving and was dying for some bacon and eggs. The need for protein was gnawing her empty stomach.

"Hey, guys! See, I told you I'd be back!" No one was in the kitchen, but plates with food were piled on the table and pans were burning on the stove.

Holy crap. Something was turning to ash inside the pan. "Hey, you gotta be careful and turn the stove off when you're done." Switching off the flame, she grabbed a potholder to move the smoldering pot off the stove.

Irritated, she swung around to search for her wayward guards. "Shysutá! Striyx! Where are you?" She went to the front room, where one of the end chairs was upside down with a black lump underneath.

Running, Sherri pushed the chair away to find Shysutá facedown with a pool of light-pink blood oozing underneath her.

Next to her lay Striyx on his back with his throat cut, white blood mixed with the pink of Shysutá's on the floor between them. His silver eyes were open, and he wasn't breathing.

"Shysutá! Oh my God!" Sherri screamed, terrified the Merkaba wasn't alive. Before she reached for her lilac friend, something jerked her in a painful chokehold. A massive, muscular arm caged her in an unbreakable grip.

"Ah, I've finally got you, you *fruking* disgusting *hysta*. You've disrupted decades of careful planning and you will pay with your life."

Thick, bruising hands spun Sherri around and enclosed her neck in a punishing grip. She couldn't breathe. Her eyes bugged as the pressure of those steel fingers tightened. In a desperate attempt to get free, she grabbed and clawed.

Oh, my god! How...what? Consciousness faded, but not before the image of her tormenter became crystal clear.

Chancellor U'unk.

CHAPTER ELEVEN

Ki

G oddess damn it! He was lost.

Not physically lost, but "where am I going in my life" lost.

Ever since he'd left Sherri...

Idiot... his unhelpful dragon grumbled....

... on Earth, Ki drifted with no clear plan what he should do next. For the past solar cycle, he'd been busy helping Qay and D'zia in their new roles within the Federation Consortium.

It was unfortunate he couldn't keep busy enough to ignore the nagging internal conflict coupled with a choking *need* that bombarded him day and night. Especially at night when Sherri's striking features appeared in his dreams. Sometimes she floated in an erotic dance just out of reach, and other times her exquisite features created a hollow ache that yanked him awake.

When he'd coolly told her he was returning to Zerin, the pain crossing her lovely face made him grimace in shame. She'd lifted her chin in defiance when he ended their conversation by declaring he had no intension of ever returning to Earth. The last he saw of her was her stony mask and folded arms. Anger bracketed her full mouth as pinched confusion clouded her big, exquisite brown eyes. Ki remained haunted by the image.

During waking hours, it was easy to ignore personal turmoil. He spent his days dealing with demands and follow-up duties needed for the continuation of the galactic government. With the vacuum of Chancellor U'unk's sensational arrest, the Special Triad Council had appointed D'zia the interim Chancellor until the nine systems conducted a normal voting process within a solar year's time.

Ki helped with the transition as D'zia and his TrueBond, Lora, moved into the Chancellor's Palace on the Space station orbiting Zerin. While there, he enjoyed being in charge of eliminating the Erkeks in high levels of responsibility and replacing them with reputable members of the Consortium.

The only real mystery to everyone on the space station was the "playroom" with its many and varied tools of sadomasochism. Who had been the lucky recipients of U'unk's malicious attention? Hard evidence of silver blood scattered along a wall belonged to a Runihura female. Where was she now? There was no listing of her in the palace records, coming or going.

One of D'zia's first orders had been to investigate who she might be and discover what happened to her.

Ki volunteered to lead the investigation, but D'zia just looked at him and said it was "covered."

Whatever that meant.

Then D'zia had the temerity to tell Ki he should concentrate on more important matters.

When Ki demanded that D'zia explain, his TrueBond, Lora, smirked with a firm command for him to "figure it out." With that cryptic declaration, she pulled her mate away and told Ki to "get going."

He refused to let the infuriating couple distract him as he left before them, going to the palace on Zerin for Qay's coronation.

While D'zia took over as Chancellor, King Abzu E'etu stepped down and Ki's friend Qay was officially invested as the new ruler of Zerin, along with his human TrueBond, Aimee.

Aimee, during the coronation ceremony, decided it was the perfect time to give birth to Prince Ryox Argent E'etu. They named the baby after one of Qay's ancestors, and in the tradition of Aimee's people, his middle name came from someone in her family. The hybrid human/Zerin resembled a typical Zerin, except with four fingers instead of the normal three. As a newborn, the colors of his eyes remained in question, but the iridescent dark skin and ears that sloped to a point were all Qay. The baby's head was full of black, straight hair with a startling white patch that began at his forehead and tapered to the nape of his neck in a smooth line.

Good thing the Zerin populace embraced their new prince with open arms. In fact, the mixed heritage of the new royal was becoming something of a fad among his people.

Once the excitement surrounding the birth and the new king settled, Ki found he didn't have a goal on what to do next with his life. His past as a mercenary had no appeal. He'd left that behind long ago when he vowed to protect Qay. However, now that Qay was no longer in exile, Ki's duty protecting him transferred to the Imperial Forces.

Not that Ki resented moving on. In fact, he usually relished the challenge change brought. The only problem was figuring out what that challenge should be. He'd never been in this situation before, unsure and floundering. Credits he had plenty of; he could live in opulent comfort without working another day. Qay and D'zia were safe and busy with their TrueBonds and new occupations. While they had no need for him in their daily lives, they'd find something for him to do if he asked. The mere thought caused him to shudder. He always took command of his life, not relying on others to tell him his purpose. Whenever life had taken a dramatic turn, the next course became clear.

Not this time.

A dragon snort echoed in his mind. *Of course the path is clear. We go back and claim our mates.*

Look, Grirryrth, we've been over this more than once. Late that night inside the luxurious room assigned to him in the royal palace on Zerin, Ki sat in a large, roomy chair and pinched the bridge of his nose. He wasn't in the mood to rehash the same old argument. In the dim light that matched his mood, he crossed an ankle over his opposite knee. For the first time in decades, he dressed in civilian clothes and kept the Solaherra battlesuit absorbed within his skin at the cellular level. The natural materials of his soft gray tunic rested over the black pants tucked into the dark boots that reached mid-calf.

With a deep groan, he tried *once again* tried to talk sense into Grirryrth about the females they'd left on Earth...

... you left...

A devastating cry seized his body and mind. A female's scream of despair sliced and cut deep as a soulful roar of pain reached across the stars...a plea to end her torment.

What was that? Ki asked, though he didn't have to.

It was Cheithe, screaming in agony. Being separated from her mate created an unstoppable force of nature that transcended time and space.

Ki froze and couldn't take a breath.

We must go to her NOW! Grirryrth roared and clawed to escape.

No, Grirryrth! You can't come out here. Ki gritted his teeth as he struggled to hold on to his form. While the room was a big suite, it wouldn't fit a three-ton dragon. *Calm down and let me think!*

Sweat popped out on Ki's brow as he struggled and grasped the arms of the chair to help focus. The heat Grirryrth created reached an unsustainable level.

Cheithe! I'm coming. I'm coming! Grirryrth gave a resounding roar and ignored Ki's demand. In reflex, Ki stood and bent at the waist to hold on to the top of his thighs. He took in deep, gulping breaths to gain control.

Grirryrth... Goddess damn it...I said, calm down!

NO! We must go to her...

Yes... okay... OKAY. Fruking stop and let me think! Ki straightened and clenched his fists to soothe his trembling body. The internal inferno dissipated as Grirryrth finally relinquished with a rumble and a growl to fade into blissful silence in the background. Ki chuckled. Looked like all his intentions to stay away from Sherri were over and he'd deluded himself it had been the right thing to do. The absence of the MalDerVon scroll wasn't a reason to stay away. Which, he admitted, was ludicrous. Some personal marking had nothing to do with what Sherri meant to him. Besides, with her being human plus his Crart heritage, the scroll may never appear.

It finally became clear...did that really matter?

Decision made. *I'll contact Elemi to head out for Earth.* He reassured his distraught dragon.

The only thing to do was tell Qay and D'zia where he was going. And let them know he had no intention of coming back. For the first time in weeks, a peaceful calm washed over him. Yes, this was what he'd been seeking. He'd just been too stupid to realize it.

Grirryrth snickered.

"Excuse me? I must not have heard you correctly." It was hard keeping his tone smooth when Ki questioned Elemi as they approached Earth's orbit. With the news that the AI ship couldn't locate Sherri, his dragon roared and clawed, trying to get out.

Calm the fruk *down, you overgrown* gnotdile *lizard. I can't think with you screaming in my head.*

A plume of smoke drifted out of Ki's nostril. It was a sure sign of Grir-ryrth's annoyance. *I will yield for now, but you WILL find my mate.*

Blessed silence followed as Elemi answered.

"As I said," Elemi's voice took on a reluctant tone. "I'm having trouble locating Sherri."

Ki pressed his lips together. "Try to connect with her personal guards." He personally hired those guards before he left. Not that he told Sherri he took that particular job on himself. Shysutá and her AoA allies were as expensive as hell.

"Unable to comply," Elemi answered. "I am incapable of connecting with them."

A back molar creaked as his jaw clenched. "All right, let's look at this in another way. Scan for Nok and Merkaba life signs to find Striyx and Shysutá." He flicked his eyes back and forth as information scrolled across his ODVU. There...a weak signal from Shysutá's life signs in a North Eastern Canadian providence. "Can you find anyone else close by?"

"No. The Merkaba female's life-force is fading. There is a dead Nok male in the same room with her. No signs of any humans in the immiate vicinity."

"Transport me to her coordinates as close as you can."

As he spoke the last word, Ki materialized into an airy room decorated in neutral colors. He ignored the surroundings and concentrated on the prone figure of the purple Merkaba female under an overturned, heavily padded chair.

He shoved the heavy armchair away. Kneeling at her side, with gentle hands he moved her head to check for a pulse at the side of her nose. He barked at Elemi. "Elemi, transport her to your medical unit and commence the appropriate healing program."

Her body disappeared as Elemi responded in his internal ODVU. "Arrived. Analysis has commenced."

Ki turned to Striyx's still figure. With a sigh of resignation, he kneeled beside the cold body of the Nok male whose silver eyes were open and glassy in death.

A deep slice across his throat was the obvious cause of death. White blood pooled around his head and mixed with the pink of Shysutá's. A thick, metallic smell perfumed the air. With gentle respect, he closed the unseeing eyes and asked Elemi to transport the body to store in a freezer unit. "Report this incident to the Imperial Forces. They need to know what in the nine systems is going on here."

"The Merkaba female is stable," Elemi reported a few clicks later. "I will keep her in stasis until we can get her to a healer on a civilized planet." The AI vessel made a sniff of disdain.

Not that he blamed her. Earth was a primitive society with backward ideas, which included their medical treatments. He'd only entrust Shysutá's health to the best the Consortium had to offer. He couldn't begin to imagine the horrors the galaxy would face if anything happened to Hayami's sister.

Ki prowled through the spacious home, going from room to room trying to uncover what happened to Sherri. After he canvassed the entire six-bedroom household, his chest tightened. There wasn't anything else out of the ordinary. With determined strides, he went back to the large room where he'd found the dead Nok and wounded Merkaba. With clenched fists on his hips, he surveyed the living space again as his eye twitched. Where was Sherri? A growl rumbled from deep within his chest.

"Elemi." Frustration made his voice harsh. Nothing...there wasn't anything out of the ordinary to catch his attention. "Scan for any anomalies I cannot detect by myself."

Zerin male! One we've scented before. Grirryrth answered before the ship could.

Ki raised an eyebrow in surprise. *Why didn't you say so?*

Grirryrth gave him no verbal answer, but sent him a picture of Chancellor U'unk. Every bone in Ki's body hardened. He fought the instinct to change into his dragon.

"Ki, dearest," Elemi piped up. "A Zerin male and human female are approaching a ship six measures away in an easterly direction."

"Transport me to them!" Ki braced himself. What the *fruk! How did that piece of damaged* puntneji *escape and wind up here?* A thundering growl rolled out of his chest.

"I'm so sorry, dearest, but I cannot transport you because of the excessive growth of evergreen plants with elongated stems and supporting branches and needles."

"Goddess curse a sacrilege slug!" Damn if a bunch of trees stopped him from saving his TrueBond. "*FRUK!*" His growl roared as he raced out of the house to the grassy clearing.

"Grirryrth, attend me!" He lifted his arms for the transformation. The dragon must have expected the call because the minute Ki stepped into enough space, he formed and flew toward the east.

With Grirryrth's advanced eyesight, they followed the obvious trail U'unk left.

The despot had stomped and smashed through the surrounding foliage, kicking leaves, dirt, and bush out of his way. Heavy footsteps meant he had to be carrying Sherri, especially since there weren't any other footprints.

Grirryrth snorted a burst of flame at the thought of another male touching his female.

They spotted the small 8-15 ship in a narrow clearing. It had the same basic "M" shape as a regular 10-15, but this smaller vessel had room for only two passengers. It carried a maximum weapon payload, primarily used for suicide missions.

How and where the psychopath got the ship was anyone's guess. Not that he cared. He had to stop U'unk before he boarded with his female.

Grirryrth flung open his impressive wingspan to gather enough air to reach the vessel before U'unk did. The dragon landed with an earth-quaking thud, breaking trees and shrubs under him.

U'unk dropped to his knees and loosened his hold on Sherri who rolled seemingly boneless on the floor of the plant-laden forest.

Her loose body flopped as only an unconscious person could.

He doubted she was dead. U'unk would hardly waste time carrying around a corpse.

Encouraged, Grirryrth sat on his haunches and lowered his massive triangular head to eye the kneeling Zerin male. The biggest problem maintaining the dragon form was the inability to converse with their prey. For now, Ki left Grirryrth in control. Sometimes people spouted all sorts of interesting things when they assumed the creature in front was a dumb animal with no sentient capabilities.

U'unk was an exception. He ignored the giant dragon and bent to pick up Sherri.

Grirryrth growled in warning and shuffled a clawed foot forward.

"No, I don't think so." U'unk pointed a disintegration blaster at the side of her face.

Her body lay in a twisted heap, her back on the forest floor, bent at the waist with one leg over the other. With her arms splayed and short hair fanned behind her, the exposed tender skin of her temple gave the maniac a clean shot.

"You come any closer and I'll kill her quicker than you can get to me." The bald Zerin twisted his lips into a sneer.

When Grirryrth didn't move, U'unk stood as he kept an eye on the massive dragon. "Get out of my way and let me leave in my ship."

Grirryrth snorted. A stream of smoke came out of both nostrils as his bulk moved to block the ship.

"Oh, so you do understand me." U'unk's tone never fluctuated. It remained flat and impersonal. "Good. Then this will be easier for the both of us."

The blaster pointed at Sherri didn't waver. "I will take her with me, for protection purposes, of course." His dead obsidian eyes showed no emotion. "If you hinder me in any way, she'll be disintegrated without a second thought."

Grirryrth chortled, his amusement clear.

The furrow between U'unk's sleek dark eyebrows deepened. "I fail to see what's so amusing. Just so you are aware, I have no issue in killing others. Even females." He gave a thin, evil smile. "In fact, I enjoy it."

"Oh, do I's bets," a singsong voice tittered behind the disgraced Chancellor.

U'unk's eyes widened before he spun around at the sound of the feminine words. From his stiff stance and redirection of the blaster, he well aware of who confronted him.

"This does not concern you, Hayami of the Merkaba Peoples," U'unk greeted her formally. "I respectfully offer you an alternative payment for your services."

Hayami's youthful exterior was deceiving.

Ki's former commander in the AoA was hundreds of years older than she looked. Grirryrth had scented the Merkaba before she made her appearance. For once he was exceedingly grateful Shysutá and Hayami had a connection deep enough that one would sense when the other was in mortal danger. It was sheer chance he'd gotten there before she did.

Her diminutive size housed a brilliant strategist whose thin frame was covered in pale, pink skin. Her large, light champagne-pink eyes framed dark magenta lashes matching her spiky deep-rose-and-black hair—short in the front with long tresses that floated past her thighs. That day she wore a brief pleated skirt with a white blouse tucked in at her tiny waist. Small-heeled Earth-style pumps with pearlescent thigh-high stockings adorned her firm legs and dainty feet.

Strapped to those silk-clad thighs were steel rods as thin as her wrists. These were energy based weapons that were lethal to whoever she aimed at.

What Ki found interesting wasn't those nor the ceremonial Katana belted at her back. It was the metal round disks she held in all four hands, each disk not any bigger than her palm. While different in design, Ki suspected he'd seen those missiles before.

"Differ begs on you."

Hayami's full lower lip curved at the corner as her eyes throbbed with an emotion Ki found familiar.

She wore the same expression just before she delivered unspeakable agony to an unwary individual. "Tried sister to kill. Trespass money erases not."

U'unk's black gaze searched the dragon—as if the larger predator would grant him the mercy he'd not get from the female.

Hayami skipped over the prone form of Sherri and stepped closer to the big Zerin.

He dwarfed her diminutive frame as desperation rolled off him in a burnt-amber scent. U'unk didn't move the closer she came. His breath was even as he swung the blaster in her direction. "I will not hesitate to do the same to you, Hayami of the Merkaba Peoples."

"Know do this I." Hayami agreed as she stopped outside his personal space. "You not." With a quick flick of all four wrists, disks flew out of her hands and spun in his direction. In mid-flight, each plate released sharp spikes that surrounded the metal.

U'unk might have been strong or flexible enough to evade one or two of the disks, but not four. Three passed him by mere inches, but the fourth lodged in the meat of his thick neck.

With a hiss of pain, U'unk pulled the small weapon out and threw it to lodge in a tree trunk next to Hayami's bright-pink head.

It shaved off a clump of loose hair around her ear without penetrating the skin.

"Bad too you for." Hayami lifted her upper right hand and waved a fore-finger in his direction as if he was a naughty child.

U'unk scowled as he wiped at the trickle of garnet-red blood that rolled over the column of his heavy neck. "Is that all you've got?" The deep voice rumbled with disdain as he raised the weapon to press the cylinder at the center of her light-pink forehead. "You should have taken the money, Hayami."

The Merkaba smiled as she clapped both sets of hands and hopped in glee, uncaring that the metallic barrel dug into her soft flesh with each bounce. "See come, Fylgir!"

"Hayami, yous gos tos far agains!" A bulky yellow Orisha male lumbered toward the petite female. Having worked with Hayami for several decades, Ki had expected Hayami's mate to be close behind.

Fylgir was a half a foot taller than Ki. A small pyramid-shaped head sat on top of a hefty body with a bulbous chin that drooped over thick jowls and neck. Out of the pointy-head sprouted bright butterscotch feathers that matched a honey-feathered eyebrow. A heavy lid blinked over his one lemon iris and thin, black vertical pupil. He wore his normal canary/chartreuse-striped kilt that reached to his knees, a section draped over his right shoulder. A tuff of canary-yellow feathers covered his split-toed feet that were dusty from running along the woodland floor.

In his two thick fingers on each hand, he carried a regulation blaster, ready to discharge in U'unk's direction.

"No down put!" Hayami waved an arm to stop Fylgir from shooting. "Fun see good now!"

With a growl, Fylgir did as she requested and lowered his beefy arms.

Grirryrth pulled his head back to get a better view of the small group. Ki had a sneaky suspicion he knew what Hayami had done to the former Chancellor. He'd seen the effects of the Void Bolt when one had attacked his friend D'zia. It caused complete memory loss, the victim retaining only the basic intelligence of a small child. Once administered, the being lost not only their memory but became a blank slate open to manipulation by others.

Fortunately for D'zia, Ki happen to be available to administer the antidote within a short period. He doubted U'unk would have the same opportunity. Even though U'unk's back was to him, Ki could tell when the mind wipe succeeded. The big body slackened, and he dropped the disintegration blaster to the forest floor.

"See you!" Hayami grabbed Fylgir's arm and yanked it in her excitement. "More yes buy keep to."

Ki shuddered thinking of Hayami having something as lethal as a Void Bolt. While she had "retired" from the mercenary life, she was still one of the most bloodthirsty individuals he'd ever met. Without Fylgir's steady influence, he'd hate to imagine her running around and using the galaxy as her playground.

"Yous sits." Fylgir told the lumbering U'unk weaving on his feet.

The large male complied with a flop without a comment.

Ki wanted to change forms with Grirryrth, but the big baby whimpered in Hayami's direction for attention.

"Beautiful oh's dragon my is I." Hayami pushed U'unk's shoulder aside to rush to Grirryrth and Ki. Without fear, the Merkaba ran to the massive dragon who lowered his snout for her caresses. She rubbed the sensitive scales between his eyes with one set of hands while the other scratched his lower jaw.

Grirryrth's bottom foot twitched with each scratch of her strong nails down his throat.

"Him missed, yes one lovely," she crooned.

Grirryrth lapped up the attention like a dragon just hatched.

Damn, Grirryrth. Ki groused. *Have some dignity, will you?*

The only answer was a rumbling purr as he butted his head into her stroking hands.

A loud female moan interrupted Grirryrth's reunion with Hayami. The dragon pulled back and changed into Ki's form between one thought and the next.

Ki clasped Hayami's upper arms to mutter, "Thank you" before he rushed around to get to Sherri, who sat up and rubbed her throat with a slight cough.

"Are you all right?" He stooped and put a hand on her shoulder while she weaved and bobbed. He gazed into her exotic brown eyes while she leaned on her elbows on the pine-needle forest floor. Her breath evened out and her color looked good, except for the purple bruises encircling her throat.

Bruises in the shape of U'unk's large fingers.

Ki's body stilled. His vision pinpointed...*eliminate the one who did this to her.*

"I-I'm okay. I guess." Sherri raised her head and her eyes rounded. "Wait! What are you doing here?" Those striking single-colored orbs narrowed as her brows snapped together. "Let go of me." With a jerk, her shoulders swiveled to make him release her.

He did, not because of her actions but because when she spoke, it forced him to abandon his murderous plans for U'unk.

The muscles along his neck relaxed. Her obstinate attitude stroked and settled something deep within. A broad smile broke as he stood with arms crossed and a wide stance. He wanted to strut and show off his female. This brilliant woman faced death and came out fighting. Instead of cowering in fear, she attacked the male she believed wounded her.

Not that she was wrong.

Too bad for her he didn't care she was furious at him. Ki was more than grateful she was alive and away from the Chancellor. She could be mad all she wanted—the better to savor the coming battle before they both surrendered to each other.

Mate, purred the treacherous male dragon. *We will claim now.*

Ki ignored the smug, self-righteous statement. He was more worried about Sherri than giving in to anything Grirryrth had to say. That would come later.

Sherri rose and didn't glance his way as she marched toward the sitting U'unk.

For the first time, Ki saw the effects of the Void Bolt on the large Zerin.

U'unk sat on the moist forest floor with legs splayed and hands hanging at his side. His slack face tilted to the right, a slight angle that added to the blank expression. The older Zerin's alien, black irises were unfocused and fixated in one place. A pool of drool was threatening to spill down his overlong thin beard and mustache.

Sherri swung a leg back to kick the prone male.

Ki bolted over and grabbed her off the ground and swept her away.

"Let me go, you overgrown oaf!" She kicked and pummeled his thighs twice with her bare heels. Thank the Goddess she didn't have any shoes on or she'd have done serious damage. "I'm gonna kick his ass!"

"No, you'll only hurt your feet." With a sigh, Ki secured a hold around her waist. Partly to keep her in place and partly to snuggle that luscious frame into his. Taking in a deep breath, he savored her unique scent. Yes, there it was—the aroma of sweet, feminine musk that was all Sherri.

Sherri continued to struggle.

With a grunt, Ki gave her a quick nip at her tender earlobe.

She went ramrod straight and stabbed a lethal glare his way.

Damn, she made him hard.

Grirryrth purred in agreement.

"Put me down." She gave a whispered command.

Ki didn't want to, but relinquished his hold. With slow, careful movements, he remained mindful of the sharp needles and rocks on the ground under her naked feet. With a lopsided grin, he stepped back and raised his arms in a sign of surrender.

She returned the gesture by displaying an upright middle finger.

He wasn't entirely sure, but he surmised he had just been insulted.

"M'alalu! Zerin my own!" Hayami waved her twin sets of arms to get his attention. "See come did I!" Her upper limbs swept to display the silent U'unk.

Hayami always made him smile with her childlike wonder at the universe, even those times when she dismembered an enemy with her bare hands.

She did everything with such gusto and joy.

"Yes, Hayami. I see." With his palms on his hips he stood between her and the slack Zerin.

Sherri walked closer and stopped next to him. "Is that Shysutá's sister, Hayami?"

"Yes." A quick nod as he kept part of his attention on her and part on the drama in front of him. "What are you going to do with him?" He addressed the question to Hayami.

She fluttered an upper right palm in a dismissive gesture. "Bah, oh. Don't him want. Weapon have I must." The effervescence of her champagne-pink eyes gleamed with avarice as her lower hands clapped. "Use, much yes."

"Yeah, but what about him?" Sherri pointed a finger at U'unk while her other hand fisted on her slim feminine hip.

"It is my duty to take care of him." An unfamiliar male voice spoke.

Ki pushed Sherri behind him at the first sound of an unknown male coming out of the forest.

"I am, after all, his twin brother." Lok walked into the clearing from the same direction that Fylgir did.

While still appearing gaunt and delicate, he looked better than the last time Ki had seen him. One of the major differences between the twins was that Lok had midnight-black hair, liberally sprinkled with butterscotch strands that denoted his advanced age. A long braid hung in a single rope down his back and reached past his ankles. There wasn't a small warrior plait hooked behind his ear as was the Zerin tradition. His gaunt face was free of facial hair except for an unshaven scruff across his jawline and upper lip.

Dual-colored irises, normal for a Zerin, stared back. A deep-jade inner circle with a lighter apple-green outer ring surrounded the iridescent green pupil. The emotions behind those expressive orbs rolled in waves of despair and resignation.

Moved by the profound sorrow coming from the male, Ki's mouth tightened. No one should have to endure such misery.

The older male gave a respectable bow in greeting. He wore a traditional soft gray tunic and loose pants tucked into black boots.

"We have not been officially introduced." Ki met him halfway. With an inborn instinct, he recognized a comrade-in-arms.

The gaunt male gave a wan smile. "My name is T'terlok Shon U'unk." He nodded toward U'unk. "As I said, I am the older twin brother of Shon T'terlok U'unk."

Ki reached over to embrace the male's forearms in a traditional Zerin greeting between warriors. "I am M'alalu Ki E'eur." With a gentle squeeze, he let go. "I saw you when you first came to Earth, but where were you before that?"

The male's mouth tightened. "Shon kept me a prisoner in the palace dungeons for the last fifty years. Since his arrest I've been in the care of Councilman Aine." Going to his sitting brother, he placed an open palm on the bald head. "I understand the weapon used against him has completely wiped his memory." He glanced nervously around the clearing. "Is that true?" With trembling fingers, he tilted his brother's face to his. "Do you know who I am?" His eyes darted over U'unk as if to find reassurance.

U'unk blinked before he answered. "No?" His face scrunched. "Should I? I don't think I do. Who are you?"

The soft note to his voice surprised Ki. He'd only heard the Chancellor speak with flat inflections.

"I am your brother Lok." The thin male squatted to sit on his heels. "Would you like to go home with me?"

U'unk broke into a wide smile. "Oh, yes! That would be wonderful!" He spoke as if he were a small child, seeking approval. "Can we have sweet cakes? I'm starving."

"Now wait just a damn minute..." Sherri pushed past Ki.

He grabbed her arm to pull her back. "Let me." He waited for her nod of agreement before he approached the sitting males.

"Lok." When he got the male's attention, he continued. "While I understand the family bond you two have, you must understand the crimes U'unk has committed against the galaxy. He has to answer for what he's done. The ruling nine systems need to conduct a trial and decide his fate."

The other male shook his head and glanced at Hayami. Without another word, Lok resumed a nonsensical conversation with his brother.

Confused, Ki blinked toward Hayami for clarification.

Sherri snorted.

"Worries M'alalu not." Hayami opened her lower left palm to activate a communication vid.

A holographic image of Aine, the Lead Councilman of Zerin and the Head of the Special Trial Council, stood next to Triad Associates Kasdeja and Tuhon on the forest ground.

"Greetings." Aine's aged face was firm with a stern expression. "If you've received this message, Chancellor U'unk has been successfully reacquired and his memory wiped. The Triad has decreed that in the best interest of the citizens of the Federation Consortium, Chancellor U'unk will 'disappear' with Hayami and T'terlok amid rumors of his death." The Onoel female and Runihura male nodded in agreement.

A strangled choke came from Sherri next to him.

Ki had to admit, this was bureaucracy at its finest.

Aine continued. "While the honorable T'terlok has suffered at the hands of his brother for the last fifty years, he has pleaded for leniency and requested to be appointed U'unk's caretaker. In the interests of preventing civil unrest and the potential galactic uprising a trial might generate, we of the Special Triad Council have granted his request."

"Let's not forget the disgusting Erkeks and Friebbigh who helped him escape in the first place." Triad Associate Tuhon spat his displeasure as his obsidian face twisted in anger. "This way, if they all think he's dead they won't go looking for him."

Triad Associate Kasdeja continued as her hands fluttered when she spoke. "We made an agreement with Hayami that she not disclose his whereabouts to anyone, including the Special Triad Council. They are allowed to leave unimpeded and without delay." Her voice was firm within the small blue-and-orange feathers lying flat on her stern face.

At that final warning, the transmission ended.

"This is such bullshit," Sherri mumbled.

Ki agreed, but they didn't have a choice except obey the Special Triad.

Hayami closed her hand when the vid finished. "Go Flygir times to." She pointed her pink face to the towering yellow Orisha. The lumbering male clumped over to the sitting brothers, now engrossed in a low conversation. "Okays yous, lets gos." He tapped Lok's shoulder with a thick finger.

"What? Oh yes, of course." Lok placed a hand on U'unk's arm. "Are you ready to go home, Shon?"

"Will there be sweet cakes there?" Shon U'unk kept the simple innocence of a small child. "Can we play *Jûn-Jûn* after we eat?" He stood with Lok's help and bounced in excitement as his large hands clapped. "That would be so fun!"

Lok nodded. "Yes, brother, we will do that." He grasped the top of U'unk's arm to lead him out of the clearing. "But first we have to go to Hayami's ship to take us home."

"Ooh, the pretty pink lady?" U'unk's guileless eyes swung to Hayami with a wide smile. "We're going with her? I like her." He nodded his bald head as his long facial hair swayed. With a shiver on his large frame, he rubbed his arms under the bell-shaped sleeves of the burgundy robe he wore. "I'm cold." A quivering chin went with the innocent gaze.

"Yes, let's get you someplace comfortable. Come, we'll find some of those cakes you want." Lok led his eager brother away.

It was a tender moment when U'unk grabbed his brother's hand like a trusting child.

Ki still wanted to blast his head off rather than watch him walk away. Even when the two males disappeared around a copse of trees, the temptation lingered. He mentally shrugged. Just as well, he had something more important to take care of.

Yes, mate.

"M'alalu." Hayami caught his attention. "Have please Shysutá ship mine to? Then you come AoA you need? Out Shysutá leader new must?" Her bright pink lips curved in a mischievous smile that matched the pulsating mirth in her expressive eyes.

"Elemi, please transport Shysutá to Hayami's ship." After his command to the ship, Ki narrowed a glare at Hayami. *Little instigator.* He appreciated her offer for him to take over as the head of the AoA since Shysutá was injured, but he'd come there for only one reason.

Sherri.

His reason stiffened beside him. "Well, now that that's over, I've got to get going." Sherri headed back to her house.

Ki promised himself not to laugh as she balanced on her toes to navigate through the forest floor with bare feet. Warmth spread through his chest as he appreciated the sway of her hips in the loose pants she wore as she tiptoed through the sharp objects on the forest floor.

"Yous goin' or whats?" Flygir demanded with a lumbering hand on Hayami's shoulder.

Whenever the two stood together, the clash of their pink and yellow colors threatened to give Ki a massive headache. "No, thanks." He shook his head with a wide smile before turning to follow the obstinate human. "I've got better things to do." *Damn,* it was good to have a clear goal again. Hayami's twinkling laughter faded as he caught up with Sherri and swooped her in his arms. Her warmth settled over him as her elusive scent calmed something deep inside.

"What in the hell do you think you're doing?" Sherri punched a fist at the top of his chest.

He gave a slight grunt to let her know he was paying attention.

"Put me down right now!"

"In due time, *yofie-na*." He nuzzled her fragrant neck without breaking his stride. With a gentle lick, he savored her ambrosial flavor of her soft skin. Soon she'd be panting cries of pleasure underneath him as he plunged into her hot, wet...

Blinding pain caused Ki to stop and grab the ear Sherri's teeth had in a firm hold. *Fruking* female bit hard enough blood seeped. "*Goddess damn* it female! What was that for?"

CHAPTER **TWELVE**

Sherri

S herri fumed. *Asshole!* Who did he think he was, anyway? Picking her up like a sack of groceries with eyes hot enough to melt off a girl's panties. Not to mention the heady fragrance coming from him in intoxicating waves.

Not. Going. To. Happen.

So what if she'd decided to go after him? So what if he came to her rescue like a freaking knight in shining armor, saving her from the evil villain? So what if the mere sight of his massive, gorgeous, pearlescent body made her want to jump his happy ass?

His smoldering, possessive gaze pissed her off. No way would she let an overgrown, alpha, too-smug-in-his-own-masculinity male take her for granted. If he knew what was good for him, he'd *back the hell off right now!* Who could blame her for administering a little physical pain so he'd get the hint? Maybe she shouldn't be proud she had to resort to primitive tactics, but the lumbering giant refused to listen.

That little snip of pain did the trick. Big baby, he didn't have to yell like that. Thank God he didn't drop her, but she had to do something to make him pay attention to her demands to put her down. His masculine mojo squirreled her insides, and it was hard to think. They were close enough to the house she wouldn't have to walk far on the rough forest floor. She'd gather whatever dignity she had left and be done with it.

"What did you do that for?"

Damn it...even his growl was sexy. His chest vibrated against her breasts, making her nipples pucker in reaction. Jeez, her body was such a hussy.

Cheithe snickered in the background.

"I told you to put me down." She wasn't going to give an inch. Arms crossed with a narrowed glare should do the trick.

Ki snorted. A whiff of gray smoke rippled out of one nostril. *Wow*, that got under his skin. "No."

Wait...what? Looked like she wasn't making herself clear. He still carried her toward the house. Sherri raised an eyebrow. "Really? You'd better rethink your caveman ways, buddy."

Ki mirrored her eyebrow expression and upped the stakes by turning up the corner of his full lips. "I do not know what a caveman is, so I cannot think differently about being one."

Obstinate...stubborn...*ridiculous* man.

She huffed as they passed the tree line and made it onto the grassy clearing. The two-story barn architecture with its cherry gable topped by a copper dragon weathervane filled her with a sense of homecoming. It represented a safe place to lick emotional wounds when the memory of the perverse man holding her became too much in her day-to-day life. The weeks apart had stretched into an eternity.

"Look, let's try this again." Arrgh, hard to speak in a reasonable tone through clenched teeth. "Please put me down. I am more than capable of walking." With a wave of her hand, she gestured to the soft grass in the warm air. "While I appreciate your help back there..."

A male snort.

"... I can take care of myself."

He stopped and surveyed the area.

Sherri took advantage of his distraction to admire the strong column of this throat. Dark, shining skin throbbed on the side of his neck and held her attention. Ki was a powerful male in his prime, ready and able to defend and protect others. Sherri wanted nothing more than to lean up and nibble the skin to see if he tasted as good as she remembered. *Damn,* now she was getting all girly and mushy.

A jolt signaled he was going to put her down. In a gentle move, he swung her feet on the springy grass.

"Now, what?"

Her companion crossed his arms over the massive chest she didn't want to leave.

She mimicked his stance. "Now, go away." She turned on a bare heel.

NO! Cheithe cried. *Do not send my mate away!*

Hush, Cheithe. Sherri reassured. *I know what I'm doing.* I hope.

A huge palm wrapped around her upper arm and held her in place. "I am not going anywhere."

Well, that was a challenge if she ever heard one. With a tilt of her neck, she glanced upward to take in all that handsome height. She just loved the blue/green combination of his eyes, especially when his iridescent pupils were wide as he gazed back. "Oh?" She cocked a hip. "Okay, I'll bite. Why not?"

The corners of his eyes crinkled and his lush mouth stretched into a small smile under his close-cropped mahogany beard. "In spite of your proclivities for drawing blood from my ears...do you really have to ask?"

What did that mean? Heat crawled up her neck and face. "Of course I have to ask. The last time we spoke, you were perfectly clear I was..." She tapped a forefinger against her lips.

As if she'd ever forget his hurtful parting shot.

"Oh yes, I was 'a wonderful person' and that you just knew I would be claimed by some lucky male very soon, it just wasn't going to be you." She clasped her hands behind her back and tilted her head to the side. "Is that correct?"

"Yes." Ki grabbed her in a soft hold and pulled her close. "And I'm the lucky male coming to claim you."

That clueless answer struck her dumb. Disbelief gave way to a surge of anger. "Just who in the hell do you think you are?" She pushed away with a raucous voice and narrowed eyes.

He didn't move as the amused smile curled higher.

That did it.

"You can't 'claim' me like lost luggage." She poked his rock-solid chest. "And what makes you think I want to be claimed by a scared, out-of-touch *child*?" She pushed again at the rock-hard chest with a hiss. "I'd rather take my chances with an evil-emperor-wanna-be instead of putting myself out there for you again."

Ki's dark skin blanched. His full lips frowned and those distinctive eyes blazed.

With a *harrumph* and a flick of her hand, Sherri swiveled out of his hold and headed toward the house, head held high.

The growl in her ear was the only warning she got when a big arm wrapped around her waist and lifted her up to face him. Time stopped as she glared back. She half expected a burst of anger and wondered how to handle him when he exploded.

A blank expression covered his face as his mouth stretched in a stern line before he lowered her slowly to the ground. With a brief nod of his head, he released her. With a blank stare, he gave a short bow and turned to walk away.

The sight of Ki's back made Cheithe lose her mind. She thundered and roared, dragging Sherri along when the dragon forced the change in order to stop the retreating Zerin.

Only he wasn't a Zerin any longer. With a masculine roar of his own, he'd changed into Grirryrth simultaneously.

The sheer determination of the female dragon shoved Sherri into the "back seat." Cheithe took full control and only allowed her the barest ability to observe.

The joyful reunion of Grirryrth and Cheithe was loud, earth-shattering, and heated. Each blew plumes of smoke and fire at the other—bathing their bodies in searing flames. Together they twined their sinuous necks to nuzzle each other's snout—burning waves of heat singed the ground beneath the claws of their hind legs.

The sounds of purring, roaring , and crooning filled the air before they pulled apart and raced to the sky as one. The freedom of flight soared around them, the balmy atmosphere a soothing cushion under their wings.

Once Cheithe established herself in the airstream, Sherri's consciousness became blocked.

The loud, steady drip-drip-drip of water woke Sherri from a dreamless sleep. Groggy, she raised her head and groaned when every muscle and bone in her body screamed in protest from sleeping on a hard ground in one position.

Good God almighty, what was going on? Sherri sat up and something sharp dug into her left butt cheek. With a hiss of pain, she lifted high enough to scrape the offending rock out from under her. *What the...?* There hadn't been anything between that butt cheek and a sharp rock.

She gaped at her exposed breasts and bare lower half. *Shit!* She was naked and sitting in...a cave? No, not just a cave but a large, damp cavern. To her left was a wide, jagged opening, letting in dim light from the outside. It was either morning or evening, hard to tell from where she sat. A slight breeze came from the opening, bringing with it the scent of dry rock and dust to mix with the mossy odor from where water dripped in the dark behind her.

A rumbling male groan made her start. Twisting at the waist, she spied an equally naked Zerin spread out on his back with all his masculine glory on full display.

Ki moaned again, and he twitched. He rubbed his closed eyes as he muttered under his breath. With a deep snarl, he pulled himself up and rested on his forearms.

The pull of his stomach muscles caught her notice as he moved—the six-pack flexing in glorious temptation. She soon became the focus of his bloodshot stare.

"Are you all right?" he asked as they gazed at each other.

She took a moment to run an internal inventory before nodding. "Yeah, I think so." She pushed back a lock of hair falling into her face. "But I feel like I've been hit by a Mack truck more than once. I'm sore all over." Especially between her legs. Her cheeks heated. If she didn't know any better, she'd swear she'd been in a sexual marathon.

She slid her glance away and squirmed. The only reasonable explanation to be this tender was because she must have had copious amounts of dragon sex. Flashes came—images of Grirryrth twining around her as he gave her a solid bite on the neck to hold her steady. Next came the image of her caught within the male dragon's massive claws as they zoomed toward earth when he penetrated her.

Cheithe...the little tramp...snickered in the background. *Yes, my mate and I have claimed each other. Look closely at yours.* She made the suggestion in a conspiratorial whisper.

Sherri drew her lower lip between her teeth and snuck a peek at Ki under her lashes. At first, there wasn't anything different about his large body shining in the low light as he ran a palm down his face. With a grunt, he pulled away and leaned his massive torso to rest on his palms. His head dropped back with eyes closed.

With his face exposed, the right side became clear. A tattoo started at the middle of his forehead and tapered to fan across the top of his cheekbone. It was an intricate scrollwork that shone in deep purple ink across his dark skin. Embedded within the middle of the swirls and lines, his temple housed a multifaceted, diamond crystal.

A wave of heat blasted through her and she became lightheaded. A MalDerVon scroll. Ki wore a MalDerVon scroll. The Zerin symbol of True-Bond mates that Lora explained to her when Sherri commented on the one Lora sported that matched D'zia's.

With trembling fingers, she touched her left temple. Did she have one?

She did!

At least something was there. It had the smooth edges of a raised diamond, but what was weird was she *sensed* her fingers touching it. It was the same as if she felt any other part of her body.

Holy Crap! Ki was her TrueBond. Sherri turned away and blinked as tears filled her eyes. Wrapping her arms around her knees, she rested her forehead on them with closed eyes. Why was she so weepy? Her inner hollowness was all about the man who had made it clear he didn't want her.

"Are you okay?"

She twitched. His voice startled her. "I'm fine." She lied to her knees. Now what? What could she do about this ridiculous situation? Tight nerves made it hard to breathe.

"Sherri, what's wrong?"

"Nothing." She continued to direct her conversation at her knees. One glance his way and she'd melt. "Go away."

A puff of dust from the dry floor teased as heavy footfalls came close. "I will do nothing of the sort." Ki's crooning voice came as a surprise. "We are TrueBonds. It is time to begin anew."

Begin anew? Who in the hell talked like that? Her face burned at the rhetoric comment. "So what?" The grip on her poor knees tightened. "You don't have to stick around."

Ki's masculine chuckle should have been a warning. She squealed when tree-trunk arms swung her up and snuggled them together.

"But I want to stick around." The last word came out muffled as he nuzzled the sensitive skin behind her ear.

Sherri jerked and glared. "Oh yeah? Since when?" She waved around the craggy cave. "Since your stupid dragon attacked mine and forced us here?"

It was my *decision to be with Grirryrth. He did not force anything and I resent you saying something that childish.*

Cheithe's admonishment shamed Sherri.

Ki frowned, but didn't say anything as he lowered them to the dirt floor to rest against the rugged cave wall. With a soft grunt, she was placed on his lap.

"Grirryrth didn't force Cheithe any more than she forced him."

Great, now two voices told her what an unreasonable bitch she was. She folded her arms.

Ki took in a deep breath.

His wide chest moved and made the skin on her back pebble with warmth.

"Look, Sherri, we should talk."

Her stomach dropped. Here it came. Now he'd go over all the reasons they shouldn't be together, MalDerVon scroll be damned. "No need to spell it out." Enough. Why endure this torture any longer? She scooted off and stood. "Let's leave and get this over with."

The irritating male sat against the ragged cave wall with a forearm resting on a bent knee. A frown matched the furrowed lines between mahogany brows. "I don't know what 'spell it out' means, but I believe we have a misunderstanding."

Sherri stiffened. To Ki's credit, he didn't ogle her naked body. Which was perversely irritating. She ignored the passing thought and shoved hurt feminine pride back. "Is that so?" She rested her fist on a cocked hip. "Enlighten me."

With a steady gaze, the alien male rose and sensually stalked forward with his dual-colored orbs and a smooth smile.

Sherri blinked as her neck heated. Ki's sexual overture tightened her nipples and created mini-spasms deep inside.

Without a touch, the warmth of his breath feathered her ear as he whispered, "I see you."

"Wha'?" Her brain scrambled, and she sounded like an idiot. A tempting male, sea breeze scent proceeded his warmth when he moved in closer.

"I see who you are inside." A large palm rested above her heart. "I see a brave, intelligent female who has captured the very heart of a dragon."

He encircled the side of her neck with one hand and pulled her close until his masculine lips were mere inches from hers. "And I see the female who has claimed me."

Ki closed the gap and rested the soft pads of his lips on hers but didn't otherwise move as he wrapped her in his strong arms.

His thick thighs rubbed against her, the coarse hair on his legs adding to her sensual experience. At the same time, the soft beard rubbing the outside of her mouth caused a shiver of appreciation. When a traitorous sigh escaped her, Ki took advantage and plunged inside. Firm lips and tongue took possession, an intense move that scrambled her senses as their flavors mixed and made her head spin. Did she taste him or did he taste her?

Oh, good God, what was he doing to me?

Cheithe sniffed in amusement. *Obviously, he's making love to you. Do I have to stay and explain things to you?*

Sherri's brain scrambled. It was impossible to concentrate while Ki's masterful seduction took over.

Do not be stubborn, child. Cheithe chided. *He is your mate. Do not let pride come between you and your happiness. Isn't he what* you *looked for when you left Earth?* With that firm reprimand, Cheithe disappeared from Sherri's consciousness.

The sudden departure of the dragon startled Sherri and allowed her to pull from Ki's devastating assault. She took a step back to clear her befuddled mind. Time to get a handle on what was going on.

"Wait, wait!" She held up a palm to stop him from following. At the hope and need blazing out of his eyes, her will almost crumbled. "I don't understand." *Okay, take a deep breath.* Instead of calm, her lungs filled with Ki's signature scent as it mixed with the moist, cold air. Her body took on a life of its own; her nipples hardened, and she shook with internal heat. Crossing her arms, she ignored the sight of his iridescent skin flushed in passion. "What made you come to Earth? How did you know the Chancellor kidnapped me?"

A grimace twisted his mouth. "I had no idea U'unk had even escaped from the Imperial Forces." He pushed a strand of long mahogany hair from his face.

Sherri blinked. Long hair? What happened to his normal shoulder-length hair? Instead of resting on his shoulders, the thick curtain played peek-a-boo with the planes and hills of his chiseled chest to rest at the top of his thighs.

"I came because of Cheithe's cry." The tips of his pointy ears flushed a cute shade of fuchsia. "I heard her, and I had to come." With a sheepish grin, his eyes caressed. "I realized I'd been fooling myself in thinking we needed to be apart."

Ki rested his large palms at the tops of her shoulders. The heat burrowed into her and relaxed tight muscles.

"Let me tell you why I left in the first place." With a rub against the back of his neck, he went to the craggy wall and sat. With a sheepish grin, he beckoned her to join him.

Sherri scanned the dirt floor between his thick thighs where his semi-erect penis lay. Rubbing the chill bumps on her arms, she gazed at his wide-eyed plea. While Grirryrth had told her the initial story, he hadn't been able to describe the feelings behind Ki's actions. She wanted to hear his side of the story and why not do so huddled within his warm comfort? With an inward sigh, she settled against his chest, the partially hardened penis nestled along the dent of her spine. His strong embrace wrapped around her and he grasped her hands in his as he told about his past.

And what a story it was. A tale of a selfish boy who'd stolen his father's battlesuit in secret to confront some bullies. That one thoughtless act left his family unprotected on a hostile mining planet known for its unscrupulous citizens. Rogue bandits ended up butchering his entire family. When he and Grirryrth escaped Reinus45 a year later, he'd vowed not to have children. He couldn't take a chance his selfish genes would pass to another generation.

Sherri zoned out as Ki's voice trailed off.

"Sherri?"

The sound of the male rumbling tone behind her made her jump.

"Don't you have anything to say?"

She found it difficult to organize her scrambled thoughts, but he deserved honesty. "It's hard to relive your sad story with you, and I'm sorry for what happened to you and your family. No one should have to endure something like that, especially at that age." She gave an amused chuckle. "I'm not sure you want to hear what I really think about everything else." No need to glance back to know he was confused. It was clear by the unyielding way his chest became still.

The firm hold tightened. "Go ahead, tell the truth."

The terse timbre caused her to smile. The oaf probably believed he was an awful person who didn't deserve love, much less have a family that included children. While she'd never planned on having kids, who knows? With the right partner, she might reconsider having that adventure...much later. But, something about his fears didn't make sense.

"Before I do that, I have a question. Don't Zerins use birth control?"

The big man tightened his hold. "Yes, but normal birth control doesn't work with me because of Grirryrth." He cleared his throat with a sheepish grin. "The Solaherra dragon would just ignore it whenever he felt like it."

Sherri's heart started racing. "You mean I could be pregnant?"

"No." He shifted behind her. "The time isn't right now."

When he didn't say more, Sherri decided to tackle Ki's earlier concern. "Ki, I have to be honest here. I believe your reason for not wanting children isn't based on logical facts, but on the insecurity and memory of a young child." With a pat to the back of his hands, she turned to look at him...yep, he was grimacing. "You know you'd make a great father." She considered not only what he said but also the feelings behind the words. "What I really think is you're terrified of giving unconditional love for fear of it being taken away."

Ki frowned and glanced away. "Maybe. I don't know." His eyes unfocused before several blinks brought him back. "Grirryrth agrees." A rumbling chuckle vibrated against her. "You've repeated something the dragon has been saying for decades. I just never wanted to believe him."

"So, what's changed? Why *are* you here?" Yeah...pick the scab and make it bleed.

A smoldering smile bloomed before those masculine lips nuzzled between her neck and shoulders. "When I heard Cheithe's cry, I realized I'd made a terrible mistake."

His light lick caused a shiver to run down her back.

"You'd already gotten past my impenetrable defenses. I am no longer whole without you." When she was silent he nudged her. "Well? Do we have a chance?"

Heat bloomed in her chest as the corners of her mouth turned up. Never in her wildest dreams did she think a man would want to have the "relationship" talk. Not only did he want to have the conversation, but he also wanted to dive deep.

How refreshing and disturbing all at the same time. However, the time had come to play "devil's advocate" and poke at the proverbial elephant in the room.

"What if I'm not sure?" The flickering light on the rocky wall caught her attention as she organized her rambling thoughts. "I was furious at your rejection. One moment you enjoyed being with me, and the next I was dismissed without a second glance. I mean, I was just getting used to being with you, then you left." She shifted her knees to adjust for the lack of circulation. While she wasn't sitting on the dirt floor, Ki's firm thighs had little give. "I have a hard time trusting people in the first place. And once that trust is broken, it takes a lot for that person to get it back."

"That's a fair statement." He shifted, but his hold didn't loosen. "And I have to admit, I feel the same way. For the most part, I've lived separate for that very reason."

Ki's massive shoulders shrugged and he rubbed a warm palm across her back. Again with the shivers.

"I believe the more time we spend together, we'll learn to trust each other. I'd like us to be partners in every way possible." He lifted her arm and brought her attention to the iridescent sheen overlaying her tan. "There is an advantage TrueBond mates share that you humans have no concept of."

Wait...was she feeling the finger caressing the top of her hand *and* feeling her skin under his finger? The twofold sensation of their shared experience tightened something low inside.

Sherri squinted at the possibilities. If she could feel what he did... *Shit*, she was way out of her league. Sucking in a breath, she rasped, "Why didn't this happen before?"

She didn't have to see the smug, male smile to know he had one.

"The TrueBond hadn't been completed before."

Warm breath nuzzled the bottom of her neck again, the sensation amplifying her responsiveness.

"Plus, because of my Crart heritage, we will revel in an intense gratification that even full-blood Zerins don't experience."

It was hard to understand a word he said. Sherri's entire focus was on the tactile pleasure of his touch. "Cart? Wha'?"

"Car-art." He nibbled her receptive skin. "I am the last of an extinct species that can cohabit with the Solaherra dragons that share our existence."

Sherri was immersed in the shared desire of wandering male hands across her lower stomach. What was he saying? It was impossible to concentrate with his mouth licking and caressing her neck and shoulders. Hang on...something didn't make sense.

"Wait." She grabbed a roaming hand before it reached her breasts. She glanced back and relaxed at his indulgent smile. "I'm not a Crart." Maybe her pronunciation didn't sound like his, but she'd gotten the point across. "So how can I change into Cheithe?"

With a grunt, he sat back and took her with him.

With relaxed muscles, she snuggled into his wide chest. Yeah, plenty of room for her to lean in warm comfort. Now all she had to do was find something for her butt...

"First, let me give you a little history lesson. Thousands of millennia ago, the Crart and the Solaherra races lived in harmony on the thriving planet of Aonia. An unexpected betrayal tore the two species apart in a devastating war. The fighting was so severe, it left Aonia uninhabitable." He paused.

Sherri closed her eyes and enjoyed his fresh male scent. The tantalizing aroma was better than the tang of sea brine on a summer breeze.

"The next part of the story is pure legend, but it's the only explanation that has lasted throughout the generations."

Sherri opened her eyes as he spoke.

"Before the last of the Crart and Solaherra died, the All-Knowing Goddess interceded. 'You have destroyed that which I have created,' she told the two remaining leaders as they lay dying. 'I will spare your lives, but each will depend on the other for your existence. From this day forward, you Solaherra will live within the Crart—and you Crart, you are responsible for the continued life of the Solaherra. From you to each generation thereafter until such time the Solaherra will be strong enough to call forth his female to begin his race anew.'"

"At this point, she infused the Solaherra battle suit on the Crart male. Since the Crart people were dead, the male left the dying planet of Aonia and wandered the galaxy until his descendants ended up on Zerin. There, they found Zerins had the ability to merge with their females in a TrueBond. That gave them the hope a Solaherra female might be born. With each passing generation, Grirryrth tried to call forth a mate, only to be disappointed."

He hugged Sherri. "Until you. Even though we hadn't completed the TrueBond process, your human heritage allowed Grirryrth to become strong enough to call Cheithe into being."

Well, that was a nice fairytale. Chock full of myths and legends, but some truth had to be in there somewhere. For now, Sherri had only one question. "Um, so how are they going to begin their race 'anew' "?

He chuckled. "Afraid you'll have little dragon eggs, *yofie-na*?"

Rat-bastard. "Well, it's a legitimate question, buster," she retorted.

There is no reason to be scared, child. Cheithe whispered. *I cannot breed for several generations since I am not strong enough to exist alone. The battle suit carries the essence of both Grirryrth and myself until I am able to be on my own. Your firstborn child will carry the battle suit after Ki transfers us. Once that child finds their TrueBond, Grirryrth and I will separate as I join their mate just as I have done with you.*

Sherri blinked. Well, wouldn't that be something to endure—two dragons inside instead of one. She couldn't even imagine.

Ki's loud laugh shook her. "I know what Cheithe told you, but remember any child we have won't carry the battlesuit with the dragons until they are mature enough to understand. Hopefully, well into adulthood." He was quiet before he spoke again. "At one point, the two dragons will become strong enough to escape the bonds of the battlesuit and separate on their own." He shrugged. "It probably won't happen in our lifetimes."

"Hmm." What could she say? Hard enough to absorb all the strange information at once. A silky caress whispered across her forearm. Startled, she gasped when a long, mahogany lock of hair wrapped around her arm. With tentative fingers, she touched it. What in the world?

She followed the tresses with her gaze to Ki's head, and a gasp escaped. Even in the dim light of the dank cave, it was easy to see the heavy curtain of his hair that pooled on the dirt floor around him. The auburn highlights scattered throughout would have cost a fortune at the expensive salon she visited. The blended hue gave the glorious tresses a combined depth.

Oh, yeah... why the sudden transformation in his hair? She scooted back and sat on her heels facing him. Not only was it longer and with an added color, but his eyes were also altered. Instead of the blue/green irises, the hunter-green ring was now interwoven with bronze—giving it a bright hazel hue. The blue ring stayed the same, maybe a little darker navy than before. His iridescent green pupils hadn't changed, but were wide as they roamed over her. If she wasn't mistaken, the dark tan of his skin had lightened underneath the pearlescent sheen.

"Why do you look so different?" She spoke behind splayed fingers. "Are you okay?" What if he'd caught a virus here on Earth? Was he sick?

Ki's eyes crinkled as his full lips curled into a slight smile under the close-cropped beard, now highlighted with auburn strands. "What you see are the effects of the TrueBond. My body has adapted some of your characteristics," he nodded toward her. "Just as you have taken on some of mine."

"Wha'?" Sherri scrutinized her arms and the tops of her legs. Sure enough, her normally tawny skin was a shade darker with a light sheen to it. She touched her face, nothing weird, thank God. But when she'd moved, her hair flowed across her shoulder and settled in a dark pile on her thigh. She picked up an inch of the wavy strand to consider its complexity. While the overall color of reddish-brown remained the same, now it held a rich blend of mahogany.

The most disturbing part was it was longer than ever before. There was a reason she'd kept her style in a short bob for years, but now the thick mane flowed past her waist. What was odd, though, was as she rubbed her tresses, her hair *experienced* the touch of her stroking motion.

With a squeak of alarm, she dropped it and landed with a thud on her butt. A puff of dry dirt wafted from beneath her and tickled her nose. After a hard sneeze, she became aware of a stinging pain somewhere. She moved her head to the side, trying to figure out where the pricking came from. The ache only deepened.

"You're sitting on your hair," Ki stated in a reasonable tone.

He'd raised a knee and rested a big forearm across it, blocking her view of those interesting man parts. "Huh?" Sure enough, she had a large chunk of hair trapped under her. Lifting her butt, she swept the pile out before sitting back down on the hard ground. Gathering the heavy mane in one hand, she put it over her shoulder to rest over her chest. Damn, long hair had always been a pain in the ass, but she doubted she'd be cutting it if sitting on it hurt.

She peered at the relaxed Zerin in front of her. "Did anything else change?"

A masculine smile came out slow and sensuous. "Of course. Your eyes look lovely with the added ring of blue around your pupil. I have to say it's quite striking."

Damn, where was a mirror when you needed one? Speaking of which...

"Can we get out of this cave anytime soon?" Sherri scanned the bleak surroundings. "Why are we here in the first place, anyway?" Loose stones littered the dusty ground, with the jagged edge of the opening several feet away. The cavern was void of any sharp stalactites, but the area retained a dampness that paired with the smell of rotting mold.

Why wasn't she cold? There was a reason she preferred the desert climate of Arizona.

Ki shrugged his massive shoulders. "After Grirryrth and Chei-the's...ah...flight, they became tired and found this place." He waved a finger, encompassing the cavern in all its glory.

"Great. Any chance we can leave soon?"

Yes, we will take you back. Cheithe's voice projected.

From the expression on Ki's face, Grirryrth had echoed Cheithe. He stood and went to the mouth of the cave.

Sherri followed right behind him, her gaze hooked on the firm globes of his scrumptious ass. Once she reached his side, she peered down the edge at the sheer five-thousand-foot drop. "Holy shit!" She jumped back. With a quick grab at Ki's upper arm for support, she leaned over. They were so far up, they'd passed the tree line as puffy white clouds dotted the sky below them.

"Do not worry *yofie-na.*"

The joy in Ki's voice surprised her.

With a gentle touch, he took her hand off his arm and kissed her knuckles before taking two steps back. "We are dragons and we own the skies!"

With that exclamation, the crazy, naked idiot ran to the edge and jumped off.

Sherri screamed and stumbled after him only to fall on her ass when the gigantic eggplant color of Grirryrth's underbelly swooped past. A bark of shocked laughter replaced her suffocating fear at watching Ki take a dive off the steep cliff.

Sherri rushed to the threshold and gawked, trying to find the crazy man. There...there he was! Just above her, his magnificent body with the enormous purple membranes of his wings caught the early morning light. He swooped and looped with a dance of masculine grace. He was the embodiment of a dominant and dangerous predator high above the clouded landscape.

Cheithe trilled her approval and scrambled to take over to join her mate.

"Damn hussy, wait a minute!" Sherri no sooner shouted the words than the female dragon had her jumping off the cliff to transform into the Solaherra dragon.

Shit! One of these days, she'd have a say in what form she kept.

The dragons played all the way to Sherri's house. First, it was a game of chase, then mock battles and ending with a competitive race. Cheithe won, but Sherri suspected the frisky male dragon had another agenda on his mind as he flew close behind.

Twilight bathed her rustic home in a warm glow. The driveway lights twinkled and gave a sense of welcome.

Grirryrth and Cheithe landed in the wide front yard before giving up their control.

Once again, Sherri stood naked next to an equally naked Zerin male. A naked and happy Zerin male. His erection was stiff, with a small drop of pre-cum seeping out the tip. Sherri flipped her eyes to his, which narrowed in response. She enjoyed his regard as shivers of anticipation made her clasp her hands behind her back and straighten her spine to thrust her breasts higher.

The lowering sun glinted on the crystal at Ki's temple and the need that blazed out of his eyes. Without a word, he lumbered to her before he swooped her into his massive arms as if she weighed no more than a child. The big Zerin locked his lips to hers and gave her a searing kiss of a lifetime.

In response, she wrapped her arms around his neck, entangling her fingers in the luxurious hair at the base of his neck. Their combined tresses mixed and stroked together. Sherri returned his passion with a dance of tongues and wallowed in his masculine flavor.

She loved the way he kissed. He was a methodical, intelligent man who was thorough in whatever he did. His kisses weren't any different. Full, sensuous lips mastered hers while his tongue worked in concert with hers. Breath became secondary as she became engrossed in the prelude to the coming pleasures.

With long strides, he gripped under her knees while the other cradled around her back.

An adept multi-tasker, his kiss scrambled her senses as he carried them into the house.

With powerful lunges, he sprinted up the stairs, his feet jumping over every other step. The jarring broke their lips apart as they approached her master bathroom.

The room was large, with a huge glass-walled shower enclosure sporting multiple showerheads and a pulsating spray on the ceiling. Once she was on her feet, he closed the door as she activated the spray with the temperature automatically programmed.

Warm, clear water washed away the dirt and grime of the cave. The soothing pulses of the showerheads lent a lush rhythm to their lovemaking. Ki's large hands caressed and stroked every part of Sherri's body, his palms filled with neutral-scented soap that filled the air with the spicy tang from the oils seeping out of his pores.

With each pass of his hands, sexual tension tightened her lower body, as her oil-soaked palms slid over him. With special attention, she grasped the silk-covered steel of his erection and massaged the soft skin.

Several times, he hissed out a breath and rumbled a male groan. The soft, warm water added to the sensuous feel of his skin against hers.

God! He was so responsive. *Yeah, baby...right there.* His big body trembled as she stroked his oval-shaped ball in a gentle motion. The ecstasy swarming through him echoed through her. As if she needed extra encouragement to continue.

Touching wasn't enough. Sherri lowered to meet his eager cock as it quivered in a happy greeting. When she opened her mouth, she became airborne and was thrown over a broad shoulder. When she squealed and thumped on his broad back in protest, she got a light smack on the globe of her ass. The water turned off as Ki took them out of the shower and headed to her bedroom.

"Female, you are not allowed to bring me yet."

With a toss, she became airborne again before bouncing on the soft mattress of the king-sized bed that might end up being too small.

"I will taste you first."

Sherri flushed at the highhanded statement. But, why argue when his warm mouth latched onto the quivering slit of her sex?

Ki pulled back and stared. "I've wanted to ask you," With a nod, he indicated her glistening pussy. "Did you mean to do this?"

Resting on bent elbows, she tried to figure out what he was talking about. Did he mean the color of her pubes not being as bright red as before? When a thick forefinger brushed along the short landing strip, she smiled. "That's how I like it groomed." Sherri wiggled her hips. "You don't like?"

He took in a deep breath and his tongue flicked between the folds. "Oh, I like very much. Such a beautiful, sweet pussy undressed just for me." Without another word, he dove in and licked, stroked, and nibbled. Not only the stiff nub but also on the surrounding sensitive skin.

Her lower core tensed as the sensual oils seeped out of her pores and her labored breaths matched each swipe. Then her toes curled when he probed with two thick fingers. Ki found her sweet spot with unerring accuracy, teasing and stroking the sensitive nest at the front of her upper channel. Her hair looped to encircle his wrists, not to stop him but to help hold on for dear life.

The explosion was coming, and she wasn't sure if she'd survive.

"Are you ready, *yofie-na*?

Cheithe whispered *my love*, translating the words Ki had been using for so long.

"Re-ready?" She stammered with eyes squeezed shut. A whipcord of strained nerves tightened, and she was more than ready to detonate.

His smug grin said he was pleased at taking her to the brink so quickly. "Yes, my own." A low croon. "You will come for me now."

His full lips wrapped around her slit while he flicked her stiff clit as his fingers scissored and probed her inner core, giving her a sense of fullness. At the coordinated plunge between his tongue and fingers, Sherri's straining nerves released in a pleasure so sharp it brought bright stars that flickered across her closed lids. "Ki-i-i..." tore through her throat on a high-pitched wail.

Before the last note left her lips, Ki shifted to widen the space between her legs. With unerring accuracy, he thrust his cock inside. Wrapping his arms under her head, he brought her lips to his in a scorching kiss and held tight. He plunged into her over and over, a male rigid with determination.

In response, she wound her legs around his waist. The move opened her wider for their mutual gratification.

As the strokes became deeper, Ki tore his mouth away. With a harsh roar, he lowered his head and latched on with sharp teeth at the tender place between her neck and shoulder. The bite was hard enough to puncture the delicate skin.

The pain caused her to catch her breath in shock before a euphoric wave burst in ecstasy. A tsunami of completion tore through and left her weak before it was over. Her legs slid off to bonelessly flop to his sides.

Ki unlatched his sharp teeth from her skin and nuzzled the wound.

He gave a hard push of his hips that woofed a gasp out of her. Above her, his large frame shook, then stilled. Raspy puffs of air escaped against her ear as the big Zerin tightened his hold. A soft masculine sigh sounded as his weight bore down.

Sherri welcomed the heavy body on top of hers. She plunged her hands into his thick, silky hair to let the strands fall through her fingers. In reaction, the mahogany tresses wound around her wrists and forearms in a gentle stroke. She nuzzled against the fragrant column of his throat, breathing in the scents of musky brine with a tinge of a fresh sea breeze with feminine satisfaction. His unrestrained lovemaking made her giddy. Sherri's heart was weightless while intense joy rushed through.

This was right. This was what life was all about. Having someone in your arms who represented everything to you...someone who complemented you in every way without being the same. A person who effortlessly filled those holes you'd lived your entire life with.

With sudden clarity, it dawned on Sherri she truly was madly and irreversibly in love with Ki. She might have guessed it before, but now there wasn't a shred of doubt in her mind.

Great, now that she'd figured that out, where to go from there? She had huge responsibilities on Earth she needed to stay and finish. Did she have the right to ask Ki to remain and join her hectic life here?

One thing for sure, she'd assume nothing. Time to take a deep breath and give him an offer he couldn't refuse.

Chapter THIRTEEN

Sherri

Sherri's opportunity to discuss her relationship with Ki came sooner rather than later. Entangled with Ki in the wide bed, she was startled when one minute he was all over her and the next he wasn't.

He'd jumped off the bed and crouched in front of the open door to her bedroom, arms and legs spread in a defensive gesture.

Sitting up, she flung away the hair hanging in her eyes and blinked at his unusual move. With a grunt, she grabbed a sheet off the floor to cover her naked self. Should she be scared or impressed by his actions? A befuddled smile crossed her face. *Eh,* probably both. She leaned over to the maple nightstand and pulled out a baby Glock. With the sheet tucked under her arms, she pointed the weapon at the open door. She had absolute faith in Ki's instincts, and his movements screamed that someone was in the house.

At first, the air was still, the wait heavy. Then a muffled, masculine voice barked just out of eyesight, "Police. Put down any weapons and raise your hands."

Sherri lowered her pistol and cocked her head as two men in black armored suits filled the doorway with the words "SWAT" across their bulletproof vests. Seeing the familiar human law enforcement unit, she put the Glock under a pillow and raised her palms outward.

Obviously, Ki did not understand who they were. He tensed as if ready to spring.

"Ki." She made sure her tone was calm. "Stand down. It's okay."

His hefty thighs trembled as his posture screamed of a man ready to engage. The SWAT team's guns remained steady, pointed in their direction.

Crap! Time to defuse the situation before it got out of hand. Sherri scrambled off the mattress, keeping the light-blue sheet plastered around her as she stood in front of Ki. "Stand down!" She yelled at the SWAT team. A low growl rumbled out of the male behind her who had a tight grip on her upper arms.

He tensed as if to pull her behind him.

"No!" She twisted out of his grip and kept an eye on the two men. She couldn't see their faces behind the black helmets, but she was sure they thought they were in a hostile situation. "Ki, don't move." She kept her attention on the threat in front of her. "I am Leader Sherrilyn Cantor. What can I do for you, gentlemen?"

Bodies stiff as marble statues, they stepped aside in unison as a third man walked in. This one was in the same black uniform as the helmeted men minus the helmet. A fit middle-aged man, well over six feet tall, his buzzed hair liberally salted with gray, exposed a hardened, craggy face.

Although he had deep brackets framing his full lips, Sherri doubted he smiled much.

Hazel eyes flashed impatience. "Leader Cantor?" The hard authority in his voice matched the no-nonsense demeanor. His wide nose pinched as he glared at Ki.

Sherri nodded. "Yes." Wrapping the sheet tighter, she stayed in front of the large, naked Zerin. "What is the meaning of this?" She swept the room with a wave of her hand to encompass them.

The man stiffened, back ramrod straight. Ice-cold eyes narrowed as he scrutinized her.

Hmm, looked like she'd been found wanting.

"We were called in by your assistant, a Ms. Basimah, who informed us your guards have not reported in as directed. In fact, they have dropped off the communication grid assigned to them."

A hard rock squeezed her stomach, and she became dizzy for a moment. No way would Basimah call in American police to check on her in Canada. Not only that, all she had to do was contact her by the communication implant Sherri had. A quick glance at the guards holding weapons at her confirmed her suspicions. They weren't from any law enforcement agency and those weren't standard-issue weapons aimed in their direction. American SWAT teams usually carried a 9mm HK MPS or a Beretta. These two both had .40-caliber Smith and Wesson handguns. She'd opened her mouth to respond when Ki placed a large palm on her shoulder.

"Our sincerest apologies," he answered behind her. "They have been replaced and I'm afraid we neglected to inform the proper Earth authorities."

Puzzled why Ki stated it that way, Sherri kept quiet. Where he was going with that statement?

"Is this true, Leader Cantor?" The spokesperson for supposed SWAT team maintained a stony appearance.

Sherri doubted it would be easy to change this guy's mind about anything but nodded. "Yes." She gestured at the man behind her, the warmth of Ki's chest covering her back. "This is Ki of Zerin who is now my guard."

The man's gaze focused above her at Ki. "I see." He stared at her with an unemotional expression. "Any objection to speaking with me alone?"

Before Ki could respond, she did. "No, not at all." He had no idea who they were dealing with and it was up to her to protect him. With a tight grip, she clasped the slipping sheet. "Allow me to change first, so please leave."

The man shook his head. "No, I'm afraid I can't allow that, Leader Cantor."

Sherri opened her mouth to protest but Ki strode from behind her dressed in the dark battlesuit of the Solaherra dragon. Bemused at the widening of the man's eyes, she watched Ki come over and wrap the sheet tighter to tuck the ends between her breasts.

"Go get changed. I'll wait here for you."

Sherri's eyes widened at the serious frown. Maybe he wasn't as unaware as she thought. "Um, okay." She glanced to the men standing at the doorway, their guns held steady in Ki's direction. "Don't do anything until I get back."

He shrugged his massive shoulders. "No promises, so I'd hurry if I were you."

The back of her neck tightened. "Yeah, okay."

Racing to the heavy, maple dresser on the other side of the room, she took out a peach-colored bra and matching boy shorts before grabbing a pair of jeans and a blue cotton pullover from the bottom drawers. Rushing to the bathroom and shutting the door behind her, she dressed as fast as she could before running a toothbrush across her teeth. Her hair smoothed out and plaited into a loose tail down her back.

Damn, that was all kinds of wonderful. She had no hair fasteners since she'd never needed one before, so she left the end of the braid alone. It would be great to see if it stayed in place without one.

She hoped nothing happened while she'd been gone. It was awfully quiet out there. With the light-blue sheet in one hand, she opened the door an inch with the other. None of the men had moved except Ki.

Who was missing.

"Where's Ki?" She hid behind the solid-wood door.

"Come out, Leader Cantor, and no one else will get hurt."

Well...shit. That can't be good. Looked like the pretense was over. Sherri slammed the door and twisted the lock. She blinked to activate her communication bud, but dead air greeted her. *Damn it!* The signal must be blocked somehow. Heart in her throat, she spun around and checked the bathroom with fresh eyes. She'd never considered trying to escape from there before. A chill crossed her spine.

Can you sense where Ki is? she asked Cheithe. The few seconds it took for the dragon to answer had Sherri shaking in worry. *Is he hurt?*

They are near and fine.

Sherri got the impression the question confused Cheithe.

I do not understand why they are not here since they are amused and relaxed.

A hard pound on the door made Sherri squeak in alarm.

"Come out now or we'll use force." A deafening male voice boomed.

"Where is Ki?" she yelled at the closed door.

The answer she got was a loud thud against the solid oak. The hardwood bowed under the stress. *Son of a bitch!* They weren't kidding. Her frantic search hadn't help much. The only window in the plush room lay above the claw-footed tub and was too small for her to wiggle through. *Fuck!* She'd wanted to expand that window for weeks now but had never gotten around to getting it done.

Another hard thwack made her jump and spin around. The door curved under the pressure. One more hit and it would splinter.

Okay, escape was not going to happen. A weapon. Yeah, that's what she needed, a weapon. *Shit,* why did she leave the Glock in the other room? The closest thing in here that might be some kind of weapon was a blunt-tipped pair of tweezers and a box of tampons.

Hardly fear-inspiring utensils.

Crash! The door split in two as the helmet-clad cretins grabbed the splintered wood and tore them free from its hinges. There it went...her last chance at defense or freedom.

Sherri stood her ground, faced the invaders with legs a length apart and arms folded. "Get out," she demanded.

Like all bad guys, they ignored her.

"Take her and let's go." The leader snapped. He turned to leave, not bothering to check to see if his men obeyed.

The two thugs grabbed her upper arms and hauled her out of the bedroom. Rat-bastards didn't even give her time to grab shoes or socks. Pulled between them, they weren't too gentle as their thick fingers clamped around her arm in a tight pinch. Sherri winced at the biting pain.

They towed her across the beige carpet of the hallway and down the steps to the wooden floors of the short pathway to the front door. It was open, showing the shaded patio and the wooden steps leading to the grass outside.

When they brought her into the blinding sunshine, she squinted and tilted her head to avoid the bright rays. They approached the leader who stood with his back to them with leathery fists on slim hips.

The guards flung her, and she landed with a painful thunk on her knees and palms with a whoosh of air. *Damn...that hurt!* Her palms and knees might sting for a while, but at least she didn't face-plant on the grassy knoll. A low growl let her know where Ki was. Sherri sat on her heels with hands resting on her thighs and jerked her head his way. There he was, a few feet to her left.

He was sitting on his knees, his fingers laced behind his head with his wrists zip-tied together. His mahogany-rich braid was draped over his shoulder, the tail curled over his lap to fan on the ground. His face was blank, lips parted with the tips of his fangs on full display. Those hazel/navy eyes skimmed over her before the skin across his iridescent cheekbones relaxed. His lush mouth curled at the ends. With a blink, the smile widened.

What did he have to smile about?

Be calm and let your mate take the lead. Cheithe chided.

Take the lead? How could he do that tied up?

Trust him.

The leader turned around to face her. "Get up."

Sherri glanced at Ki, who nodded. Resisting the urge to roll her eyes at his odd behavior, she rocked back on her heels and stood before the black-clad terrorist. "Let me guess... Basimah didn't send you, did she?" She wasn't going to show fear to this ridiculous asshole. "And you're not the police either, are you?"

A sneering glare. "You were an embarrassment to the human race before, but now you are an abomination." He walked over, grabbed her chin, and jerked her head to the side to stare at her MalDerVon scroll. "What is this shit? You've marked yourself up to fuck this alien?" He tossed her face aside in disgust. "You think making yourself look like him will somehow save you?"

"What do you want?" She stepped back and rubbed the abused jaw.

The older man leaned in with teeth bared and spittle flying. "I want you to die."

When the words came out in a whisper, Sherri shivered at his fanaticism.

"Tom!" He straightened and barked at one of the guards who'd brought her outside.

"Yes, sir!" The young guard scrambled over and gave a sharp salute.

"Let's get this over with. Set it up."

"Right away, Headman Addison!"

The slim guard pulled off his helmet and dropped it on the ground. The fresh-faced boy who couldn't be over twenty scrambled with bumbling feet to the black SUV sitting in the curve of her driveway. With jerky movements, he opened the door and grabbed a small video camera before rushing back.

Tom rushed to stand next to his leader, trembling so hard the camcorder shook. The guy might be nervous or excited, but that didn't stop him from pointing the thing at her.

Well...crap. Sherri's stomach dropped. She tried to take comfort in the serene expression on Ki's face, but it was hard. She stepped back and hit the solid wall of the other guard. *Damn*, she'd forgotten all about this other bozo.

Addison grabbed her and forced her to her knees.

She squealed in protest.

"Stay down, whore." A wet hiss came from his scowling mouth and he maintained his firm grip until the guard with-no-name came over and retained the punishing hold.

Sheesh...up or down? Damn idiot should make up his mind.

"Anytime, Tom," Addison commanded from next to her.

Tom nodded and the little red light on the camera came on.

With narrowed eyes, the leader spoke while staring at the lens. "Fellow Humans of Earth, my name is Headman Paul Addison, the leader of NARF—The North American Resistance Force." He puffed out his brawny chest and stood tall.

"I am here today to usher in a glorious revolution to take back our country and planet Earth. Not only from these traitors." Grabbing a fistful of Sherri's hair, he snatched her head back.

A wave of agony shot down from her scalp to the base of her spine. She yelped in response and tried to yank his hands off.

He jerked harder. "But from the alien oppressors who've taken our God-given right to choose our own leaders." He nodded at Tom to put Ki in the camera sights.

Tom swung to point the lens toward Ki before swinging back.

"As Americans, it is our duty as the only superpower on the planet to lead the way to victory. We will show our fellow nations how to eliminate traitors." He waved a large, serrated knife in his free hand and placed it across the vulnerable skin of Sherri's neck.

Sweat rolled down her back and her temples as she quivered. She tried to catch Ki's attention, but he wasn't in the same place he'd been only seconds ago. Out of the corner of her eye, a dark blur passed behind Tom and his camera, moving too fast for her to track.

Sherri held her breath, waiting for the guard or the pain-in-my-ass leader to react to whatever she spotted. Maybe someone was there to help. Between the burn of her hair being pulled, and the fiery sting of the knife against her throat, she'd had enough. Even though she wasn't in the most dignified position, she glowered at her tormentor as he blabbed his nonsense.

"Only a male weak in character will hold a defenseless female captive and brag about killing her for others to witness," the husky, deep tones of her TrueBond announced. A large, three-fingered hand grabbed Headman Addison by the throat and hauled him away from her. Ki threw a hard punch at the man's jaw.

The middle-aged leader fell with a thud next to the other unconscious guard sprawled on the grassy ground.

Tom, the camera-holding dolt, squealed and dropped it on the ground. He moved to run but Ki's voice stopped him.

"Boy, you will pick up that vid device and continue."

Tom hesitated for a nanosecond before he scrambled and fumbled with the camera to point it in their direction.

That feed wasn't going to make good viewing, with all the shaking the kid did.

Addison groaned.

Ki picked the man up by his neck and dangled his feet off the ground.

The man struggled, scratching and punching the hand around his throat as his face turned purple.

"I am putting the people of Earth on notice." Ki plopped the man back on the ground, but didn't release his firm hold.

The natural beige color returned to the man's face as he gulped for air even as he continued to tug at the hard grip.

"My name is M'alalu Ki E'eur of the planet Zerin. Leader Cantor is my TrueBond and under my personal protection," he snarled, fangs on full display. "And I will *not* allow any harm to come to her. Nor will I allow violence to befall the rest of humanity as Earth gains admittance into the civilized galaxy."

Ki released his hold before he clipped the man on the back of the head. The Headman flopped unconscious at his feet. With a self-satisfied smirk, Ki went to help her stand. His eyes narrowed as he examined her face before he lowered his mouth to cover hers.

The warmth of his kiss was deep and soul shattering, assuring her he would always be there for her.

He stroked a firm, masculine claim.

Sherri, in turn, twined her arms around his neck and pressed as close as she could to his wide chest and staked her own claim.

He rumbled an approval and rested his massive palms between her bottom and waist.

The nubs at the side of his tongue burst with the spicy flavor she craved.

Ki eased back and smiled when he rested his forehead against hers.

She returned his blatant display of love before she claimed him in a kiss that devastated them both.

EPILOGUE

The Royal Palace of Zerin—one solar year later

Ki leaned back into the deceptively soft cushions of the lounger in the personal suite of his king and friend, Qay. He had always liked this particular family room. It housed their small group in understated opulence. The colors were neutral, the flooring a high sheen of natural wood overlaid with heavy, colorful rugs in a range of jewel tones. The walls were a relaxing hue of beige with an undertone of the royal emerald green. One side of the room boasted a long, tan couch big enough that six individuals could relax in comfort. On the side of the room where Ki relaxed sat three lounge chairs in thick faux animal hides. Their hues varied from whimsical almond to brunet brown.

On his right sat his long-time friend, King Qay, in his favorite chair.

Qay had his feet planted firmly on the ground as he clutched a mellow amber drink in one hand. Occasionally, he'd take a sip.

To Ki's left, the new Chancellor of the Federation Consortium, D'zia E'etu, relaxed, absorbed in the conversation. The male was Qay's cousin and all-around pain in Ki's ass.

D'zia sat on his own acorn-brown lounger with his feet up and crossed at the ankles.

Oddly enough, D'zia wasn't enjoying any alcoholic beverage but instead abstained throughout the evening. A quick glance at the heir crystal nestled in D'zia's temple confirmed Ki's suspicions. The color was changing at a slow pace. One click it was a dark emerald and the next it was a light green. Well, well, well. D'zia's TrueBond had conceived and now carried twins—a boy and a girl. Ki hid a smirk with a sip of his drink.

One thing D'zia hadn't given up was his habit of teasing and finding humor in most situations. That personality trait usually grated on Ki's nerves, but tonight he'd let the annoying *norakthed* get away with whatever nonsense he spouted.

A quick movement on D'zia's shoulder drew Ki's attention to the spybot, JR10. While the bot might resemble an Earth spider, he was anything but. He was one of the most sophisticated AIs around, and his caustic temperament made D'zia look demure in comparison. Even now, the bot was going on and on about some adventure he'd just experienced with the AI ship, Elemi, in the Estraa sector. Something about joining Shysutá and her merry band of AoA mercenaries in recovering a kidnapped royal from a ruling house of the Consortium.

Apparently, the Erkeks who'd done the deed hadn't wanted to give up their captive to a small spider, a self-aware ship, a pissed-off Runihura male, and a bossy human female. Too bad the disgraced species hadn't known whom they dealt with when they took the princess. Not only did the little group save her, but they also destroyed an important sector of the Erkek Empire.

A trickle of feminine laughter from across the room caught his attention. Sitting with the other females on the long tan couch sat his TrueBond, Sherri, with her two friends, Aimee and Lora E'etu. Lora's AI companion, JR11, a smaller version of JR10, rested on one of Lora's shoulders.

The females' heads were close together as they whispered in hushed tones.

Ki frowned. Nothing good could come from them plotting in lowered voices. The only interruption in their conversation was when his Royal Highness, one-year-old Prince Ryox Argent E'etu, ran away from the grownups...without garments on his lower half. With a squeal of maniacal baby laughter, he avoided his human mother who chased after him with outstretched arms and a red face while calling out for the escaped toddler to stop.

"... and then Elemi zapped him on the ass!" JR10 was winding down his narrative with a wave of a slender foreleg.

Both D'zia and Qay chuckled at the punch line.

Ki raised an eyebrow. No reason they had to know he hadn't been paying attention.

"D'zia, how does it feel now that you've been officially voted in as the Chancellor for the next ten solar years?" Ki took another sip of his fiery drink.

The startling color of D'zia's turquoise eyes filled with humor while the deep dimples at the sides of his smile warned of the smartass answer coming. "I'm living the high life, my friend." D'zia deadpanned. "Good thing there's plenty of time for things to go sideways."

While Ki had no idea what "sideways" meant, two could play the smartass game. He gave the other male a slight nod with a stony expression. "Your acknowledgement of the inevitability is hereby noted."

JR10 whooped and landed on his back with his twelve legs waving in the air as he laughed. "Ya see, dude? This guy is mega funny!" The bot laid on his torso with his legs folded under him and the colors in his compound eyes reflected the room's light as he swiveled his attention between the three.

Qay gave a snort and rolled his eyes as he took another sip. Living with his human TrueBond was affecting his friend's mannerisms.

Ki's frown expanded. Did he display human behaviors as well? Something to think about...

D'zia's smile turned into a flat line when he scrunched his face. "Actually, things are a hectic mess. I get thousands of demands every day to 'fix' something or someone U'unk screwed. And they all want it now." With thin lips, he continued. "You wouldn't believe the illegal things that he'd been doing for the last fifty years. There's enough evidence to keep the lawgivers busy for decades."

The younger male narrowed his eyes at Qay. "Good thing he 'conveniently' died on Earth, isn't it?"

Qay shrugged. "The male's in an unknown location and is quite harmless in his present mental condition."

D'zia snorted. "I still don't understand why you let that *fruking puntneji* live. He should be tried and executed for his crimes."

"Well—" Qay took another small swallow of his drink and sat back. "—two reasons." He rested the round glass on the flat of his belly. "First, a trial would uncover everything U'unk has done in the last fifty years. The deep scandal would tear the fabric of the Federation Consortium apart." He nodded at D'zia. "Only now are you scratching the surface of what he was capable of. Can you imagine a trial uncovering not only what he did but also how he did it? Zerin and the nine systems would fall into a civil war because there isn't a member system he hasn't harmed or taken advantage of in some way."

Qay tapped a finger on the rim of the glass. "And secondly, we owe Lok for the way U'unk made him disappear without anyone being the wiser." A slight flush stained his prominent cheekbones. "The Special Triad is going to look into how easy it was for U'unk to replace Lok in the Senate before he became Chancellor. Anyway, the Triad and I agree the decision was Lok's—whether U'unk lived or not. He said all he wanted to do was take care of his brother for the rest of their lives. The only stipulation was he didn't want to worry about finances nor have the threat of anyone looking for them." Qay shrugged and his eyes became unfocused. "I tried to talk him out of it. I told him he should live his own life, but he insisted it was too late for him. Said he'd been out of circulation far too long and had no desire to reenter civilization." He blinked and brought his focus back. "Lok has a way to contact us if he changes his mind."

Ki took a healthy sip of his own drink and enjoyed the smooth, slow burn. "Do you think he'll abuse U'unk? As retribution?"

Qay shook his head. "No, and that's the unbelievable part. For some reason, Lok loves his brother and wants to take care of him." He pursed his lips together. "Not that I would blame him if he did want revenge."

"And what about you?" D'zia turned the conversation over to Qay. "Is being the king everything you'd hoped and dreamed of?"

"Well, I wouldn't go that far." Qay's voice was muffled in his drink glass as he took another sip. "While the day-to-day responsibilities are hard enough, it's the toll on Aimee and Ryox that bothers me."

Ki frowned. "Is there a problem?" He rested the tumbler on a nearby side table and leaned forward. He didn't like the pensive look on Qay's face when he talked about his TrueBond and child.

"Yes and no." The answer came out in a slow drawl as Qay watched Aimee wrestling with their rambunctious toddler as she tried to put clothes on his naked lower body.

Aimee laughed at her baby as Lora and Sherri playfully argued what type of restraints to use.

"While our people have for the most part accepted Aimee, there is a growing unrest at having a human in the ruling house. The council has had several vigorous debates already, but so far the consensus has been in our favor." He shrugged and brought his attention back to their small group. "Nothing we can't handle, but I'm working on contingency plans if needed."

"You can count on us to help whenever!" JR10 emphasized from D'zia's shoulder.

Qay nodded in acknowledgment. "I appreciate that, JR10."

"So, Ki, my man." JR10 turned his bulbous multi-colored eyes his way. "How's it goin' on Earth?"

Ki tilted his head as he considered his answer. "As well as can be expected, I suppose."

Qay narrowed his eyes with a frown. "Are you still having problems there?"

"I deal with humans every day." Ki gave an uncharacteristic snort. "Of course I'm having problems." He shrugged and leaned back while he retrieved his glass and took a sip of his own beverage before crossing an ankle over bended knee. The Braliader mix in the bottom of his glass was a beautiful swirl of red and black liqueur that would kill anyone else after the first taste. Without his Crart/Solaherra heritage, Ki couldn't drink it. However, Grirryrth loved the fiery liquor and Ki had no problem indulging him whenever he was at Qay's palace. Especially since it was the only place in the Federation Consortium to find the illegal liquid.

Qay kept the rare bottle under personal lock.

Ki appreciated his friend never questioning his ability to enjoy the poisonous drink. Of course, it helped when Ki finally let his friends know Gryrrith and Cheithe's history. Both of his friends had peered at him before they shrugged and went on to discuss other things. "But, I have found my purpose in life not only in being with Sherri but in helping her fledgling species survive. Every day brings new challenges, and more often than not, I find myself in the middle of a paradigm shift on my long-held beliefs." He devoured his gorgeous TrueBond with his eyes as he spoke. She was the reason he'd finally become a whole male. He who had once been a two-dimensional creature of habit. Watching her speak to her friends with a slight smile on her gorgeous face gave him a deep sense of belonging.

D'zia was asking Qay about a procedure involving humans wanting to visit other planets when a tantalizing scent twitched Ki's nose. His dick hardened and his heart raced. What was that? Grirryrth rumbled as Ki's skin flushed with the mating oils. He gripped the sides of the chair until the thick leather ripped. He gave a startled glance at the others, and was relieved that no one noticed his lack of control.

Except his mate. Sherri sent him a slumberous gaze, her glorious lips pursed. Her hand found the bottom of her loose auburn braid and twirled it around an elegant finger. She tilted her head and licked her full lips with a pink tongue. The clear crystal in her MalDerVon scroll twinkled in the low light.

Ki's gut seized. What was that aroma?

An image of Sherri plump and ripe with his child clouded his vision. Ah...that's what was different. His TrueBond was ovulating. Ki waited for the crushing sensation to arrive...the one that told him to run as fast as he could to avoid fathering offspring.

It never came. Instead, a profound joy flooded and stole his heart. Yes, he wanted a child...a child with Sherri's intelligence and beauty. A sense of completion and purpose filled him. Ki slid her a slow look. His hands itched to touch her soft skin. He took in a deep breath to inhale the spicy-sweet scent of his aroused female. The distance between them irritated him as the mating oils persisted in seeping out.

Enough.

"Excuse me, gentlemen." Ki interrupted the conversation, put the glass on a nearby table, and stood. "It seems I have a previous engagement." Ignoring the knowing smiles and smirks of his friends, he crossed the room focused on Sherri.

When he came close, her exotic eyes narrowed and her sensuous lips curled upwards at the corners. She straightened, which thrust her breasts in his direction.

No male alive would ignore the invitation she sent. Ki stopped in front of her with an extended hand. "Come, TrueBond. Time to go home. There are things to discuss."

Sherri beamed and enfolded her warmth and strength with his.

Perfection settled deep within...a sense of wanting to go home that he'd missed for so long.

Then things became clear. He didn't need to go home, he was home. The TrueBond he held in his arms embodied his sanctuary; his place of refuge, of solace, and most of all...love.

She was all the redemption he'd ever need.

A SMALL ASK....

I hope you enjoyed ***Ki's Redemption***! Before you go, please take a minute to leave a review **HERE.** Good, honest reviews are worth their weight in gold to an author. It helps others find my works and lets them know it's okay to take a chance on my stories. Not to mention, it makes my day when I hear from readers!

Thank you :)

ACKNOWLEDGMENTS

No writer has a better group of folks that help to make a dream come true:

The great team at Barany's School of Fiction. You keep me on track and motivated better than anyone else.

To the cheerleaders at WSB - I really appreciate that none of you roll your eyes when I yet again bring the conversation around to my writing.

To Jacqueline Sweet (sexy... sexy covers), ELF the editor, and Sidekick Jenn. As always, you're right there with what I need. You are invaluable and irreplaceable.

To the awesome Goobs, you are a constant source of inspiration. To Barb... what can I say? I wouldn't be me without ya!

To all my friends and family - I am nothing without you. You make me whole, me make me viable, and most of all... you make me crazy!

Damn... life is good!

ABOUT AUTHOR

Keri Kruspe, award-winning *"Author of Otherworldly Romantic Adventures"* loves nothing more than to write about romances that feature "feisty heroines who are afraid to take a chance on life... or love". Her writing career started when she became irritate that most SciFi Alien Romances had women kidnapped before love found them. Determined to create something different, she turned "the alien kidnapping trope upside down" (Vine Voice) and the **ALIEN EXCHANGE** trilogy was born.

Keri's latest SciFi Romance series, **ANCIENT ALIEN DESCENDANTS**, is taking the Ancient Alien motif and mixes it with a sensual, romantic twist.

A native Nevadan, Keri is a lifelong avid reader who lives in northwestern Michigan with her hubby and the newest member of the family, a Jack Russell Terrier named Hestia. When not immersed in her made-up worlds, she enjoys discovering the fascinating landscape of her new home and pairing red wine with healthy ways to cook while indulging in her classic rock collection. Most of all, she loves finding her next favorite author.

If you want to know when Keri's next book will come out, please visit her at her website where you can sign up for her mailing list. You'll get a FREE copy of the novella, *The Day Behind Tomorrow* that is a prologue to the **ANCIENT ALIEN DESCENDANT SERIES**. Not to mention being kept updated on the life of a dedicated, obsessed author.

Join the fun on Social Media:

Facebook

Twitter

Instagram

ALSO BY

An Alien Exchange Universe:

An Alien Exchange

D'zia's Dilemma

Ki's Redemption

Chloe's Turn

Ancient Alien Descendants

Alien Legacy: The Empath

Alien Legacy: The Shapeshifter

Alien Legacy: The Psychic

Alien Legacy: The Vampire

Alien Legacy: The Mage (coming 2022)

Made in the USA
Middletown, DE
04 July 2023